How Sweet
the Sound

THE REWINDING TIME SERIES
Inspirational Novels of History, Mystery & Romance

book 3

DEBORAH HEAL

Copyright © June 2015 Deborah Heal

ISBN: 1514152355
ISBN-13: 978-1514152355

This is historical fiction. While every effort was made to be historically accurate about the real people, places, and events of the past, they were fictionalized to one degree or another. Readers may find more about the history behind *How Sweet the Sound* on the author's website.

As for the contemporary characters, any resemblance to actual living persons is purely coincidental. It should be emphasized that any characters associated with Cave-in-Rock State Park are totally fictitious, as are those of McKendree University. (Furthermore, real faculty meetings at this wonderful and historic institution are undoubtedly always useful and riveting to those attending.)

Other Novels by Deborah Heal

Available in e-book and paperback, The Rewinding Time Series:
    Once Again (book 1)
    Only One Way Home (book 2)

Available in audiobook, e-book, and paperback, The History Mystery Trilogy:
    Time and Again (book 1)
    Unclaimed Legacy (book 2)
    Every Hill and Mountain (book 3)

For my brother Marvin Woods who loves caves,
rocks, minerals, and other geological curiosities
even more than I do.

Amazing Grace, how sweet the sound,
That saved a wretch like me.
I once was lost but now am found,
Was blind, but now I see.

—John Newton

CHAPTER 1

After a leisurely walk across campus on a pleasant July morning, Merrideth Randall pushed open the glass door of Holderman Library, fully expecting to find the place empty. Most students were gone on summer break. Only relentlessly dedicated students—or desperately behind ones—attended the summer term at McKendree College. And even those would be gone the moment the last classes ended that afternoon, eager for the four-day weekend in which to celebrate the nation's independence by eating barbecue and blowing things up.

But the freshman committee meeting she had come to supervise was apparently already in progress. Surprised, she checked the clock over the circulation desk. No, she was not late. Actually, she was twelve minutes early.

Even from across the room, it was obvious the meeting was not going well. That part was not a surprise, given that Alyssa Holderman was its chairperson.

Alyssa's sarcastic comments in Merrideth's classroom had been hard for her fragile ego to take in her early days at McKendree, but by the time the semester was half over, Alyssa had grown more respectful and *she* had toughened up. The girl had even put several nice notes about her class in the school's *Compliments and Comments* box. Nevertheless Alyssa Holderman's self-importance was best experienced in small doses. Odds were that she had already reminded the committee that the library they sat in was named for her great grandfather.

Despite Merrideth's reservations, the head of the history

department, Arthur King—or King Arthur as the students affectionately called him—had appointed Alyssa as the freshman chairperson for the *History of McKendree College* book project. The deadline to get the manuscript to the publisher was August fifteenth, and there was still work to be done, summer break notwithstanding.

The students looked up when Merrideth approached their table. Dane Walters, wearing his usual nerd-wear, smiled warmly. Fortunately, he had outgrown the crush he had had on her first semester. Before the break she had noticed him walking around campus in the company of a cute freshman girl. Joe Diego slumped sleepily in his chair but mumbled a greeting. He, too, had been in her first-semester class. She no longer made the mistake of thinking that his demeanor was an indicator of apathy or a lack of intelligence. Behind those half-mast eyes was a sharp brain.

At the head of the table, Alyssa smiled impatiently, as if annoyed to be interrupted, and shuffled a stack of papers.

"Looks like you got an early start, Alyssa," Merrideth said. "It's not even ten yet."

"She told us to be here at nine forty-five," Dane said, looking puzzled.

"As chairperson of this committee—"

"A fact that no one is ever likely to forget, Alyssa," Joe drawled.

"As I was saying," Alyssa continued, "As chairperson, I determined we couldn't afford to waste a single minute. The deadline looms, and we have tons of work to do."

The girl was right, of course. But changing the meeting time was also a power play, plain and simple. As the adult, Merrideth should remain professional and get on with what she was hired to do. But the Imp of Perverse demanded that she make the little tyrant wait. Sitting down next to Dane, she casually picked up the library book that lay on the table in front of him. "This looks interesting."

"It is, Dr. Randall," he said. "I brought it to show you. I thought you might like to add it to your suggested reading list. You know, for your History of Southern Illinois class."

"Thanks, Dane. I'll consider it." The book was called *Haunting Hardin County*. Thumbing through it, Merrideth saw that the topics included encounters with ghosts, bloody Indian atrocities, spells by witches and warlocks, mysterious crop circles, and infamous outlaws, including pirates on the Ohio River. Her students would like the book all right. The question was whether there was any truth among the sensationalism to justify adding it to the list.

"My favorite part was about the pirates." The excitement in Dane's eyes made him look about twelve.

"How could there be pirates in Illinois?" Alyssa asked disparagingly. "The state is landlocked."

"No it's not," Dane ventured cautiously.

"Well, there are no high seas," Alyssa said. "You know what I mean."

"River pirates," Joe said. "If you'd give him a chance to explain, Alyssa, he would tell you that there were pirates on the Ohio when the settlers came downriver on their flatboats. I saw it in a movie once."

Alyssa sent him a withering look. "Well, you can't believe everything Hollywood tells you."

"Well in this case, Hollywood got it right," Merrideth said. "Unless the moviemakers gave the pirates eye patches and wooden legs."

Joe chuckled. "No, and no pirate ships with skull-and-crossbones flags either. The movie is *How the West Was Won*, Dr. Randall. They've got it at Family Video, if you're interested."

"As a matter of fact, I'm looking for something for tonight," Merrideth said. "My friends' little girls are coming over for our weekly movie night."

"Then if the pirates didn't have ships, how did they rob the settlers coming down the river?" Dane asked. "The logistics, you know?"

"I don't know. It's an interesting question, isn't it?" Merrideth said. "But right now we need to discuss our project."

"Yes," Alyssa said. "So if we're finished talking about boys' pirate fantasies, we should get back to work."

"I'm not—" Dane sputtered.

He was distracted from whatever he was about to say when Alyssa thrust a red ink pen into his hand and slapped a copy of the manuscript on the table in front of him. It was neatly labeled with her name, beneath which she had added *Chairperson* in bold letters. "I found over twenty typos in your report on the Methodist Circuit Riders that founded the college." She slapped another copy down in front of Joe. "And I lost count in your Bothwell Chapel piece."

Merrideth decided it was time to wrest control of the committee proceedings from Miss Know-it-all. She took her own copy of the freshman reports from her shoulder bag and laid it on the table. "Alyssa is right. It is important to make sure our part of the project is absolutely typo-free when we turn it in. Our pride demands it. But even more important is that we lay out the information in a logical manner that the reader can easily follow. And most important of all, is that we get the facts right. And where could it be more important than with our illustrious McKendree bell? I found several inconsistencies with the dates that we need to clear up."

Dane and Joe shared a satisfied look and then turned to smile smugly at Alyssa who was the author of that section. No doubt they would rub it in later. Hiding a smile, Merrideth opened the manuscript to the first date in question.

When Professor King had given her charge of the freshmen, he had stressed that she was to let them do the work and not to give in to the temptation to do it for them. At the time, she had not understood what he meant, but now she did. It would be so much faster to correct their mistakes and be done with it. She would not have to worry about getting the work done on schedule or wrestle with Alyssa at every turn.

But the even bigger temptation was to put her *Beautiful Houses* software to work on the project. She and her friends Abby and John had found the program on her computer sixteen years before. With it they had been able to virtually rewind time, uncovering all manner of intriguing historical details about the people who had lived in her house—details that had never made it into the history books but should have.

The three of them had kept the software a secret ever since because they did not want some unscrupulous person to misuse it. But it would be easy enough for Merrideth to sneak her laptop into the bell tower some night when no one was around and let the software take her back until she got the answers to their questions about the McKendree bell, and anything else they wanted to know about the college's early years. No doubt she could discover many interesting facts to jazz up the freshman reports. As a historian, didn't she owe it to posterity to preserve as much of the college's history as possible?

But every time she was tempted to use the software, she

reminded herself that the students would learn best by doing, not by her handing them the information on a platter. Besides, unless she found substantiation they could not use the information anyway.

She worked with them for over twenty minutes. When she felt confident they knew what needed to be done to get the freshman portion of the project ready for prime time—and that they were working amicably together—she wished them luck and rose from the table. Once she checked out the *Haunting Hardin County* book she could get back to her own work.

Meghan Ashton was manning the circulation desk. And Andrew Heuer was manning *her*. The couple stood next to the filing cabinet lost to the world in a lip-lock. Since they were seniors and Merrideth only taught lower-level history courses, she did not know either of them well, but well enough to know they were good kids.

However, public displays of affection were frowned upon at McKendree, and faculty members were supposed to do their part to remind students about proper decorum and being considerate of their classmates. Most of the time her colleagues turned a blind eye, and so Merrideth did, too. But PDA was getting out of hand, especially since the summer term started. Everywhere she turned someone was getting affectionate.

Or did it only seem that way because she was not in a romantic relationships herself? It was her own fault, of course. She had decided to put dating on hold until she got well established on the faculty. And now that she felt fairly secure in that regard, she was far too busy with her classes to figure out how to get back into the dating game. Where did an introverted, socially stunted, twenty-six-year-old go man-hunting anyway?

Andrew and Meghan's kiss went on and on. She did not want to be a Nazi about it, but if she kept standing there doing nothing, she would look like a pathetic voyeur who got her thrills from vicariously watching other people's romantic interludes. She was about to clear her throat when the library door whooshed open, and Brett Garrison strode in.

Oh, great! Perfect timing.

He smiled when he saw her, and as usual her stomach jumped. Her reaction was even worse than usual because she had not seen him for over three weeks. As a tenured professor, he was not obligated to teach the summer term, and physics and higher math were not on the schedule then anyway, which was why he had left town to spend time with his aunt on her farm.

At least Brett's arrival had caused Andrew and Meghan to finally snap out of it. But now they watched his arrival with curiosity, as did the freshman committee members. Everyone on campus seemed to take an inordinate interest in her and Brett. They were the youngest professors on campus, and the only unmarried ones, so it was natural, she supposed, that everyone tended to watch their every move. And Brett's obvious attention to her from the first day she had arrived on campus had not helped things at all. He was majorly attractive and completely out of her league, not that he seemed to realize it. But even if he were suitable for her, she had known, even before her mentor Marla White had lectured her on the subject, that dating Brett Garrison would be a stupendously bad career move, especially in a college the size of McKendree.

Now she needed to escape the library before he reached her and caused any more rumors to fly. She turned to leave.

"Wait, Doctor Randall," Meghan said. "I have to check that book out to you."

"Right." Merrideth handed her the book, and Meghan scanned its bar code into the system.

It only took her a second, and the moment she was done, Merrideth grabbed the book, put her head down, and aimed for the door like a wide receiver running for the end zone. And bumped into Brett.

"Whoa, Nelly," Brett said, grabbing her arm in support.

"That's what you get for sneaking up behind me. And did you just allude to me as a horse?"

"Sneaking up on you? You nearly knocked me down." He made no move to turn loose of her arm. Speaking of PDA! Merrideth stared at the offending hand until he removed it and put it into the pocket of his tan chinos.

"I would never, ever compare you to a horse," he said, lowering his voice to a library-appropriate whisper that made her shiver. "Cross my heart." His heart along with the rest of his upper half was clad in a crisp white shirt, open at his tanned neck. His green eyes gleamed at her with interest. "I heard you were in here and thought I'd walk you to your classroom."

"Why not just put an engagement announcement in the school paper?" she whispered desperately.

"Don't be ridiculous."

She tipped her head toward their audience.

After a glance at the students staring at them he added, "I see what you mean. Okay, let's get out of here," he whispered out of the side of his mouth. "You leave first and I'll stay here and pretend I'm reading up on..." He pulled a random book from the nearest shelf and glanced at the title. "...*Primate Sociology*. Then, I'll slip out when no one's looking and meet you in the quad at 10:45." He looked down at his wrist. "We'd better synchronize our watches."

"Don't be annoying."

He grinned annoyingly. "No, I suppose that would be a little too dramatic. The secret is to play this casually." He sauntered over to the circulation desk and leaned nonchalantly against it. She knew she should just leave the library, but, like a moth to a flame, she followed him there.

"Can I help you with something, Doctor Garrison?" Meghan said it in a perfectly normal, even professional tone of voice, but beside her Andrew wore a peeved expression. Everyone knew that half the girls on campus had a crush on Doctor Garrison. Like Indiana Jones, he often had to wade through throngs of admirers waiting outside his classroom.

"No thank you, Miss Ashton. I'm just here to tell Doctor Randall an amusing anecdote about my sojourn in the country."

Merrideth followed his lead. "So how's your Aunt Nelda's latest project coming?"

"She converted half her barn into a craft workshop last year," Brett explained to the students. "And this year she turned her attention to the other half, which is now a completely refurbished abode for the menagerie she's collecting."

"Professor Garrison is being modest," Merrideth said. "He did the remodeling."

"Really?" Dane said from the table. The tone of his voice indicated that his hero-worship was still in full force. He got up and came to the counter.

"And did you know that besides her crafts and hand-crafted jewelry, his aunt is the famous poet N.A. Garrison?" Merrideth said.

"Really?" Meghan said. "I love her work."

"Sorry, it's too deep for me," Andrew said.

Brett grinned. "Me too, but don't quote me on that. Even if you're not into her ambiguous modern stuff, I'm sure you'd like her latest poem, *An Ode to Free-Range Chickens*. It's a hoot."

"Chickens now, too?" Merrideth said.

"Yes, but Lilliput and Miniscule are still the main attraction at Rancho Garrison. And that leads me back to *my* latest creative endeavor." He scrolled through the photos on his phone and then held it for her to see. "Voila! Behold their new patio."

"Those are goats, Doctor Garrison," Dane said.

"Yes, they are, Dane. Pygmy goats, to be exact."

"And you made them a brick patio?"

"Naturally. Lilli and Mini dislike getting their hooves wet. Or so Aunt Nelda tells me."

Dane laughed. "I never figured you'd have an aunt named Nelda, Doctor Garrison. Much less goats named Lilli and Mini—or anything else for that matter."

Merrideth grinned at Dane. "Me neither."

Alyssa, who had left her important duties as chairperson to come over, took a quick look at the photo and then disguised her curiosity by pretending to be interested in a rack of flyers on the counter. Joe still slumped in his chair at the table half asleep, but Merrideth knew nothing escaped him.

"That looks like a speaker on the side of their barn," Andrew said, leaning in for a closer look.

"Oh it is," Brett said. "Pygmy goats also dislike sudden loud noises."

"Fourth of July coming up," Joe mumbled from the table.

"Give the sleeping man fifty points," Brett said. "Last year, Odious Ogle—that's my Aunt Nelda's horrible neighbor—set off so many firecrackers her ears are still ringing. She didn't want Lilli and Mini to be traumatized for life. Who knows what goats with PTSD would do?"

"How are speakers supposed to help?" Alyssa said.

"We'll be piping in music to calm the goats. At least take their minds off the racket."

"Sounds like a fun way to celebrate the Fourth," Merrideth said, grinning.

"You should come," Brett said.

And just like that the students were back to watching for hints of a romance between them. The invitation had been light and friendly, but she knew full well that beneath his breezy jokes he was a determined man. Sometimes she forgot how dangerous he was. He wanted things from her—emotional things—that she was not prepared to give him.

He seemed to realize he had blown it. "Well, anyway, Doctor Randall, I just thought you'd find my goat story amusing. Walk me to my car, will you? We need to discuss the faculty meeting next week."

As far as she knew there was no earthly reason they needed to discuss the faculty meeting, so she gave him points for trying to salvage the situation.

Not looking to see how the students took that, Merrideth followed him to the door and out onto the quad, which was thankfully still mostly empty. They sat down at a patio table outside Ames Hall. The purple and white umbrella overhead gave them just the right degree of shade for a summer morning.

She set the book on the table. Brett picked it up and studied the title. "What's so special about this?"

"What makes you think it is?"

"Well, you seemed bent on sneaking away without checking it out."

She thought it best to ignore his question. "You might like it. There's a section in it about 18th-century piracy on the Ohio River that has me intrigued. I may do more research on the subject so I can add that to my History of Southern Illinois class."

"The kids would love it, I'm sure. But don't forget your primary purpose in life is to churn out academic papers. Write a journal article and it'll keep old Publish-or-Perish Peterson off your back for a while."

"Oh, I plan to. Kill two birds and all that. Actually, three birds, because anything I find will also go into my book."

"You're writing a book?"

"I was hoping to write a whole series of them about Southern Illinois. But I'm having trouble finding a publisher interested in even the first book. So far, the ones who have bothered to respond to my queries have only sent form letters with no explanation of why they were rejecting the project."

"I guess you have to have some shtick to catch their attention."

"My angle will be to focus more on the common people of the time—their motivations, problems, stuff like that—and not so much on the dry facts and figures. Make history really come alive for people."

"That would be great, Merri. I hope you find a publisher."

"I'm not waiting around for one to give me permission to begin it. I've already started writing about Fort Piggot—your Garretson ancestors, too. And the Cherokee Trail of Tears."

"All of those are good topics. If only you could go back in time. Think of all the nitty-gritty details about the common people's day-to-day life you could find for your book. But if I had a time machine, I'd want to go forward in time and see—" He stopped and looked curiously at her. "What's wrong?"

"Nothing." She calmed herself and put on what she hoped was a bland smile. He was just joking around as usual. He couldn't know about *Beautiful Houses*, nor would he find out, if she could help it. He would go wild if he ever found out about a program that defied the laws of physics. And he would never agree to keep such a thing secret.

"I've missed you, Merri. Phone calls just don't cut it."

His comment was a touch too personal to be considered one a mere a friend would make, but she decided to pretend that it was. "Me too. Campus is too quiet. With everyone gone, there's no one around to tell me funny goat stories."

The umbrella fluttered over their heads. In the distance a student played Frisbee with a golden retriever. Brett smiled at her, making the day more beautiful still. "I'll have more pastoral stories from Rancho Garrison," he said. "I'm going back to Aunt Nelda's after this."

"Tell her I said *hi*."

"I will," he said and went back to watching the dog.

Usually Brett seemed content to play it her way. She had placed him firmly in the *Friend* category, and so far he had agreed to remain there, even though he had made it plain that he wanted there to be more between them. His occasional personal comments were undoubtedly intentional and meant to remind her of that fact. Trial balloons, as it were.

It wasn't that Merrideth did not want more, too. She wanted to marry. Someday. A therapist had once told her that she had commitment issues stemming from her father's abandonment.

Maybe it was true. Or maybe she just had not met the right man yet. But as for Brett Garrison, even if he were Prince Charming in the flesh, he did not qualify as long as they were colleagues. She was not about to endanger her career with a campus romance.

Her mother despaired that she would ever get married. Just yesterday, she had called to tell Merrideth that her twenty-seventh birthday was in thirteen days—as if she needed the reminder—and to ask her why she still had not managed to "snag a man." Merrideth had no illusions that her mother was overly concerned for her happiness. Her main reason for wanting her married was so she could leave her daughter's security to a husband and expend even less energy thinking about her welfare than she now did. She would have been relieved to know of Brett's interest—if she had chosen to tell her of his existence.

She turned to say something about the unusually mild weather they were having and was surprised to see that Brett's perennially pleasant expression was gone. She had never seen him look sad before, and she found that she did not like it at all. Perhaps she had come to rely on his cheerfulness just a little too much.

"What's wrong?" she said.

"I don't know."

"You don't know why you're sad?"

A little smile quirked his lips and was gone again. "I don't know what's wrong with Aunt Nelda. I've never known her to be so … needy. When I first got to her place three weeks ago, she presented me with a mile-long list of things she wanted me to do. And she keeps adding more things to it every day."

"That isn't so unusual, surely. You always do things for her."

"But not build patios for goats, for crying out loud. And she's cranky, too."

"Now *that* is unusual." Brett's aunt was one of the nicest women she had ever met, even if she was an inveterate matchmaker. Or at least with her nephew, she was.

"Anyway, I've got to get back and see what's next on her list—a bathroom addition to the chicken house, an in-ground swimming pool for the cats. Who knows?"

Merrideth laughed. "And I've got to get back to teaching."

"Come for a visit, Merri. You're sure to be amazed by all the improvements."

"We'll see. Have fun."

They rose from the table and he gave her a long look. "You, too. Talk to you soon."

She watched him stride across the quad toward the faculty parking lot. The sun glinted off his black hair and made his shirt glow radiantly white.

In answer to his unvoiced question, yes, she had missed him, too. She had missed him entirely too much during the past three weeks. And she knew that the invitation to come visit him would play in her head in the coming days, tempting her to be foolish.

CHAPTER 2

The DVD was cued up, the popcorn was made, and icy cold bottles of carbonated grape juice—a treat Abby allowed Lauren and Natalie only on rare occasions—stood ready on Merrideth's counter top. Furthermore, the girls' Cinderella tent was erected next to Merrideth's bed, ready for when the movie was over or the girls conked out, whichever occurred first.

Merrideth got three red cereal bowls out of her cabinet. "Lauren, can you pour the popcorn into these while I get the tray?"

"Sure."

Merrideth smiled at her serious look. She was a conscientious worker, whether it was doing her third-grade homework or pouring microwave popcorn into bowls. Merrideth had every confidence that the amount each of them received would be scrupulously equal, almost down to the kernel.

"I want to help, too, Aunt Mewwi," Natalie said. She was six now and her adorable lisp had disappeared for everything but the name she called her. As far as Merrideth was concerned, she hoped that never went away. "How about you get the napkins, Bug?"

Affection for the girls sometimes nearly overwhelmed her. She was only their honorary aunt, but at the rate she was going, they were probably the closest she would ever get to having children of her own. Abby had finally given up trying to pay her for babysitting them when Merrideth had told her she should pay her and John for letting her be a part of their family.

"Okay, movie time!" Merrideth picked up the tray and headed for the living room. When they were settled on her lumpy couch, a girl on either side of her, she aimed the remote at the TV and then paused. "If you're sure you want to watch this. We could always do something more kid-appropriate. We haven't watched *Frozen* yet this month."

"That's because it's only the first day of July," Lauren said reasonably. "Animated movies are okay, but we like old-people movies, too, Aunt Merri."

"You're so kind. What about you, Natalie? Last chance to vote."

"You said it's about pirates in the olden days?"

"It is. Among other things."

"Then I want to see it."

"Okay, then so be it." She clicked the remote and the opening credits of *How the West Was Won* began. As Lauren had said, it was definitely an old-people movie. By the time Merrideth was born, it had already been around for over twenty-five years. With its all-star cast and narration by Spencer Tracy it was a movie classic, and it was about time she got around to watching it. When she had asked for it at the video store the clerk had looked dubiously at the girls and tried to talk her into getting a children's movie instead. The woman obviously didn't know the Bugs.

They had a healthy curiosity for learning about any subject that came up, and a special fondness for history that John said they inherited from her. Ha Ha. Whatever the reason, Lauren and Natalie were getting to be as obsessed with finding out about "the olden days" as she was herself. It made her proud.

The movie began and they were introduced to the Prescott family who were leaving their home in New York, bound for the Western frontier, which in 1800, Spencer Tracy explained, was the Illinois Country. The major highway west was the Ohio River, a much easier and faster mode of travel than overland. Thousands of pioneers like the Prescotts came down the Ohio on flatboats loaded with everything they owned. They had to contend with storms, river currents, and sand bars. If they went ashore, there were Indians, bears, and cougars to worry about. But there was another danger they had not counted on—pirates. And the most dangerous stretch of the river was at Illinois' southern border with Kentucky.

Merrideth paused the movie. "Okay, girls, we're getting to the pirate part. If you get too scared, just close your eyes."

Lauren gave her a long-suffering look. Natalie said, "Okay," and snuggled closer to Merrideth's right side.

As Joe Diego had said, the moviemakers had not given the pirates the stereotypical trappings of the trade. The pirate leader was played by Walter Brennan, and he and his gang used a large cave as their base of operations. From there they had a good view of the river and could spot prey coming for miles. As for the Prescott family, a hero played by Jimmy Stewart rescued them from the clutches of the evil pirates and together they continued on their way west.

"When can we see the pirates?" Natalie said.

Merrideth paused the movie again and pointed to Walter Brennan's image frozen on the screen. "We already did, sweetie. See? That man is one."

"He looks too mean."

"Well, pirates *are* mean, Bug."

"Not BBS pirates."

"She means VBS," Lauren explained. "That stands for Vacation Bible School."

"That's what I said," Natalie protested. "BBS. At my friend Cynthia's church they're having a Pete-the-Pirate BBS this year. And we're going to go."

"If Mom lets us," Lauren said.

Merrideth felt her eyes bulge. "They're having a pirate-themed VBS? For impressionable little kids? That's horrible!" Realizing she had just insulted their friend's church, she shut her mouth. "I'm sorry. I shouldn't have said that."

"Don't worry. Mom got mad about it, too," Lauren said. "She doesn't care for pirates much either."

"That's because pirates were murders, thieves, and ra—. They were very bad people. They didn't sing songs about Jesus, okay?"

"Some pirates do, Aunt Mewwi," Natalie said. "I know 'cause Cynthia's got the Pete-the-Pirate CD. Can we watch the rest of the movie now?"

Merrideth sighed. "Okay, Bug." She un-paused the DVD, and the saga of the Prescott family resumed as they left the river and continued westward overland via covered wagon.

The girls seemed to enjoy the movie, but Merrideth had trouble getting back into it. She was stuck thinking about the pirates. The Hollywood movie producers of 1963 had not glorified them, as more recent ones had Johnny Depp and his a band of Caribbean pirates. But the movie had not really answered Dane's question about logistics. If the pioneers were out in the middle of the river, and the pirates hid in the cave, how had they gotten their greedy hands on the booty? Was the cave hideout even real or just a fictitious invention of the screenwriter?

Lauren and Natalie began to wilt after the first hour. By the end of hour two of the three-and-a-half-hour movie, they had fallen asleep, slumped like rag dolls on either side of her. She woke the girls and guided them first to the bathroom to brush their teeth and then to their Cinderella tent. She crawled in after the girls and kissed them good night.

"I'm sorry. I should have rented a better movie. Next time we'll get something for kids."

"I guess we better," Lauren said. "That was really long."

"What's for breakfast, Aunt Mewwi?"

"If you're very good, I'll feed you gruel. Maybe a few crusts of stale bread if I'm feeling generous."

Natalie giggled sleepily and turned over on her side.

"Good night, Bugs." Merrideth blew them more kisses and backed out of the tent. When she got to the door, she heard Lauren ask what gruel was.

"It's what witches give to children lost in the woods," Natalie explained.

"Aunt Merrideth wouldn't ever give us that," Lauren said indignantly.

"It's a joke," Natalie said.

"Oh, I get it," Lauren said with a yawn.

Merrideth stifled a laugh. Lauren was the older of the two sisters and her test scores were off the charts, especially in math, but she was still more literal in her thinking than Natalie.

Still smiling, Merrideth retrieved the library book she had found that morning and went back to the couch to read the short section in it about the river pirates. It did not satisfy her curiosity. She set the book aside on the end table and went to get her laptop.

A quick Google search told her that the cave was real, not a product of the movie scriptwriter's imagination. It was called Cave-in-Rock and was located two miles from a town of the same name in Hardin County. The cave was currently owned by the state of Illinois and overseen by Cave-in-Rock State Park. Stories about it had been around for over three hundred years. In the late 1600s, French explorers made vague mention of the cave. Then in 1766, a Philadelphia merchant named John Jennings, who saw it when he was taking trade goods to Fort de Chartres, wrote about it, giving a detailed description, including evidence that indicated Indians had used the cave in the distant past.

The first reported criminal use of the cave was in 1796. Through the years afterward it became the headquarters for a variety of crooks, counterfeiters, horse thieves, prostitutes, and murderous pirates. The books were full of lurid stories. The accounts were contradictory and, like the movie, frustratingly vague about the details. One website was more scholarly and purported to tell the real truth of the pirates of Cave-in-Rock, but even so, she came to the disappointing conclusion that there was no way to separate the legends from the truth or get a clear picture of what had gone on there.

It was only a little after ten o'clock, but she should get to bed, too. The girls were notoriously early risers, and she wanted to surprise them with blueberry pancakes. She started to shut the laptop, but then a thought percolated to the top of her brain. Since the cave had been used for human habitation surely it would count as a house, at least for the purposes of *Beautiful Houses*. The software only went into what she called *miracle mode* if run in an old house, one with enough history—or *soul* as Mrs. Arnold had called it back in the day. If the cave qualified, she could get a first-hand look at the pirates.

She dug in her pocket for her phone and called Abby.

"Hi, Merri," Abby said. "How are the girls?"

"Fine. They're sleeping like babies. How would you like to go on a pirate adventure with me? If we left first thing after breakfast, we could be there by nine or ten."

"You did get the right grape beverage, didn't you? The non-alcoholic, no-sugar-added kind?"

Merrideth laughed. "Oops. That must be why Lauren and Natalie are sleeping so soundly."

Merrideth explained why she had developed a sudden urge to research the river pirates and her plan for satisfying her curiosity. She ended with, "I could publish a journal paper about the pirate cave and also put it into my book."

"It sounds fascinating and I'd love to go, Merri. But I don't

17

have anyone to watch the girls. John's in the middle of a big trial, and I have to—"

"Maybe it's time we took them time-surfing. Natalie would get that stupid Pete the Pirate out of her head quick enough."

"She told you about that, did she? I'm sure the man means well, but come on! Christian pirates?"

"So let's take the Bugs on a real pirate adventure."

"They're too young, Merri. John and I have talked about it. Natalie, especially, would never be able to keep the program a secret. Besides, we want them to experience the joy of learning the good old-fashioned way first."

"You're right, of course. I'll let you know what I find out."

"I don't think it's a good idea for you to going exploring a cave alone. Wait and John and I will go with you another time."

"It can't be too dangerous. After all, Cave-in-Rock is a tourist destination. And I won't have another four-day weekend off until I don't know when. Forever, I think."

"Why don't you ask Brett to go with you?"

"You're kidding, right? How do you think he'd interpret it if I asked him to spend the weekend with me? Out of town. In a motel."

"He would understand perfectly well that you were just asking as a friend."

"I doubt there's a man alive who would take such an invitation that way. And I'm surprised you'd suggest something that had even the merest whiff of impropriety. I can only imagine the wagging tongues around McKendree if—when—they heard."

"I wouldn't have suggested it with just any guy, but I have full confidence in him. In the jargon of education, Brett Garrison meets and exceeds standards."

"Glad you approve of him, my meddlesome friend, but how could I get any work done without him seeing the software? The moment he did, he'd call a press conference and announce *Beautiful Houses* to the world."

"I doubt that he would be so rash."

"Maybe, maybe not, but I don't want to risk it."

"I'm telling you right now John's going to be worried sick about you."

"John's turning into an old fuddy-duddy. Remind him that I'm a big girl now."

CHAPTER 3

The town of Cave-in-Rock was tiny. Only 346 people currently called it home. According to her research, it had been settled in 1816 during the height of the area's outlaw period, the majority of its founding citizens on the run from the law in Kentucky and Virginia. For a town with such a history, it looked pretty tame. Merrideth did not see a single bar, but did pass two small cafes and three of the five churches listed on the Hardin County website. A vintage false-front building labeled River Front Opry House caught her eye, and she wondered if there would be live music while she was in town.

It was a quarter to eleven when she reached Park Street. She was to turn there and drive two more miles to the state park. But she did not turn, because straight ahead was the Ohio River, the morning sun reflecting off its surface. Five or six cars were lined up heading straight for the river like lemmings determined to dive in. Then she saw a sign and realized they were waiting for the ferry to take them across to Kentucky.

It called to mind another ferry further up the Ohio at another small river town called Golconda. She had watched—courtesy of her software—as White Dove and thousands of other Cherokee used it to cross from Kentucky into Illinois in the dead of winter. How the people had suffered! It had indeed been a Trail of Tears.

But that had been in 1838. Golconda's ferry was long gone, and who knew how long Cave-in-Rock's would continue to operate? Maybe she should make the trip across the Ohio River while she was in town. It was bound to be a more pleasant experience than

White Dove's family had.

A car came up behind hers, startling her out of her reverie. She turned onto Park Street and drove on to the lodge. Its exterior was a nice mix of stone and brown siding. Inside, the lobby was paneled in knotty pine. A family was checking in. The desk clerk was a pretty middle-aged woman in a bright pink smock. She looked up and smiled at Merrideth and then went back to talking to a man at the counter. The man's wife, with a sleepy toddler on one shoulder and a huge diaper bag on the other, was riding herd on two boys who were determined to put their hands on everything in the room, including fragile items on the gift shop shelves in the corner of the lobby. A preschooler in glasses, cowboy boots, and drooping red shorts followed the mother, tugging on the diaper bag and asking when they were going to see the pirates.

It looked like it was going to be a while before the clerk got to her, so Merrideth set her overnight bag down and went to look at two glass display cases that hung on the walls. The first case held a collection of minerals—coal, galena, and fluorite crystals in purple and golden yellow. A sign informed her that fluorite was the state mineral, which she vaguely remembered from school. It went on to explain fluorite's importance in making steel, pottery, optics, and plastics, which she had not known, and that Illinois was the primary producer of fluorite in the United States, the largest deposits being in Cave-in-Rock and nearby Rosiclare.

One of the boys went racing by to show his dad a one-eyed pirate action figure he "needed" to buy. Sidestepping him, Merrideth crossed the room to see what the other display case held.

Her pulse picked up when she saw that it contained historical artifacts recovered from the cave. There was an assortment of arrow heads, and a small squatting human figure carved of stone, believed to be a religious icon belonging to one of the Mississippian Mound Builders who had once visited the cave. Next to it was a rusty iron mold for making counterfeit coins. A placard explained that the lead and silver necessary to make them had been procured at the nearby Saline River. There was a tarnished silver cup, looking completely out of place, its ornately engraved garlands of stylized flowers and leaves making it entirely too fancy to actually drink tea from. It was probably a gift meant to be displayed on a mantel or shelf. And last of all was an antique, long-barreled pistol that was not actually from the cave, as its label was careful to point out, but the type of weapon the pirates might have used during that time period.

"May I help you?"

Merrideth turned and saw that the family had gone while she was lost in thought. The smiling desk clerk was ready for her. On her pink smock she wore a button that read *Official Member: Zombie Defense League.* Next to it was a plain brass tag indicating that her name was Shirley.

Merrideth returned the woman's smile. "I'd like a room for tonight, please. Maybe tomorrow, too."

"Why sure, honey. Would you like a cabin or a room in the lodge?"

"A room, I guess."

She signed the credit card slip, and the woman handed her an old-fashioned brass key. "Thank you, Ms. Randall. Go through that doorway. The restaurant is on the right. On down the hall are the rooms. Yours will be on the left. I hope you enjoy your stay."

"Thanks. I can't wait to see the cave."

"I'm sure you'll find it fascinating. Everyone does."

She found the room easily and set her things down beside the bed. The room was paneled in the same dark knotty pine as the lobby, which probably made it appear smaller than it actually was. But the bed was comfortable and the bathroom was immaculately clean.

What she thought at first was a picture window turned out to be a sliding patio door leading to a little deck. The view from it was equal parts spectacular and boringly utilitarian. On the right were the lodge's air-conditioning units and a section of the parking lot. But on the left was a portion of the well-kept park and beyond that the luxuriant growth of trees and shrubbery that Nature tended. Through the trees she caught a sliver of the river in the distance.

Retrieving her small lightweight purse and not-so-lightweight backpack, which she rarely let out of her sight because it contained her laptop and other time-surfing equipment, she stepped out into the hall, locked the door behind herself, pocketed the key, and went in search of the cave.

In the lobby, Shirley was busy checking in another family, so Merrideth stepped out onto the front portico and looked for a sign to indicate how one got to the cave. The day was bright without being oppressively hot, and a gentle wind stirred the leaves and made the state and national flags flutter against the flagpole. Several crepe myrtles were in bloom. Their deep red blossoms paired with the green grass gave the landscape a Christmas-in-July color scheme.

Less flashy, but of more interest to her, was a state-park-brown sign with a yellow arrow and the word *CAVE*. The sign was posted at the junction of the front sidewalk and a bark path that led past the guest cabins and disappeared into the deep green shadows of the trees beyond. A pleasant sense of anticipation filled her as she started down it.

At the first cabin, the little boy with the glasses and cowboy boots solemnly watched her approach. His red shorts were still askew, but he was shirtless now. Behind him the cabin door stood open, and the toddler of the family was trying to get himself over the mountainous obstacle of the threshold to follow his big brother outside. The mom appeared at the door and scooped him up. "Oh, no you don't, buddy." She smiled distractedly when she saw Merrideth and took him inside, leaving the door open.

Merrideth gave the little cowboy a wave.

He waved back. "I got wings."

She looked closer and saw that he had Scotch-taped feathers to his shoulders. He shrugged first one shoulder and then the other to emphasize the fact.

"They're real, too."

"I like them," Merrideth said, hiding a smile and wondering which role he was currently playing—cowboy, Indian, eagle, or combination thereof. "Listen, you're not going to jump off something, are you? You know you can't really fly."

"I might." Then he grinned and she was reassured that he was only pretending.

"Okay, happy flying."

She waved again and went on her way down the path. When she got to the end of the manicured lawn, the chipped bark came to an end, replaced by concrete steps leading steeply down through the trees. After a short distance, the green vegetation gave way to a wall of limestone that reared up alongside the path. The cave couldn't be much farther.

But when she came around a curve, the path suddenly disappeared into the muddy Ohio River. She could not tell how deep the water was, and she was not about to risk her life—or her computer's—to find out. Twenty feet away a set of wooden stairs with sturdy guard rails rose out of the water and continued on around the rocky bluff where presumably the cave entrance was. So close and yet so far. She felt like kicking something.

Merrideth retraced her steps and came, huffing and puffing, to the upper level. A khaki-clad park worker carrying a black garbage bag and a litter spear was working near the path. He was white-haired and thin, his back crooked, either from age or from years of stooping to pick up other people's trash.

"Excuse me, sir. Can you tell me about the cave?"

He did not look up, and she wondered if he was deaf. Then she saw the cords dangling from his ears. She walked into his line of sight. He startled and then pulled out his ear buds.

"Sorry," he said, smiling sheepishly. "Listening to an audio book. What can I do for you, Miss?"

"The path to the cave is under water, and I was wondering—"

"Sorry about that. All those rains up north last week have caught up with us."

"No need to apologize for the weather."

"We do try to keep the tourists happy," he replied with a grin. "But we haven't yet come up with a way to control the rain. But if you wait a while, the water will go down. The Ohio's a mercurial beast. The water level changes by the hour."

"Oh, I hope it goes down. I'd like to get a first-hand look at the cave. I teach history up at McKendree College and thought my students might enjoy learning about the pirates."

"Well, Miss, as my daddy always used to say, there's more than one way to skin a cat. While you're waiting for the water to go down, you could take the ferry across the river and get a look at the cave that way. The ferry runs 'til 9:30. It's free and all."

"Thanks. I'll take your advice. And let you get back to your work. And your book."

"I must admit I'm anxious to. It's a cowboy shoot 'em up, and the sheriff is just about to get the horse-thievin' outlaws cornered in the canyon. But, Miss?" His face turned serious. "When you go to the ferry, stay in your car. See, there's something they should have told you up at the desk. Hellhound Homecoming is this weekend."

He seemed to think she should be familiar with the event. When he saw that she wasn't, he said, "Hellhound—you know, the rock band."

"Sorry, I've never heard of them."

He grinned. "They'd be shocked to hear you say that. But in my opinion, you're not missing much. They own a campground just north of town and have a huge festival there every summer. They rent it out to other groups when they're not around raisin' Cain." He looked at his watch. "Speaking of which, the Road Hogs should be gettin' here any time now."

"I'm sorry. I don't know them either."

"It's a motorcycle club. They crash the Hellhound party every year. And a decent woman, 'specially a pretty young one like you, shouldn't be out and about alone."

She must have looked dubious, because his expression became resolute. "Really. Be careful, Miss. You don't even want to know what goes on there. You might say they're our modern-day outlaws of Cave-in-Rock."

"Thanks, but don't worry. I have absolutely no intention of going to Hellhound Homecoming. All I'm interested in is the cave."

"Good. Have fun, then."

The ferry ride *was* fun, once the panic of driving her car onto a floating deck subsided. Three other cars made the trip to Kentucky with her, their drivers seemingly blasé about the experience.

Once they pulled away from the shore, the bluffs on the Illinois side of the river became visible, and shortly thereafter, the cave came into view. Its mouth was an almost perfect ellipse, which according to the information she had read was fifty-five feet wide at the base and some thirty feet high. It was set in a massive block of limestone over ninety feet tall. There were trees on top of the bluffs, and a few others managed to survive on the stony riverbank at its feet.

It didn't take long to reach the Kentucky shore. There was not anything of interest within sight, unless you counted cornfields, and she didn't, so she stayed on the ferry and waited for the return trip to Illinois. Once they docked, the ferryman opened the gate, and she drove off the ramp onto the street. At the stop sign she waited as three motorcyclists slowly rode by. So the bikers had arrived.

The three men were clean-shaven and quite normal-looking. The first one wore a leather jacket and chaps. When he passed through the intersection, she saw that the back of his jacket was decorated with a banner reading *Road Hogs* and beneath that, a wild boar with beady eyes and blood-tipped tusks. The emblem on the second man's leather jacket was an American eagle with its wings outstretched to show off flag-like feathers of red, white, and blue. She was so struck with the beauty of it that she didn't see what, if anything, was on the third biker's jacket.

Maybe the men were military veterans. Didn't a lot of them ride bikes? In any case, they did not look too scary to her.

In the next block someone had erected a cheery yellow pavilion while she was gone. A banner saying *Welcome Hellhounds & Road Hogs* spanned the front, and two or three people sat at a table with bottled water and stacks of books. They obviously were not afraid of the big, bad bikers either.

The old man at the park was probably one of those straight-laced types that panicked at the sight of motorcycles and leather jackets.

She got back to the lodge just in time to order a sandwich before the restaurant closed for the afternoon. She ate it quickly and then hurried back down the trail to see if the river was ready to cooperate with her.

It was. When she reached the bottom she saw that the water had indeed receded. The concrete steps were a little slippery, although someone had scraped most of the mud from them. She jogged up the wooden staircase and rounded the curve of the bluff. And there was the cave. Up close, it was so much more impressive than from her vantage point on the ferry.

The cave's gaping mouth let in an abundance of light. The interior did not look anything like the spooky meandering cave in the movie. She huffed in annoyance. Why did they include the cave at all if they were not going to present it accurately?

The real cave was a single room approximately forty feet wide by one hundred and sixty feet deep. The article she had read said it had the equivalent square footage of about three average three-bedroom homes. By that unit of measurement, the cave was large enough to comfortably house at least fifteen people. But it was not so large that it would be creepy for its occupants. As Goldilocks would have said, it was just right.

A hole in the ceiling formed a natural skylight. It must have made a handy chimney for campfire smoke back in the day. It also provided natural ventilation, which explained why the air was fairly fresh with only a faint smell of mold. There were no stalactites nor stalagmites to watch out for, and the floor was relatively level. All in all, it was a very nice cave. No wonder so many people had sheltered there through the years.

Unfortunately, many of them had felt the need to let the world know they had been there by defacing the cave's walls with graffiti. She had read that the earliest names carved there purported to date from the late 1790s. More recent vandals had used felt-tipped markers and included crude limericks to go along with their signatures. If she had time she would try to sort through all that to find some of the oldest ones.

But first things first. She slipped off her backpack, took out her laptop, and sat on a stone ledge that was conveniently chair height. After the computer booted up, she clicked on the *Beautiful Houses* icon, and the program began to load. The moment of truth had arrived. If her theory about the cave proved true—that it would count as a human dwelling just as any house of wood or brick—the software would do its thing. And she would be able to see the cave's pirate occupants and watch their history unfold. If she were wrong—well, then she would have to be content that she'd had an interesting road trip and the chance to see the infamous cave in person.

Finally it finished loading, and the familiar logo filled the screen, its banner inviting the viewer to "Take a Virtual Tour" emblazoned across the top. A series of featured homes began scrolling past. An Elizabethan manor house near London came into view and after a few seconds was replaced by a house of turquoise mirrored glass located south of Los Angeles. She scrolled through dozens of other dwellings. Not a single one was a cave. She sighed. Well, it had definitely been worth a try.

The sound of voices came to her. The little cowboy and his family stood in the cave entrance. After a moment of stunned wonder, the boys came whooping into the cave.

The cowboy wore a shirt now and Merrideth smiled, wondering if his "wings" were still in place beneath it. He had added an Indian headdress to his ensemble. It was made from a brown grocery bag, the feathers brightly colored with markers, and made her think of Lauren and Natalie's craft projects.

The dad, carrying the toddler, hurried after his other three boys. "Be careful, Sherman. Your boots will be slippery on the rocks."

The mom came over to where Merrideth sat. "Sherman insisted on wearing his cowboy boots. I don't think he's had them off more than an hour since his birthday." She hoisted her diaper bag and extended a hand to Merrideth. "I saw you at the lodge. I'm Brenda, and that's my husband Keith with our four wild things Shawn, Shane, Sherman, and Shield." With each boy's name she held a hand to show their relative heights.

"I'm Merrideth. Looks like they're really into caves."

"They're into everything, literally and figuratively," Brenda said, smiling. "We're homeschooling the boys and always try to hit as many educational spots as we can wherever we go. We're on our way to my little sister's wedding in Nashville."

On the other side of the cave, the father was telling the boys something about counterfeiters. They did not appear to be listening. Instead, they seemed to prefer a more kinesthetic approach to learning. Like little monkeys, they were running their hands over and climbing onto every geological features of the cave they could reach.

Voices came Merrideth's computer speakers and she jerked in surprise.

The cave! It was there on the screen. Four or five people sat around a campfire eating. They were discussing something about boats—flatboats. At the bottom of her screen, the time counter indicated the year was 1780. The program was definitely working. She smiled in satisfaction. The fact that it didn't require an actual, traditional house in which to work could open up all sorts of possibilities for future research.

"Are them pirates?"

Merrideth jumped. The little cowboy had somehow made it across the cave without her noticing and stood behind her, studying the computer screen.

"*Those*, Sherman," Brenda corrected. "Are *those* pirates?"

"No," Merrideth said, closing the laptop. "Just a website about people camping out in caves."

"That must be some computer you have there," Brenda said. "How do you ever manage to get a Wi-Fi signal this far from the lodge?"

Across the cave, one of the boys fell and began to wail. The father, still juggling the toddler, helped him to his feet. "Brenda, we've got to get this knee cleaned up and bandaged."

The woman hurried over to her family before Merrideth could come up with something plausible that didn't involve telling her about the nifty little app that piggy-backed off other people's bandwidth half a county away. Or about the military-grade battery she had found so that the energy-sucking *Beautiful Houses* program could run for hours on end. The family left amidst a flurry of cranky recriminations, soothing explanations, and Sherman's plaintive, "But we didn't get to see the pirates."

Merrideth waited a couple of minutes to make sure they were gone and then re-opened the laptop. Yes, the cave and its inhabitants were truly on the screen and not a figment of her imagination.

She zoomed out to see more of the cave. There were more people there than she had first thought. Forty or so men, women and children crowded around several smoky fires. Outside the mouth of the cave rain came down in sheets. They obviously weren't pirates. Probably just travelers taking refuge from the rain. It was difficult to tell what they were saying. Even without interference like the noisy rain, it was always difficult to hear well without going into virtual mode.

She zoomed back in, and the details of the people's clothing and equipment came into sharper focus. And so did their faces. Everyone looked tired, worried, and hungry. Several men were cooking some kind of small game—rabbits or squirrels maybe—on spits over the fires. Women stirred something cooking in iron pots. It didn't look like nearly enough food for that many people.

It was tempting to lock onto one of them and go virtual for a while. It would not take long to find out who they were and where they were bound. But Merrideth had learned long ago to discipline herself to focus on the project at hand. And right now, that was to learn as much about the pirates of Cave-in-Rock as she could, not get sidetracked by other random visitors to the cave.

A man wearing buckskin stepped toward the fire and began to address the group. He looked familiar. She squinted at the screen and then zoomed in on his face.

"Captain Piggot!" Her squawk echoed off the cave walls, and she looked up to make sure no one had come in to hear her outburst. Fortunately, she was still alone.

It was actually Captain James Piggot. She was sure of it. When she was researching Brett's Garretson ancestors, she had learned that the Piggots had played a major role in the Illinois Country. Fort Piggot had been the largest, most fortified of all the forts along the Kaskaskia-Cahokia Trail. Her discovery of its location—with the help of the software—had been a satisfying moment and a feather in her professional cap.

But the Piggots had settled along the Mississippi River, not the Ohio. Perhaps they were on their way there now. But the chances were astronomically low that she would open up *Beautiful Houses* miles away in the cave and find on her screen the exact moment in time when James Piggot had stayed there. Unless her theory about the software program was true: like Google, it "learned" her search habits and then helpfully supplied what it thought she would like to know more about.

How then could she not take the time to see just a little of Captain Piggot's time at the cave? She set the lock on the captain and clicked *Virtual.*

✳✳✳

APRIL 14, 1780

"I know you all are cold and tired. And truth be told, we'll not go to sleep this night with full bellies. But don't lose heart. Providence has provided us with this good cave, and the hunters will have better luck once the rain stops."

"But the Indians, Captain Piggot. What about the Indians?" Jacob Gratz held up a stone hatchet head for all to see. "My boy found this in the back of this *good* cave. They'll be back and murder us while we sleep."

"From the looks of things, this cave hasn't been used for quite a spell," Piggot said. "Maybe not since the olden days. But I've posted six men to stand guard outside the cave, and others down at the boats."

"Sit down, Jacob," Larkin Rutherford said angrily. "And do cease giving the women and children cause for nightmares." Jacob did not obey Larkin's command to sit, but at least he moved away from the fire looking somewhat chastened.

"How much farther, Captain Piggot?" Jesse Gude called out

from across the cave.

"Colonel Clark's map says that from this cave we've got another ninety mile to the confluence. Then it's only five mile down the Mississippi to the site he had in mind for us to build Fort Jefferson."

Jacob Gratz came forward again, belligerence written all over his face. "And how are we going to get the corn planted if we're building a fort?"

Larkin Rutherford glared at him in disgust. "I should think you'd be eager to get walls around you on account of how afeared of the Injuns you are, Gratz."

Piggot gave Rutherford a quelling look and then turned back to the people. "As I already explained plenty of times, Jacob, we'll need every able-bodied man to fell the trees. But after we get the stockade built, the families can get started with the tilling and planting while my militiamen work on the fort—and a cabin for your family, I might add."

Jacob muttered something he did not catch and turned away again. Piggot gritted his teeth and thought how satisfying it would be to go knock the man upside the head. If he hadn't needed him to meet the numbers Colonel Clark insisted on for the mission, he never would have asked the lack-wit to come with them.

Eleanor brought William, Levi, and Jacob and came to stand at his side in a show of support—or more likely to keep him from doing something foolish. As always, his wife calmed his frazzled temper. He squeezed her hand to convey his thanks and then turned to smile encouragingly at the others. "You all just keep thinking on that land you're going to get. Four hundred acres each and so rich you can grow doorknobs if you have a mind to. You'll harvest plenty to supply your families' needs and fulfill your obligation for the militia."

One of the women called out from the rear. "The food's ready, Captain."

"Then let us eat it with gratitude for God's kindness toward us."

::*

THE PRESENT

Merrideth pulled herself out of 1780 and back to the present. It always took a few minutes to shake off the disorientation and emotional overload that came whenever she used virtual mode. Sometimes she had difficulty figuring out which were her own thoughts and emotions and which were those of the people she had encountered. She had picked up on the captain's weariness and worry because she had been locked onto him. But several others standing nearby, especially his wife, had oozed enough fear that she had picked that up as well.

After a moment, it sank in that the Mrs. Piggot on her screen was not the same wife she had seen at Fort Piggot in 1788. The captain's common-law wife Frances Ballew had been made of sterner stuff than this Eleanor. Merrideth had watched Frances preparing to do frontier surgery on a man who had been scalped and left for dead.

But that was in the future. She had not realized that Captain Piggot was involved with the Fort Jefferson project. George Rogers Clark had ordered it to be built at the confluence of the Mississippi and Ohio Rivers. It was a strategic location, to be sure, but the environment had not been hospitable to the settlers. After only a couple of years, the fort was abandoned due to sickness, Indian attacks, and a series of other catastrophes.

But Captain Piggot did not know that yet. Now he was trying to encourage his tired, cold people, not knowing that very soon the wife at his side would be gone. By the time Captain Piggot left Fort Jefferson and moved up into the Illinois Country he probably would not be thinking God so kind.

If she followed Piggot and his people, she would be able learn a lot more about Fort Jefferson than historians currently knew. Even more interesting would be to go back farther in time to see the Indians who had left the artifact that Jacob Gratz' boy had found in the back of the cave. Perhaps it had belonged to one of the Mississippian Mound Builders who had once lived throughout the whole Mississippi River Valley. How amazing it would be to finally discover the purpose of their mounds and how they built them.

Talk about a good journal article!

So many intellectual trails to follow. So little time. Merrideth sighed. It was time to say goodbye to Captain Piggot and get to work finding the pirates. She would have to go forward in time another fifteen years or so, when westward migration was in full swing and the pirates were there ready to prey on the settlers. She typed the year *1797* into the date box. The image on her computer screen scrambled into incomprehensible pixels and then became a racing data stream.

When all the pixel dust settled, the cave was empty. But there was plenty of evidence that it was being occupied. A small fire crackled beneath the cave's natural chimney where the earlier travelers had cooked their meager meal. But otherwise everything was different. Pitch torches had been added along the walls for more light. Near the entrance, a log counter top had been built. Something was painted on the front of it. She zoomed in and found the crudely painted words: *Wilson's Liquor Vault and House for Entertainment.* So, it was a tavern. But was it a pirate's tavern or some other clever entrepreneur's? Behind the counter were several spigoted barrels and stacks of wooden tankards. Caribbean pirates always drank rum, at least they did in movies and books. Merrideth wondered what Ohio River pirates favored. Whiskey maybe? Near the bar was a table with several log stools. A deck of cards waited to be played. The only other home improvement she could see was a rough log partition at the back of the cave, built to create a private compartment.

She turned her eyes from the eighteenth-century cave on her screen to the one she sat in and wondered how likely it was that someone would come in while she was time-surfing. There was little danger of one of the Road Hogs stopping by. They were probably only interested in getting drunk and disorderly, not sight-seeing at historically significant sites. And she had not seen any tourists other than the one family. But there were bound to be a few around who might decide at any time to come for a look at the infamous pirate cave. She would have to do her work with an ear open for approaching explorers.

A sudden squawk from her computer speakers told her the cave of 1797 wasn't entirely empty after all. Zooming in, she saw that several rustic twig cages at the end of the bar held chickens. Hopefully they were laying hens and not roosters slated for the frying pan.

Crates and wooden chests were stacked haphazardly around the perimeter of the cave. The amount of clothing hanging from pegs and littering the floor indicated the cave was home for quite a few people. But where were they?

She didn't have time to sit around like Goldilocks waiting for the three bears to come home. She fast-forwarded a little, and then a little more. Red and orange light of a setting sun streaked the sky beyond the arched cave entrance. And then six men stood outlined against the colorful backdrop. The pirates had come home.

She paused the action and studied them. They were a rowdy-looking bunch, wearing rough clothing of leather or homespun on their bodies and even rougher expressions on faces weathered by hard living.

Except for the man at front and center. He was dressed almost elegantly, with a touch of lace at his throat and cuffs. On the young side of middle age, he looked fit and handsome. Natalie would have said he did not look like a pirate. He certainly did not look like Hollywood's conception of one, except for the spyglass he held.

His expression was pleasant, as if he had just been discussing bird watching with his companions before she froze him in place. But if he were indeed the leader of the Cave-in-Rock's pirates, as she presumed, then he was no innocent. Today, he would undoubtedly have a rap sheet a mile long, maybe even show up on the FBI's Most Wanted list.

Merrideth dreaded getting inside his head. But it would be the quickest way, maybe the only way, to learn what really went on in a pirates' den, including how they preyed on their victims.

Taking a deep breath, she locked onto him and switched back to virtual mode.

✵✵✵

1797

Collapsing his looking glass, Samuel Mason strode happily into the cave. "Set the stage, men. You know what to do. Floss! Mabel! Get out here. Visitors are soon to come knocking upon our door, figuratively speaking."

The two women came stumbling out from the back room, rubbing their eyes and pouting at being awakened. He didn't begrudge them their nap. They'd had a long night.

He softened his voice. "We've got a big fish to land, ladies. Word from upriver says it's a big broadhorn, loaded to the gills with barrels of whiskey."

"Tempting fish, indeed," Floss said.

"Can we have chicken instead, Samuel?" Mabel said. "I don't care much for fish."

"Sure, darlin'," Mason said. Unlike Floss who was sharp as a tack and received a commensurate share of the booty, Mabel was too simple to understand most of what went on.

"How are we playing them, Samuel?" Floss said, patting vainly at her frizzy red hair. "Rough or nice?"

"Only an hour until full dark, so they'll be looking for a place to dock. Convince them this is the place."

"So, no damsels in distress this time, then?"

"Those men will be ready for liquor and skirt, no offense meant."

"None taken." Floss pulled her bodice down another inch and turned to Mabel. "Come on, sweetie. We'll remind the men how thirsty they are."

Mabel, biddable lass that she was, followed Floss outside to do her part in making sure the boat stopped.

CHAPTER 4

THE PRESENT

"Miss?"

Merrideth jolted back to the present.

"Hey there, Miss?" It was the groundskeeper from the lodge. His white hair stood out against the darker cave wall.

"Yes?" Merrideth said. "Sorry. I was into my research."

"You must have been," he said with a grin. "I came to warn you that the beast is on the move."

"I'm sorry, sir, I don't—"

"The river's rising again," he explained. "The lower path will be covered before long. Name's Fred, by the way. No need for sirs."

"Thanks, Fred. Mine is Merrideth." They shook hands. His palm was leathery and callused. Hers was sweaty.

"I thought you'd want to know."

"Thanks. As much as I am enjoying your cave's hospitality, I have no wish to spend the night here. At least without a nice fire to cook my supper like the settlers—like they probably had."

Stopping right when the pirates were in view was frustrating, to say the least. But even without the rising water, it was getting too late to continue much longer anyway. When she stood to follow Fred out, her vision went weird for a second and then her head

35

began to throb. Sitting inside a cave on a rocky ledge for over an hour could not be good for a person's posture. She must have thrown her neck out of place. Or maybe she was allergic to mold. The cave was fairly dry, but it was a cave, after all.

The little aspirin bottle she kept in her purse was empty. She tried the lodge's gift store in the lobby, but they were sold out. Shirley apologized and suggested that she try the Casey's north of town.

On her way there, Merrideth kept her eyes open for the restaurants she had spotted when she first came to town. Rose's Kountry Kitchen had looked promising, notwithstanding the annoying spelling of its name. But now the whole place was dark and the parking lot empty. A paper sign fluttered on the door, but she did not get out to go read it. The River Front Opry House was also dark, as was Dutton's Cafe on Canal Street. The lights were on in a building up ahead. The sign said *Reed's Grocery.* Good. She could get the aspirin and pick up something to eat in her room. But just as she turned into the parking lot, the lights winked out and someone pulled the window blind down. At least there was still Casey's. They had pizza and sandwiches. She should fill her gas tank anyway.

Fortunately, it was open, its parking lot nearly full. The franchisee was reaping the benefit of everyone else's early closing time. She got the gas pump started and realized a second later that it was one of those kind that went ka-thunk, ka-thunk, ka-thunk as if it were pumping molasses instead of gasoline. The people at the other pumps didn't seem to be having any trouble with theirs. No, she was the lucky one. Resigned to a long wait, she leaned against her car, hoping the pizza did not sell out.

A distant buzz came to her from somewhere to the north on Route One. The buzz grew into a roar. And then a double line of motorcycles came into view. Forget the trio of tame motorcyclists she had seen earlier. *Now* the Road Hogs were in town.

They slowed their bikes to a crawl. Even so, the sound was deafening. As the lead biker passed Casey's, his motorcycle's chrome reflecting the light from the overhead lamps, he hooted and pumped his fist high. Riding behind him, a woman hugged his waist and smirked at Merrideth as if to say, "This is my man. Just look how dangerous he is."

They were indeed scary-looking, and she mentally apologized to

Fred for dismissing his concerns. Most of the men had beards and wore black leather or blue denim, which caused them to blend into the dusk. But some had painted their faces as clowns, the white grease paint standing out in sharp contrast to their dark clothes and surroundings, giving them the appearance of disembodied heads floating by. Diabolical Stephen King clowns. Not the kind that entertained at children's birthday parties.

Fred had said the Hellhound's campground was north of town, but the bikers continued south on Route One. In two blocks it turned into the town's main street. Maybe they knew a short cut. Maybe they wanted to share the window-rattling noise of their engines with the residents of Cave-in-Rock first.

She should already be tucked safely into her room at the lodge, but the pump was still lazily ka-thunking along. The gauge registered a whopping 7.6 gallons of gas pumped so far.

At the house next door, a man mowing grass shut off his lawnmower to watch the spectacle. Two bikers peeled away from the rest of the herd and came to a stop in the street in front of him. They revved their engines, and Merrideth wondered if they intended to race. Instead, the bikes stayed put, and black smoke billowed from their rear tires.

The smell of burning rubber made her nose burn, but it seemed to impress the homeowner who clapped, as did the smiling young man pumping gas next to her.

"What are they doing?" Merrideth said.

"It's called a burnout, ma'am. They do it by accelerating their engines while at the same time braking."

That was *how* they did it, but not *why*. He was so pleased by the demonstration that she didn't ask.

"They have a contest every year. I'm going to enter it if I can get off work in time."

It seemed like a guaranteed way to ruin a tire. But to each his own. "Good luck."

"Thanks. I'll need it."

One of the burnout artists eased his way back into the line and continued on toward town with the other bikers. The other one pulled out what looked like a heavy chrome flashlight and bashed in the homeowner's mailbox before he rejoined his comrades.

The young man next to Merrideth cursed, then mumbled an apology to her.

"Wow!" Merrideth said. "Why did he do that?"

"Maybe he thought Keith was dissing him. Or it could be he just felt like it."

The homeowner didn't shout and wave his fist at the vandal, as Merrideth expected him to do, just stood there watching him go. Then he restarted his lawnmower and went back to mowing his yard.

"Isn't he going to call the police?" Merrideth said.

"No, Ma'am." The young man replaced his gas cap and got into his truck. "You don't want to cheese off the Road Hogs." The last of the motorcycles passed by, and he pulled his truck into the street behind them.

The pump clicked, telling Merrideth her tank was finally full. She paid with her credit card, then parked her car beside the building. It did not seem like a good idea to leave her laptop in the car, so she shouldered her backpack and purse and locked the car. She would just grab the aspirin and a slice of pizza, maybe some snacks for later. And then she would get out of there.

On the other side of the door, a young red-haired woman wearing a Casey's smock stood looking out. She opened the door for Merrideth and gave her a warm smile. That and the yeasty smell of pizza went a long way in dispelling the sense that she had entered the Twilight Zone.

"Hi. Welcome to Casey's." Her name tag said *Casey*.

Merrideth smiled, and the woman's hand flew up to cover her name tag. She grinned good-naturedly. "No, they didn't name the store after me. And no, I don't I wish I owned the place."

"I bet you get tired of that," Merrideth said. "Do you sell aspirin?"

Casey gave her a commiserating look and pointed. "Over there. Aisle three."

"Thanks."

She found the aspirin easily enough. It was not as easy to take the outrageous price tag, but if the aspirin got rid of her headache it would be worth it. There was a line at the pizza counter, but the cook in back was doing a heroic job of keeping up with the demand. Merrideth did not have to wait long to get her slice of pepperoni.

Casey was at the cash register when Merrideth paid for her things. "Hope that does the trick for you," she said. "Have a good night."

"Thanks. I will once my headache is gone."

At the door, Merrideth saw that the Road Hogs, finished with their pass through town, were coming back down Main Street toward Casey's. She would have to wait for them to get past, and who knew how long that would take? Maybe they intended to do several more victory laps before heading for the campground.

Figuring she might as well stay put, she turned to eye the store's three tiny tables. They were all full, but miraculously, a teenage couple was just leaving one of them. She hurried to it and slid into the seat the second the girl was out of it.

As the couple left the store, the boy politely held the door for someone coming in. A biker in a worn brown leather jacket, jeans, and lace-up work boots sauntered in, giving the room and its occupants a steely look. For a moment his eyes seemed to lock with hers, but then he went on to the pizza counter where he selected several slices from the warmer.

His face was bare of the creepy clown paint some of the bikers favored, and yet she might have felt more comfortable had he been wearing it. He was too good looking by far for her peace of mind. Actually, he was similar in height, build, and coloring to Brett, and Heaven knew *his* looks had set her nerves on edge when she first met him.

It was not that she did not find handsome men appealing. What living, breathing woman didn't? But in the presence of one, the confidence she had worked so hard to build flew right out the window, and she started feeling like a small gray mouse again. A chubby, plain-Jane sort of mouse. And she hated feeling like a mouse. Still, she could not make herself look away from the biker.

Maybe it was her biological clock asserting itself. Her mother was constantly after her to get married, and her mentor Marla White, who had repeatedly cautioned her that it would be career suicide to date Brett, was always telling her that there were other fish in the sea and she should go out and catch one.

But logic said that if you wanted a decent man you did not go looking among the sort who hung out at nightclubs and bars, and certainly not those that attended Hellhound Homecoming. So the reason she couldn't stop looking at the biker must be because her intellectual curiosity had kicked in. It would be interesting to study their world, to know what made them tick, what they got out of driving in herds to Cave-in-Rock every summer. That had to be it.

The biker finished paying and turned to look for a place to eat. He would see that the tables were all taken and leave. He would probably be in a hurry to catch up with his buddies, anyway. Just as it occurred to her that he would not be able to eat pizza while riding a motorcycle, he began walking straight toward her.

Did he mean to sit in the one empty seat across from her? Should she invite him to? It was certainly the polite thing to do when tables were in short supply. No, that would be entirely too weird. She dropped her eyes so he would not think she was open to the idea of sharing a table. She would just eat her pizza and get out of there.

But then he was there beside her table, his jean-clad leg in her line of sight. She glanced up. He was not looking her way after all, just concentrating on balancing the flimsy paper plate in his hand while he ate.

His nearly black hair was on the long side. From the glimpse she'd had of his eyes, they were a deep, almost purple blue, and serious, not at all flirtatious. His mouth was a sculpted masterpiece, but it, too, was serious and unsmiling. On the side of his neck, a tattoo peeked out of a faded, army-green T-shirt. From what was showing, she could not tell whether it was a cross or a swastika.

A man edged past him carrying a case of beer, and the biker held the plate closer to his chest and hunched his shoulders—his broad shoulders—as if trying to take up less space in the aisle. His leather jacket made a pleasant scrunching sound when he moved.

"Would you like to sit?" Merrideth had not known she was going to ask. But then the words were out there, on the table, as it were.

After a pause he said, "Thanks." He set the plate down and shrugged out of his leather jacket, then hung it on the back of the chair and slid into the seat across from her. His denim-covered knee grazed her bare one and then moved away. The look on his face told her he was aware of the contact and that it had not been intentional. He went back to eating his pizza.

Tattoos nearly covered his arms. She wanted to study them closer, but it seemed impolite, so she averted her eyes and was immediately annoyed at herself for being unable to look at them. Surely people who got tattoos wanted them to be noticed.

The silence drew out. Was he being rude or politely waiting for her to say something first?

"I was glad this place was open," she found herself saying. "For a while there I thought I'd be going to bed hungry." She mentally kicked herself as soon as the words were out. Just saying the word "bed" would be construed as a come-on by a lot of men.

He didn't give any indication that he saw it as such, and she was relieved.

"Are you vacationing at the lodge?" he asked.

Her relief disappeared. "What makes you think that?" she said rather more sharply than she intended.

A small smile touched his perfect lips. "It's the only lodging in town."

"Maybe I live here."

"If you lived in Cave-in-Rock you wouldn't sound so relieved this place was open. You'd surely have something in your refrigerator and wouldn't have to go to bed hungry. And if you were just passing through, you could find a restaurant soon enough down the highway."

Okay then. He was definitely not the semi-literate, meathead biker stereotype portrayed on TV. Knowing he was intelligent only compounded the unease his good looks had already caused. The irony wasn't lost on her. Intelligence would be one of her top-of-the-list requirements when she got around to looking for those other fish in the sea. Of course even Marla would agree that just because a fish landed at your table while you were minding your own business eating pizza at Casey's did not mean it was a keeper.

She felt a nervous laugh coming on and put her napkin to her mouth, converting the laugh into a small cough at the last moment. What was wrong with her? He would be appalled if he knew the stupid thoughts running through her head. For all she knew, he already had a wife and three kids in Peoria and had no intention of being anyone's catch, especially a small gray mouse's.

He seemed to be waiting for her to speak. It would be rude not to say something, but she had no intention of revealing too much about herself to a stranger, especially where she was spending the night. She tried to think of a non-answer.

"Sorry," he said. "That probably sounded like I'm some kind of serial killer scoping out my next victim."

And instantly, her assessment of him shifted once again. She had been too busy thinking about fish in the sea for the thought of serial killers to enter her mind. Now that he had put the idea there, her brain was shrieking for her to leave. Without delay. Because, it reminded her, having good looks and intelligence didn't prevent a guy from being a serial killer. Hadn't Ted Bundy been handsome and charming? Gathering her trash, she stood and smiled weakly at the biker. "Enjoy your weekend."

He stood, too. Somehow he had finished four slices of pizza in the time it had taken her to eat one. "I'll walk you to your car."

Merrideth's eyes felt as if they were in danger of popping out of her head. "No need."

"Really, Miss. It's not safe out there."

No kidding. She dumped the grease-stained paper plate and napkins into the trash bin and then fumbled in her purse for her keys. His arm brushed hers as he reached in to dump his own trash. She must have looked as panicked as she felt, because he took a step back and put up his hands in the universal *Don't-Worry-I'm-Harmless* gesture. She had a can of mace in her suitcase back at the lodge. If she had listened to her mother and kept it in her purse where it belonged, she would probably be pulling it out about now.

He did not follow, but when she got to her car and looked back, he was standing at the door watching her. Thankfully, the other bikers were gone. But the eerily empty street only made the Twilight-Zone feeling worse. She nearly dropped her keys trying to get her car unlocked. She did not waste any time leaving the parking lot.

***

Merrideth sat on the cedar rail of the little deck outside her room, trying to calm her nerves enough to go to bed. With the sun down, the pretty view was gone, but lights from the parking lot kept the deck from being too dark and creepy to use. It was a good place to contemplate life, namely, the uncomfortable realization that she had behaved badly.

She had had absolutely no reason to assume the guy at Casey's was anything other than a polite stranger, and yet she had bolted out of there like he was a plague carrier. She knew full well that it was not his good looks that had caused her to run away. And he had obviously been joking when he said the bit about serial killers. It was only because he chose to decorate himself with tattoos and

42

ride around on a Harley that his comment had completely spooked her.

And now he thought she was a big, fat bigot. Just like the sort of white people who panicked when they saw a black man walking down the sidewalk toward them wearing a hoodie. Had she also been guilty of stereotyping the other Road Hogs? Just because they enjoyed a more flamboyant lifestyle didn't mean they were bad people. Of course they looked scary to her. She was an introverted mouse.

Suddenly Merrideth wanted—needed—to hear Brett's voice. He knew that she was not actually a bigot. He would not be her friend if he thought otherwise.

She went inside and got her phone. He had not called or texted while she was in the shower. She could certainly call him, but she avoided being the one to initiate contact. She did not want to look too needy, and she sure did not want to encourage him to get any ideas about advancing their relationship beyond the *Friend* category.

A red and yellow glow appeared on her sliding glass door, and a second later came the popping sound of fireworks going off. She stepped back out onto the deck in time to see a second burst of red and green brighten the sky and the scrap of river visible through the trees. According to Shirley, the Hellhounds' campground was over that way. Someone there must be getting a head start on Fourth of July celebrations.

She stared at her phone, willing it to ring. It didn't. She should just call him. That was what friends did. He would find her adventures in the wilds of southern Illinois amusing, and she could ask him how Nelda was. More importantly, a dose of his humor and normalcy would help her get her bearings. She scrolled to his number, and right before she clicked it, the phone rang. It was Brett. She smiled in satisfaction.

"Hi, Brett. How are Lilli and Mini liking their new patio?"

"They are living the high life. Just as I suspected, they're jazz fans. I've got Billie Holiday playing in their barn and they didn't bat one goaty little eye when Odious Ogle started in shooting off his guns and firecrackers a few minutes ago. Speaking of firecrackers, that's why I called."

"Oh?"

"Bill and Kevin and some of us are going to the St. Louis Landing to watch the fireworks Saturday night. I thought you might like to come along."

"I'm not sure."

"It's considered one of the best pyrotechnic shows in the country."

"I know. I used to see it when I was a kid. And from the best observation post ever—the Old Dears' third-story widow's walk. But I might not be back in time."

"Back from where?"

"Listen," she said, holding her phone out to the night.

"Is that fireworks?"

"Yes, someone is setting them off over the river, not that I can see much from where I'm standing."

"Which is where, exactly?"

"On my deck."

"As far as I recall, you don't have a deck. I meant which *river*?"

"Oh. The Ohio. I'm in a little river town down here called Cave-in-Rock."

The phone was silent for so long she thought the call had been dropped.

"So what made you suddenly decide you needed to visit a little river town called Cave-in-Rock?"

It occurred to her that normal people—people who were used to having friends—probably mentioned their travel plans before they executed them.

"Or is that another of your secrets?" he added.

So he was offended. "No, not at all," she hurried to assure him. "Remember the river pirates I told you about at the library yesterday? Well, there's a cave here that was their hideout and base of operations. I'm here to learn as much as I can about it. For my classes."

"Really? I've always wanted to go spelunking. If you'd mentioned it, I would have joined your team."

He had covered over the hurt with a pleasant jokey tone of voice, but the subtext still read: *I thought we were friends, so why didn't you ask me to come with you?*

"Team? I'm not here with anyone else. It's just me."

"Are you crazy? You can't go wandering around in caves without at least one partner."

"Calm down, Brett. I'm perfectly safe."

"Don't tell me to *calm down*, Merri."

"Well, don't call me *crazy*."

He let out a breath in her ear. "I apologize. But, Merri, surely you know that people get lost in caves. People die in caves. Do you at least have a good light and emergency food and water?"

"It's not that sort of cave, Brett. It's just one large room. Tourists are in and out of it all the time."

"Okay, I guess I'll just have to trust your judgment."

"Thank you." It seemed like a good time to change the subject. "I meant to ask you about Nelda right off. How is she?"

"All right, I guess. But she seems to get tired easily."

"I hate to mention it, but she is not getting any younger."

"You're right. I guess I'm having trouble coming to terms with that. Anyway, I made her go in and take a nap while I finished Duke's fence."

"Has he been off chasing squirrels in Odious Ogle's woods again?"

"No, he's been raiding the garden. So next up on Aunt Nelda's to-do list today was for me to fence it in. Duke favors bell peppers, but he's been known to pilfer carrots and sweet corn."

She laughed. "Duke, the vegetarian Rottweiler."

"Who knew, right?"

They hung up soon after that, and Merrideth stood on the deck watching the last of the fireworks.

Brett had said that phone calls just did not cut it. He was right. Talking with him had only made her miss him more. But that was dangerous thinking, and so she stepped away from that precipice and focused on what she would do in the morning.

.

CHAPTER 5

Merrideth awoke feeling unusually sluggish. The mattress was not as comfortable as she had thought it would be. And odd noises had awakened her periodically throughout the night. She had finally figured out that it was a combination of acid rock music mixed with the roaring of motorcycle engines coming from the Hellhounds' campground. Each time the sound intruded, she wondered what the tattooed man was doing. She told herself that she thought of him only because of her intellectual curiosity about the biker culture, but then her inner voice pointed out that if that were her only interest she would have mentioned him to Brett.

She felt more alert after her shower but then realized she had forgotten her hair dryer. Resigned to bad hair days for the duration, she sat out on her little deck in the sun until her hair was mostly dry and then gathered the whole mess into a twist and restrained it with a tortoise shell clip. It actually didn't look too bad.

Shirley greeted her when she entered the lobby. Today she wore a huge yellow button on her smock that read, *Certified Ninja.* "I have good news and good news."

Merrideth smiled. "Okay, I'll take the good news first."

Grinning, Shirley held up one finger. "First, Fred was just in here and said to tell you the river's down so you won't have any trouble getting to the cave today. Second, biscuits and gravy are on the menu all weekend."

"Thanks for the heads up."

She should order something low-cal, but the smell coming from the restaurant was too tempting to resist. So she splurged and had the biscuits and gravy. After breakfast, she shouldered her backpack and headed for the cave.

The door to the first cabin stood open again, but today instead of a little winged cowboy on the porch, there was a service cart. As she passed she saw a maid inside stripping the beds. Sherman was gone, on to other adventures with his family.

She did not see indications of any other vacationers. However Fred was there, busily trimming a hedge. He did not appear to notice her when she passed. She saw the tell-tale cords dangling from his ears and smiled. He was probably still vicariously chasing bad guys and rescuing the honest folk of Dodge City.

At the cave, conditions were good for her work. There was plenty of sunlight inside and not a sightseer in sight. A solid day of time-surfing should get her lots of good material, and then she could be home in plenty of time to go with Brett to see the fireworks. It would go a long way toward patching up his hurt feelings and their friendship.

She started *Beautiful Houses* and then rewound to the point where she had left Samuel Mason and his band of pirate preparing to fleece the boatmen who had just docked. The stage was set, and Mason waited for their prey to step into his spider web.

Now if only she could tolerate being inside the head of such a man. Taking a deep breath, she locked onto Mason and clicked *Virtual.*

***

1797

Samuel Mason went to the bar, rubbing his hands in anticipation. "It sounds like a good one coming our way, doesn't it?"

George Stanley, grinned, his white teeth shining wolfishly out of his black beard. "That it does, Mr. Mason," he said, handing him a whiskey.

"Thank you. And keep the whiskey flowing for our guests, too." Mason sat back down at the table and picked up the cards to play while he waited to see what would unfold. Outside, Floss and

Mabel began calling out, cajoling the boatmen to stop. Tommy took up his fiddle and began to play "Soldier's Joy."

Fleming released two of the cocks from their cages and the blood-thirsty little beasts commenced taking out their aggression on each other. Mason found cock-fighting a disgusting pastime, but the boatmen tended to like it and were willing to lay down substantial amounts of money. His men liked the sport, too, and they gathered round to watch while they waited for the real show to begin.

The women had stopped calling out. Either the fish had been successfully hooked and landed or it had warily swum on down the river.

The question was answered a few moments later when Tommy stopped fiddling and stepped aside to allow three strangers into the cave. Floss and Mabel were at their sides, batting their eyelashes and smiling. The men looked around with interest at the entertainment laid out before them.

Smiling, Samuel Mason rose and went to them. "Welcome to Wilson's Liquor Vault and House for Entertainment. Are you docking for the night, men?"

The youngest of the three grinned happily. "We sure are." He was but a lad really, much younger than his friends, and deliciously ripe for the picking.

"Then I hope you'll enjoy your stay. Are your companions going to come up for refreshment, too?"

The oldest of the three men looked at him shrewdly. "Maybe."

The young one piped up. "Captain says we have to take turns. Me and my friends here drew the long straws."

Mason kept his smile in place. The captain must be a canny one. They had their work cut out for them.

"I reckon you've worked up quite a thirst on the river," Floss said, smiling flirtatiously.

"I sure have."

"Well, step right up then," George called from the bar. "We've got what you need."

"We sure do." Floss ran her hand down the boy's arm.

He licked his lips and looked longingly at Floss and Mabel, starting at the hems of their garish dresses and ending at the bosoms spilling out of their bodices.

The man at the boy's side pulled Floss' hand away. "Thank ye kindly, ma'am. But Billy's not interested. Captain says the boat's too crowded to pick up anything else along the way."

When the insult sank in, Floss huffed and flounced off to watch the cock fight. She, too, was a bloodthirsty little creature. Faithful as always, Mabel followed her, looking confused. Billy looked as if he'd just got word his favorite hound had died.

The third stranger laughed and pulled Billy to the bar. "Come on, lad. I'll buy you a drink. It's killing me to have all that whiskey on board and Captain won't let us sample any of it."

Mason smiled jovially. "Then sample some of our whiskey, lads. And give them our best, George. Anyone laboring to take a rich man's cargo of whiskey downriver ought to get a taste of the good stuff once in a while."

"Right you are Mr. Wilson," George said, taking up three tankards. "Only first show me your coin, lads." He smiled at them to show he meant no offense. "Dare say this be as good or better'n what be on your boat anyway."

The boatmen dug in their pockets and came out with palms covered in a respectable number of coins. They set their payment on the bar and carefully tucked away the rest. Sending Mason a look, George filled their tankards from the spigot and set them on the counter in front of them.

The men drank and then heaved satisfied sighs. "Now that's good sippin' whiskey," one said.

Fleming, knowing his part in the game, called out, "Care to bet on the birds, gentlemen?"

The boatmen took their tankards and joined the circle of men watching the bloody sport.

Mason went back to his cards. After a moment, Jack Hughes came in and sat down across from him as if his greatest pleasure in life was watching a man play Patience. Mason had cause to know his favorite pastime was not nearly so innocent and did not involve a deck of cards.

"Tell me what you've learned about our guests," Mason said softly as he put a red three on a black four.

"I figure maybe sixty barrels of whiskey. And I heard 'em mention apple-jack, too."

"Excellent news."

"Bad news is they's eight of 'em, counting the three over there." Hughes nodded toward the cockfight. The three strangers were watching it as if *their* lives and not the roosters' were at stake, which of course they were. It would be easy enough to overpower them and take the money they carried in their pockets. But Mason would never be so short-sighted. No, he wanted it all.

"The five down at the boat ain't leaving. And one's standing guard with a musket. But we can take 'em, Mr. Mason. I could go get Frank and Seth off the bluff. Then we could for sure."

"Maybe," Mason said. "Or maybe they'll get away with all that lovely whiskey and make such a ruckus up and down the river no one will stop at our establishment ever again. Never mind the boatmen. They'll be up shortly to spend their money with us."

"But that's just a few shillings. What about all the whiskey?"

Mason laughed drily. "I look at it this way, Hughes. If the good captain is willing to go to the trouble of hauling all those barrels of whiskey to the New Orleans market for me while I sit here enjoying life, then I'll let him. But don't concern yourself. The captain and his men will stop back this way on their way home. They'll be plumb giddy about stopping here, seeing as how we're going to give them a really good time tonight. And when they come again, their guard will be down and their purses full to bursting. Much simpler all around, don't you think?"

Hughes snorted. "You've got your wits about you, Mr. Mason. That you do."

"All right then. Go pass the word to the men. And buy a round of drinks for our three guests."

✢✢✢

THE PRESENT

The cave was empty and the sky outside was bright, so Merrideth knew that she was firmly back in her own time. But the scent of chicken blood, whiskey, and unwashed pirate still lingered unpleasantly in her nostrils. The poor chickens had suffered and bled as pawns in the pirates' plans, a worse fate, surely, than ending up in the stew pot. It was stupid to think of them first when the humans' lives and livelihood were in such jeopardy, but as usual after time-surfing, her brain was a jumble of confusing emotions.

In the mix was a sense of guilt. Mason had not felt the least bit guilty for what he was about to do. But even so, having been privy to his thoughts, she somehow felt culpable on his behalf.

Mason's name had been prominent in the material she had already read. He came from a respectable Virginia family and had been an officer in the American army during the Revolutionary War. He had served heroically, and several of his exploits had helped the cause. No one could explain why he had turned to crime after the war.

Even with only the small slice of his life that she had just observed, it was easy to see that Mason was a very clever man and a natural leader. He commanded his pirate band with a light hand, and yet his men—and women—obediently carried out the shrewd plans he set before them.

He was not as evil as she had expected a pirate to be. Some might find his attitude toward the whores almost enlightened. The one called Floss actually got a cut of the spoils. Nevertheless, being inside Mason's head as he cold-bloodedly plotted to rob the boatmen had left her feeling decidedly dirty. She took three cleansing breaths and then pulled out her notebook to jot down a few details about what she had seen and what topics she would follow up on later.

After she recorded as much information as she could, she set aside her notebook and stared at the cave wall, trying to recall what else she knew about Mason from her reading. Through the years there had been several outlaw gangs at the cave for short periods, and all the stories were mixing up in her head. So much of it had been sensational junk anyway. But if she remembered correctly, it was Mason and his gang who were run out of the cave when a consortium of Pittsburgh merchants sent undercover agents to discover why their shipments kept disappearing along a certain stretch of the Ohio River.

What Merrideth most wanted to discover was what happened to the families who had disappeared. For over two hundred years only God knew. Now, if she could steel herself to go back inside the pirates' lair, and back inside Mason's mind, maybe she would know too.

But then her stomach made itself known, and she realized that she was hungry, despite the hefty breakfast she had eaten. But time-surfing was hard work, and it was nearly one o'clock. She put everything back in her backpack and went blinking out into the sunshine.

The peaceful scene before her revealed no clues about the violence once committed there. The majestic Ohio flowed calmly by on its way to the gulf. Beyond the river, the Kentucky shoreline was green and lush. In 1797, before civilization's imprint, the landscape would have been even more magnificent, although it was doubtful the pirates had cared about anything other than the tactical advantage of the spot. There was an unobstructed view of the river for miles both upstream and down. For lookouts posted on the bluffs above, sighting prey would have been even easier.

The flatboats had ranged from small rafts to the 100-foot-long broadhorns, and every size in between. The larger ones had included enclosed cabins that allowed passengers a certain degree of protection from the elements—and no doubt made them more visible to Mason's men.

And once a promising boat was spotted, Floss and Mabel had stood where she did now, like the sirens of Greek mythology, waving and calling to lure unsuspecting travelers into their clutches.

Grimacing at the thought, she started down the path.

✻✻✻

Merrideth blotted the sweat flowing like a small river off her forehead and marveled at her stupidity. She could have been enjoying a nice lunch at the lodge if she had not made the spur-of-the-moment decision to walk the two miles into town to try out one of the restaurants there. At the time it had seemed like a good idea. The day was mild, a rarity for July. She would get in a little exercise, expel the fusty smell of the cave from her nostrils, and assuage her guilt about the biscuit-and-gravy breakfast. But she had not taken the hills into consideration, nor that the old sneakers she had worn for mudding around in the cave were not exactly up to par for hiking, nor that an industrial grade laptop weighed eight pounds and three ounces. And she especially had not taken into consideration that it had been a while, a rather long while, since she had last visited the gym.

Logically, hills by definition had to both ascend and descend.

But the hills she had just climbed had only gone forever up, defying all the laws of physics. Had he been there, Brett would have scoffed at her, but then again, he still believed the laws of physics precluded time travel. Finally the town came into view. At last the road actually began to descend, and the going got easier.

At the stop sign she paused to take a breather. Dutton's Cafe was to her right two or three blocks away. Two streets ahead, three scofflaw bikers went through the intersection without bothering to stop. At least they were going fairly slowly.

Down the street on her left, other bikers were parked in front of the sunny yellow welcome pavilion and seemed to be looking at items on the table. Beyond them at the river the ferry was docked. It must have just arrived; a line of cars waited to board, and none had yet exited.

Merrideth adjusted her backpack and turned toward Dutton's. A car passed by, and then a motorcycle came purring up behind her. Only it did not pass, just slowed to her speed and stayed level with her. Merrideth kept her eyes forward, hoping the rider would get the clue she was not interested.

"You need a lift?"

It was the tattooed guy from Casey's. He steered his bike closer to the curb. She was surprised to see that he wore a helmet, although it did nothing to diminish his dangerous aura. He flipped up the visor and trained his laser blue eyes on her. As before, he did not smile, just studied her seriously. But at least he was not looking at her in disgust for being a bigot.

It was all well and good to be unbiased toward those different from oneself, to presume innocence until proven otherwise. But he was, after all a stranger, and she was not about to be stupid about it. She studied him back. Surely if he *were* a serial killer or even just a slime ball looking for a new notch on his bedpost, he would turn on the charm and give her a nice big smile, wouldn't he? On the other hand, if he were a nice guy, he would not seriously think a woman he had just met would be willing to hop on his bike.

"Where are you going?" he said mildly.

She had a chronic reluctance to share information about her life even with friends and acquaintances. It annoyed the heck out of Brett. It probably would Tattoo Man, too. And if she refused to answer his simple question, he would really begin to think she was a snob. She should not care what he thought of her, but there was no getting around the fact that she did.

"To Dutton's Cafe," she said at last.

"For lunch?"

Why else, she thought and almost blurted out, "duh." But then she remembered his mental acuity the night before. Maybe she was the one being slow.

"Because if you're wanting food, you won't find it there. I don't mean to jump to conclusions, Miss." He nodded toward her backpack. "Maybe you're hiking there to meet someone or—"

"Why don't they have food?"

"I'm sure they do have food. But they're closed."

"Still?"

"Most everything is closed while the Hellhounds are in town."

The growl of motorcycles came from behind her. A pack of six or seven riders were coming up the street, three abreast as if they owned it.

"You'd better let me give you a lift."

"No thanks." Her heart did a weird gallop, and she was back to thinking about serial killers. Or creepy guys in panel vans offering to let little kids look at the cute puppies.

"It would be better if they thought you were taken. I mean mine. With me. Not with me, but with me."

Indignation replaced suspicion. "Yours? Who do you think you are?"

"Someone concerned for your safety."

She shook her head in amazement and then resumed walking, calling over her shoulder. "It's broad daylight. I assure you I am perfectly safe."

He continued purring along beside her. "Where are you going?"

It was a good question. A crowded restaurant might be the safest place for her, but if they were all closed there was no point in continuing the way she was going. And even if he was lying, any restaurant open would probably be packed with bikers anyway.

The motorcycles passed, each rider giving him a nod and one of those weird biker salutes they did, which Tattoo Man politely returned. On the back of one man's leather jacket was the American eagle emblem she had seen the day before. Either it was the same biker, or he was another patriotic citizen.

"Like I said, it isn't safe for you to be—"

"All right. All right. I'll forget about eating in town." Merrideth pivoted and headed back the way she had come.

"Good," he said behind her.

"Goodbye." She glanced over her shoulder and saw that instead of continuing on his way, he had turned his bike her direction as if he intended to follow her. She tore open her backpack and began digging for the can of mace. "I have mace in here, and I'll use it if you come any closer, Mister." Assuming she could find it.

"I'm glad you have sense enough to have some." Unperturbed, he pointed up the street. "You might need it for them."

The pack of bikers had wheeled around and was coming back down the street toward her.

At last she found the can of mace. But if she pointed it at Tattoo Man...well, there was no going back on something like that. So she kept it at her side and walked faster. He kept pace with her.

The bikers reached them and fell in alongside Tattoo Man, their engines idling at a low rumble. Then the man with the patriotic eagle on his jacket rode up onto the sidewalk in front of her, and the parade came to a halt. He smiled, revealing lots and lots of bright white teeth. "Is this dude pestering you, Miss?"

Now she did not know whom to point the mace at. It occurred to her that there might not be enough to go around. A purse-sized can was probably intended for a single attacker, not a crowd of them. What if instead of debilitating the men it only riled them up? Like when you sprayed Raid at a few mild-mannered wasps but missed, and they turned into a swarm of stinging psychos.

She tried for a calm, assured smile. "No. I'm fine. Really."

"I'd be more than happy to give you a ride," Patriotic Guy said. One of the men behind him snickered and said something which Merrideth could not hear, but did not need to.

She looked into Tattoo Man's serious eyes and then back into Patriotic Guy's smiling ones.

"No thanks," she said. "I'm with...with..."

"Trevor Dalton," Tattoo Man said.

"Right," Merrideth said, swallowing her pride. "I'm with Trevor Dalton." After another look at his eyes, she stepped down from the sidewalk, threw her leg over his bike, and climbed on behind him like it was something she did all the time.

Patriotic Guy's wolfish smile didn't waver. Trevor Dalton nodded to him and the other men, revved his engine, and took her away. Merrideth did not look back to see the pack's reaction.

Years before during John's brief motorcycle phase, he had taken her for a few rides on his small bike. He had driven it cautiously, and they had both worn regulation helmets. Even so, Merrideth had not cared for the sensation that other people apparently found exhilarating. The whole time she had pictured herself flying off the bike and becoming just another greasy spot on the pavement.

Now, with no helmet, she had the added worry of kamikaze bugs imbedding themselves in her eyeballs, or the wind whipping her hair right out of her scalp.

To make matters worse, she did not know what to hold onto. She had not even thought about it when riding with John because he was like a brother to her. But the man on the bike in front of her was a stranger. When he turned at the intersection, however, she had no choice but to wrap her arms around his middle or risk falling off. Even with the bulk of his leather jacket it was obvious Trevor Dalton did not carry an ounce of spare fat. If she had not been worrying about dying—and wondering whether she had just been rescued or kidnapped—she would have found *that* sensation exhilarating.

Whatever the case, he was the lesser of two evils. And if things went south, she still had her can of mace firmly in hand. He probably felt it digging into his stomach.

But he brought her back to the lodge safe and sound. He did not stick around for chit-chat, not even to ask *her* name. When she got off the bike he just gave her a little salute and rode away.

She stood under the portico, watching him go and savoring the relief that she had come out of the encounter unscathed. Relief turned to regret when she realized that she had not even thanked him.

She sighed. Now what did he think of her? Since there was nothing she could do about it now, she went inside to get lunch. Unfortunately, the restaurant was already closed for the afternoon. Shirley apologized for the short hours of service and offered to share her tuna sandwich with her. Smiling, Merrideth thanked her for her generosity but declined. Instead, she got peanut butter crackers from the vending machine in the hall and ate them on her way back to the cave.

After sweating in the sun for the past hour or so, the cave's cool environment was a welcome relief. Hopefully the tourists would stay away for the whole afternoon. She had a lot of history to scroll through.

When the program finished loading, it was to a different scene. According to the time counter, over two months had passed. Although she had done nothing to the settings, she was not surprised. *Beautiful Houses* had always had a mind of its own about what it wanted her to see.

Several new people—two men, three women, and two infants—had joined Mason and the others in the cave. Babies at the mercy of pirates! It was a horrifying thought. But after studying the newcomers' body language and listening in on their conversations, she changed her mind. They were not settlers about to be victimized. They were new members of Mason's gang. And either it was *Bring Your Baby to Work Day* or they actually lived there in the cave.

Taking a deep breath, Merrideth locked onto Samuel Mason and switched to virtual so she could find out.

CHAPTER 6

✧ ✧ ✧

1797

Mason heaved a disgusted sigh. Big Harpe was explaining the art of bobbing to Frank and Seth. Apparently, it was quite his favorite pastime. Little Harpe said little, but he was grinning his approval. How a man could torture another man's privates was a mystery to him. Mason shuddered, picturing Harpe's naked victim tied on a badly constructed raft, his privates lodged between two shifting logs as he went bobbing down the river until he overturned it in his frantic attempts to free himself. Or until the raft fell apart. Mason put a hand to his own jewels to reassure himself of their well-being.

Big Harpe ended the lesson with a big laugh. "Do you perceive? Either way, he drowns."

Susannah, Big Harpe's wife, stood nearby smiling broadly. Her sister Maria, the one Big Harpe called his spare wife, stood at his other side, her smile less enthusiastic. Sarah, Little Harpe's wife, sat leaning against the wall looking like she might bring up her dinner. She probably would have put her hands to her ears if she hadn't been holding both her baby and Maria's, too.

At first, Mason had assumed the Harpes' women were whole-hearted cohorts of their husbands. Maybe Susannah was, but lately he'd begun to feel a little sorry for the other two. It seemed to him that a person ought to have a choice about which path in life they traveled—the straight and narrow or the life of crime. It was, after all, a free country.

Frank and Seth walked away, shaking their heads. George, Floss, and Tommy paused their card game and sent disgusted looks the Harpes' way. Mabel smiled and waited patiently for the game to resume.

Mason sat down on a stump at their table. "What do you think of our new colleagues?"

"They're killers, Mr. Mason," Tommy said. "That's what I think. Born killers."

"And from what they've let slip, they've left a bloody trail behind them," George said.

Floss shook her head. "They're going to bring the Kentucky Regulators right to our door, Samuel."

"Autumn's nearly gone," Mason said. "I'm loath to turn them away on account of the babes."

"Poor little babes," Floss said. "Think of it. Born in jail. All three of them."

"Three?" Mason said. "I only count two."

"There was another," she said. "Susannah *said* her babe got sick and died."

"Said?" Mason said. "Lots of babies die, especially in the wilds of Kentucky."

"There was something about the way she said it made me wonder if its pa had something to do with that."

The babies in Sarah's arms began to whimper. She struggled to her feet and hurried to the far side of the cave. Maria went to Sarah and took her baby from her. The mothers settled themselves onto wooden chests and began to nurse them.

"Sarah looks terrified half the time," Floss said.

George glared at the Harpe brothers. "Something tells me when the preacher asked, that woman said, 'I don't.'"

"I rather doubt anyone asked her opinion about it one way or the other," Mason said. "I suspect they kidnapped those girls."

Charles Fleming and Jack Hughes appeared at the cave entrance. "Mr. Mason, we got company coming," Fleming said, out of breath and grinning excitedly.

"What do we have?" Mason asked.

"Signalman says it looks to be two families, maybe some

extras," Hughes said. "It's a middling size boat, but packed to the hilt."

Mason went outside and considered the sky. Lots of daylight left. They wouldn't be thinking of docking for the night. And family men were not likely to stop for their sort of entertainment.

Floss came out and stood by his side. "What's your call?"

"What's yours?"

"Depends on what I see. Maybe the poor stranded damsel. Haven't done her in a while." Grinning, she pulled her bodice up to a more respectable position and patted her hair.

"Good lass." Mason stepped back inside. "George, you stay out of sight in the back until you're needed. The rest of you come with me. And wait for my signal this time, would you?"

Leaving Floss waiting in front of the cave, they went down the path and then separated to hide in the trees along the shore. The sound of a cow's distressed mooing came to Mason before he could even see the boat.

"Hello," Floss called from above. "Are you wanting supplies? My husband has most anything you might need here in the cave."

So no damsels in distress today. Floss was good at improvising and a good judge of character. Something about the approaching strangers had told her they were not the type to be overly compassionate toward a poor stranded woman, so she had switched to another of her other favorite roles, the kindly shop keeper.

A man's voice came from the river. "No, thank you, ma'am. We're well stocked. But we have a mind to dock for the night. If that's acceptable with your husband. We wouldn't be a bother. Our stock needs to graze. One horse has gone lame and needs a spell on solid land."

"You're most welcome. No bother at all. My husband Sam's good with horses. He'll help."

Yes, Floss was a jewel. Through the trees, Mason watched the boat float closer and closer until it came up alongside his own skiff and then bumped into the dock. As Fleming and Hughes had said, it was not overly large, but it was stuffed full, a nice plump duck waiting to be plucked. Four horses, a bull, and the mooing cow were tethered on the deck. Chickens in crates added their voices to the cow's. Farm tools took up nearly every other spare inch on the outside deck. An old man and what appeared to be his two sons, one young but full-grown and the other a lad of about fifteen, were staring up at the cave, or more likely at Floss. The old man's stern-faced wife stood by the cabin door, wiping her hands on her apron. A little girl peeked out of one window. They all looked tired, as indeed everyone did who came down the river, but also leery. Floss' act apparently wasn't doing the trick to alleviate their mistrust.

Mason tucked his pistol into his back waistband, put on his best smile, and stepped out of the trees. "Greetings, sojourners. I'm Sam Wilson, proprietor of this establishment. As my wife said, you are most welcome to dock. As long as you like. And please do let your poor cow come ashore for refreshment."

"We thank you, sir." The old man said it politely but still looked wary. And when Mason held out his hand for the rope, he pretended not to see and gave it to the lad, who jumped down into the shallows, reeled the boat in, and tied it expertly to the dock.

"Mind it's snug like I showed you, Tobias."

"I know, Pa."

Judging by their worn and patched clothes, the family was not prosperous, so it was not likely they would have ready money to shop in the cave. But Floss knew as well as he did that appearances could be deceiving. They might be rich as Croesus and have all sorts of interesting things hidden away. And if they carried treasure, he would relieve them of it. Or rather, his men would when they got down the river a ways. It would not do to have them connect the robbery with the kindly store keeper and his wife at the cave. It was an art. It really was. If travelers only knew the pains he took not to kill them.

Mason smiled at the little girl still looking out the window and then nodded at the younger man, presumably her father. "It happens we have a little doll your girl might fancy. Up in the cave."

"It came all the way from Boston, they say," Floss said, smiling encouragingly from the mouth of the cave.

The young man's face lit up. Then his expression turned resigned, which Mason interpreted easily enough to mean he wanted to get the doll for his daughter but wasn't sure he could spare the coin to buy it. It was another clue of the family's lack of wealth. But he reminded himself not to assume the worst. It could just be that they were miserly. The frowning older couple looked it.

The little girl came out of the cabin and peeked at Mason

DEBORAH HEAL

through the rails. "Betsy falled in the river," she said solemnly. "She drowneded."

Mason tipped his hat. "I'm sorry for your loss, folks. The river is treacherous, indeed."

The old man lost his frown and chuckled, and the girl's father grinned and said, "Julianne's meaning her doll baby."

"I am quite relieved to hear that it wasn't her little sister." Covering a smile, Mason gave a little bow to Julianne. "Still, a tragedy to be sure."

"Don't you dare buy her that doll, Erich. Julianne needs to learn her lesson," the woman said. "I told her not to hang it over the rail. And besides, you oughtn't go up to that place. I know the kind of entertainment they have."

Neither Erich or his father paid her any heed. "Let's get the stock to shore, boys," the old man said.

"Do hurry, Lars," the woman said. "I've got to milk Daisy."

"And you will, Martha, in due time."

The two brothers began maneuvering the boat's ramp into position. When it was in place, Tobias, the younger one, led the cow down it and onto the riverbank.

Mason turned his attention to Lars. "Here, let me help." He didn't say no, so Mason went on deck and untied one of their horses, a well-made chestnut mare. He led her onto shore, and she whickered her appreciation of being on terra firma. Tobias smiled shyly at him.

Mason tied the mare, then held out his hand, man to man, and the lad took it. "I never did hear your surname."

"Hoffman, sir. Tobias Hoffman."

"Where do you hail from, Mr. Hoffman?" Mason said. "We're always on the lookout for folks coming down the river...with news from home."

"Monongahela Valley," he said. "Pennsylvania."

Tobias' dour mother Martha arrived, carrying a bucket and milking stool, and Mason knew he had lost the chance to get more out of him.

"Don't just stand there jawing, boy. Go get my stove a-going. I reckon you do want supper?"

"Yes, Ma."

Martha sat down alongside the cow, now happily grazing on the grass under the tree. "Don't think because of Daisy's fussing she's

62

a bad cow."

"No, ma'am," Mason said, rubbing the beast's rough flank.

"She doesn't have much milk now," she added defensively. "But it's rich. I'll have butter to sell you, Mr. Wilson, if you're interested."

"My wife and I would like that. Haven't had any in quite some time."

"She'll have her calf in the spring. Then you'll have lots of milk, won't you, Daisy?" The cow continued chewing as Martha sent a rhythmic stream of milk into the bucket.

"Where do you plan to settle, ma'am?"

"We're aiming for the Illinois Country north of Kaskaskia. Heard the land is good."

"Then you're only ten days away from your new home."

"None too soon, Mr. Wilson. None too soon. We intend to claim four hundred acres and get a cabin up before first snowfall."

"Did you work that many acres back in Pennsylvania?"

The woman turned away. "I've got to get this milking done. We do thank you for your hospitality."

"Then, I'll leave you to it and go see if I can be helpful elsewhere."

Martha looked up. "The magistrate said we were on the neighbor's land, not our own. Said we had to move on. That's what happened."

"I'm sure things will be better for your family in Illinois." Her story had the ring of truth. Land disputes of that sort occurred often enough on account of shoddy surveying and changing politics. But was it sadness he'd seen on the woman's face? Or nervousness, like she realized she had just revealed too much about the family's wealth and was trying to retell the story?

He met the unsmiling Lars leading a limping gelding and carrying a wooden tool box.

"He's a beauty, Mr. Hoffman," Mason said. "Shame he went lame. We see it quite often."

"Well, the Creator didn't mean for horses to ride on boats, did he?"

Mason laughed. "No, I suppose not. Other than Noah's, that is."

"No matter. After I treat this boy he'll be right enough for travel come morning."

"I'm partial to Dr. Steer's Liniment for mine. We've got some for sale up at the cave."

The man's face turned proud. He nodded at the wooden box he carried. "I have my own remedy, thank you, Mr. Wilson."

"I'm sure it's superior in every way. I'll go help with the other livestock."

"There's no need to trouble yourself. Erich and Tobias will get them."

Mason tipped his hat and smiled. "No trouble at all." He figured it was the least he could do.

He passed Tobias lugging a little cast iron cook stove to shore. It would take time for him to gather wood for the fire. When Mason got back to the boat, Erich was just leading the bull onto shore. Mason saw Floss watching from the cave and nodded to her. She knew to keep watch.

The little girl stood at the rail solemnly watching the activity around her.

Mason tipped his hat to Erich Hoffman and smiled. "If you want the doll for your girl, you'd best go up to the cave. My wife will give you a good price."

He looked tempted but didn't answer.

"Or barter. We can barter."

Erich's face brightened. "Maybe later, when my chores are done, I'll take a look at it." When he got the bull to shore, he glanced back and waved at his little daughter.

She waved back with a sad little smile. Mason felt a tug of sadness himself. He would give the doll to Julianne, whether her papa had the coin or not, if he actually did have one, which he was fairly certain he did not.

He nodded again to Floss, then continued on to the deck and pretended to busy himself with the remaining horses. There was a pretty little bay mare he would not mind having for himself and a magnificent black stallion. Lars Hoffman most certainly did know good horseflesh. Together they would bring fifty dollars at least in the New Orleans market.

When Mason was sure the travelers on shore were occupied, he ducked into the boat's cabin. It was tidy and efficiently packed with the essentials for settling on the frontier, and for traveling until they got there. The thrifty family had planned well for their journey. Gunny sacks of flour and cornmeal sat on the floor. There were barrels of brined meat, hardtack, jerky, beans, coffee, tea, sugar, and even dried peaches and apples, a particular favorite of his. Cunningly built shelves on the walls prevented supplies from falling. The cabin was altogether better outfitted than most he had seen. More like a real ship's cabin than the usual flatboats they sold to settlers up the river. He wondered if the Hoffmans had built it themselves.

There were a lot of places a person could hide valuables, but he was not worried. He knew them all. Folks always thought they were being so clever. He took a quick look out the door to reassure himself and then got to work searching. He found only food and ordinary supplies in the outer room. But there was a gunny sack curtain partitioning off a part of the cabin on the far wall that promised more. He pushed the curtain aside.

It would be difficult to judge who was more surprised—he, or the pale-faced woman who lay looking up at him from a pallet on the floor.

"Sorry, ma'am. I didn't mean to frighten you. I'm just helping with the livestock." The woman was clearly ailing and feverish, which probably explained why she didn't notice the absurdity of his statement.

"Thank you kindly," she said in a raspy whisper.

Alarmed at her appearance, he took a step back.

"It's not catching." She smiled reassuringly and then, as if that had been entirely too much effort, closed her eyes. "It's the ague. Been sick almost the whole way." Shivering, she pulled the counterpane up under her chin.

"You should take Calomel. They say it cures whatever ails you."

She didn't answer. Mason took another small step into the cabin and studied her white face. Her eyes were still closed, and she began to snore softly. He turned his attention to the tiny space. Like the rest of the cabin, it was efficient in its storage. He looked through everything within easy reach but found nothing remotely interesting. A storage box was built into the far wall. He eased carefully around the woman's pallet and opened it. No gold or silver sparkled up at him. Just clothes, ragged ones at that. Floss called something from the cave. After a glance at the sleeping woman, he retraced his steps and hurried to the horses.

Erich was just coming up the ramp. Mason led the stallion to him and then went back for the little mare. He consoled himself about the lack of treasure. At least he'd have the fine horses. And the cattle if he wanted them. Perhaps he should leave Martha her cow. She was so partial to Daisy. But then he thought of the babies up in the cave. They looked scrawny and could probably use the extra milk. What to do? What to do?

The mare went calmly down the ramp and up the bank. Mason tied her to a tree and took note of each family member. Martha was cooling the bucket of milk at the river, the little girl at her side. Lars was still fussing over the lame horse. Tobias was building the fire in the stove, and Erich was on his way back to the boat, maybe to sit at his sick wife's side.

Mason slipped into the trees and went up the trail. He stopped after a short while and whistled. Tommy materialized suddenly before him, ghost-like. After a moment Hughes, Little Harpe, and Fleming joined them.

"Where are the others?"

"Frank and Seth went back up to the bluff," Hughes said. "Don't know where Big Harpe be. He's as independent as a hog on ice."

Little Harpe glowered at the slur on his elder brother's good name. "What are we waiting for?"

"For morning," Mason answered calmly.

"Why in Hades would we do that when we can go down there and get what we want now?" Little Harpe said.

Charles Fleming rolled his eyes and sighed deeply. "Because if we did," he explained impatiently, "they'd be sure to tell other travelers. And then the Regulators would come and we'd have to leave our cave."

"And we're rather fond of our cave," Mason added. "So saddle up and get yourselves to the bend in the river. Be ready by sunup. I'll give the signal when they've left here."

"Why there?" Little Harpe said.

"Hughes will explain it to you on the way."

Little Harpe crossed his arms over his chest. "Tell me now."

Mason sighed. "The bend is the easiest place for them to land their boat." Little Harpe opened his mouth, and Mason put up a hand to forestall his question. "And they'll land it there because they're nice folks who will feel sorry for the poor lady crying on the shore. They'll be anxious to save her from the Indians."

"What poor lady?"

"Susannah. I'll send her down shortly. Floss will tell her what she has to do."

"If it's such a great plan," Little Harpe said, "why don't you send your woman?"

"First of all, Floss is not my woman. And second, the Hoffmans have already seen her." He put up a hand again. "And before you ask, you will be wearing masks. They'll not likely ever connect the robbery to us."

"It's a stupid plan," Little Harpe said. "Then we'll just have to tote all their stuff back here."

"Don't worry about it. We're just taking the horses, and they'll walk their way back here. I haven't decided about the cattle yet."

"What about everything else?"

"That's all they have worth taking. After you get the horses, leave the family be to go on their way." He started back down the trail but then stopped. "And, Little Harpe? Find your brother and make sure he knows the plan."

He didn't answer, but nodded his assent before turning away.

When Mason got to the cave, Floss was waiting for him. "Anything good? Lots of nice shiny guineas, or jewelry perhaps?"

"The only shiny things they have are those fine horses, which we'll take off their hands at the bend. Where's Susannah? She's going to be our damsel this time."

"She and the others are in back. I told them to keep the babies quiet."

"Get her ready to go. The men will want to leave shortly."

"It's about time she started earning her keep."

Floss went to the back. Mason helped himself to a tankard of whiskey and sat down to play Patience. It helped when his own patience wore thin. There wasn't much to do until morning.

CHAPTER 7

***

THE PRESENT

Merrideth pulled herself back to the present and stopped the action. But then she could not remember why she had. Time-surfing in virtual mode always took a toll. And just as she had figured, the after-effects of experiencing a pirate's mind made it worse than usual. She took several cleansing breaths to clear Mason's thoughts away. And then she remembered. Notes. She wanted to take notes while she fast-forwarded to the morning.

She set the laptop on the ledge beside her and picked up her backpack intending to get her notebook and pen out. But then everything went wobbly. Mason grinned at her from his makeshift card table and lifted his tankard of whiskey in a toast. She closed her eyes in alarm. Her first realization was that she was not entirely rid of 1797. And wasn't that an interesting new development with the software? The second realization was that she was going to lie down whether she wanted to or not. And then her body melted right off the ledge and onto the floor of the cave.

Well then. She would lie there for a while until the feeling passed. It was more than a little disturbing to retain such a clear reading on a subject once back in the present. It had never happened to that degree before. At least not to her. Maybe Abby and John had experienced something similar and she just had not realized it.

She heard the sound of boots coming across the stone floor. She was not ready to see Mason again, so she kept her eyes closed.

Hands touched her breasts. Now that was getting entirely too realistic. Merrideth's eyes flew open and shoved the marauding hands away. The arms attached to the hands were covered in tattoos, primarily variations on the skull and crossbones theme. The arms belonged to a wild-haired man who squatted beside her.

Had she actually travelled physically back in time to the pirates' cave? She blinked twice, but he was still there. He was not Samuel Mason or any of his men. This one's eyes were glazed with the effects of alcohol or maybe drugs.

At her sudden movement his eyes widened and then he grinned. "Whoo-ee! A cave girl!" He turned and called over his shoulder, "Hey, dudes, come see what I found."

More boots thudded on the cave floor and then two more men stood there grinning lasciviously down at her.

She started to sit up. The movement caused her head to spin alarmingly. Worse, her vision began to narrow to a tunnel. She gave up the idea and remained prone. It would not do to pass out again.

"I thought she was dead at first," the man with the busy hands said.

Another man laughed and punched his shoulder. "Aren't you into that sort of thing, Melvin? Oh, wait. I forget. You prefer sheep."

The one called Melvin staggered under the friendly assault, but he took no offense, just smiled slyly and took a sip from the can of beer he held. "Only when I'm not nailing your mama."

"Too bad the cave girl is already taken," the third man said sorrowfully.

A fourth man pushed his way through the others. He squatted beside Merrideth and ran a fingertip over her cheek. He looked familiar, even to her jumbled brain. Then he smiled a wolfish Hollywood smile. Even though he was no longer wearing the jacket, she knew that it was Patriotic Guy.

"Actually, I don't believe she is taken. But she will be." He smiled even wider at his play on words.

Her backpack was on the ledge behind her. She turned her head subtly to her left and saw that its leather strap hung down next to her shoulder. How quickly could she pull it from the ledge, find the can of mace within its jumble of stuff, and spray it into the man's loathsome smiling eyes?

When he rose and just stood there eyeing her with the rest of them, she felt a glimmer of hope. Maybe they were just after a little game of cat and mouse. When they were done scaring her, they would laugh and let her go. That hope died a little when one man went to the cave entrance to look out. It was obvious he wasn't admiring the scenery.

"Anyone coming?" Patriotic Guy said.

When the man turned back from looking, he was smiling with satisfaction. "Nope."

They were going to do it.

It had been a long time since she had prayed. She had given up the practice years ago when it became clear God wasn't interested in answering her petitions. But now a spontaneous and genuine, "God, help me," sprang silently but fervently into her brain. At the same moment, she pulled her backpack off the ledge and stuck her hand in it for the mace.

Patriotic Guy's booted foot came down on her wrist.

With her other hand she clawed at his boot, but it didn't budge. She reached up under his jeans and sank her nails into his hairy calf. He just laughed and pressed his boot down harder until she let go.

Another man pulled her free arm down and stood on it, too. If they applied much more pressure, her wrists would break. Even so, she kicked out with her legs, heaving her hips up off the ground. The two men standing on her arms didn't budge. Merrideth heard the other two arguing like boys vying for the last popsicle in the family freezer. She was going to vomit. She hated to do it in a state historical site. Then she nearly laughed at her misplaced concern.

"What's going on?"

Merrideth lifted her head and saw that an angel stood outlined against a glowing, orange-tinged sky at the mouth of the cave.

Patriotic Guy's perpetual smile morphed into a frown. "Nothing that concerns you. Go on back to handing out Bibles and leave us be."

Merrideth blinked, and then the sky went back to blue, and it was Trevor Dalton standing there. He came forward, and the pressure let up on her wrists. New pain speared into her hands as blood began to circulate in them again.

Apparently that left her head in short supply of oxygen, because the cave grew suddenly dim, and Patriotic Guy and the other men seemed to fade away. Then Trevor stood there looking down at her. Had the others left, bowing to his supposed ownership of her? Was he now planning to claim her on the cave floor? She scuttled away, crab-like, until she was against the cave wall.

"It's all right. You're safe." He cautiously extended a hand out to her. "Will you let me help you?"

The thought of being touched filled her with revulsion. But then he put his hands in his pockets, and she knew he wouldn't touch her unless she gave him permission.

She searched his face and saw no malevolent intentions there, only compassion. He seemed to know the moment she had reached the correct conclusion, because he took his hand from his pocket and offered it to her again. She latched onto it, and he pulled her to her feet.

And then she began to cry.

After a moment, Trevor drew her against his chest and began tentatively stroking her back.

"I'm sorry," she blubbered.

"You're not going to be one of those stupid women who blames herself, are you?"

She pulled away indignantly. "No way."

"Good."

Her tears resumed. "I'm sorry... because...I'm... crying... all over you."

"I don't mind."

And so she leaned into him again and continued crying it out. It was a relief, although at the same time embarrassing to lose control. She hardly ever cried. The analytical part of her brain told her that the reason she did so now was because she had not had the chance to recover from time-surfing before the men had cornered her. The emotional center in her brain insisted that she continue crying until she washed out the shock of so narrowly evading being raped.

Her legs turned to rubber, and Trevor eased down until he sat leaning against the cave wall with her on his lap. She should have felt embarrassed about that, too, but for some reason she didn't. That he was a complete stranger, did not seem to matter in the least. She had prayed, and God had sent him to her rescue, plain and simple.

Gradually her tears let up. She realized she was hiccupping in his ear and turned her face away. But she could not make herself pull away entirely. The sound of his heartbeat against the soft cotton T-shirt was too comforting to give up just yet.

"Okay," she said at last. "I think that's all." She hiccupped again.

"Boo," he said softly. "Did that help?"

"Maybe," she said and hiccupped again. "No. Sorry." She wiped at her eyes with her bare forearms and then winced at the pain.

His brows drew together in a frown. Then he pulled up his T-shirt and used it to blot away her tears. She got a glimpse of more tattoos on his torso.

"How did you know?" she said.

"Actually, I didn't come here intending to rescue you. I heard some of the bikers daring each other to dive off the top of the cave into the river. Most of them are too stoned to think straight. A couple of years ago one ended up paralyzed. Another time a guy drowned. So I followed those idiots to make sure they didn't kill themselves. I'm glad I did."

She hiccupped again. "Me, too."

"Do you think you can walk?"

"I think so."

He stood, helping her up as he did. She felt better than she had figured she would—until she saw that the pirate scene on her laptop still played out for all the world to see. Anyone who took the time to look would recognize the interior of the cave by the distinctive shape of its mouth. The bikers had probably been too drunk or stoned to notice, but Trevor Dalton had had plenty of time to look while he was playing nursemaid to her. She snapped the laptop closed and glanced up at him. His expression was cool and reserved, but there was a tiny bit of emotion showing. It was difficult to know if it was curiosity about her computer or just concern for her.

She returned the laptop to her backpack and he took it from her and put in on his own shoulder. "Come on, let's get you back to the lodge, so we can call the police."

So much had happened, in her own time and the pirates', that when they got outside she was surprised to find that it was still afternoon. Trevor took her hands and studied her wrists. They were red and raw from her struggles to escape and filthy from the bikers' boots. Trevor glared at her arms, his nostrils flaring, but she knew his anger was aimed at the bikers who had put the marks there.

"I'm all right." To prove it, she started down the trail ahead of him.

She was not really all right, of course. She could not even remember the walk back to the lodge, yet suddenly found herself there and being fussed over by two waitresses from the restaurant and Shirley the desk clerk, who kept apologizing for not warning her about the Road Hogs and for the fact that the lodge manager Mr. Carlson was out of town. Shirley called the police, and the next hour was even more of a blur. Sheriff Mitchell came, gruff but concerned. He examined her arms and then commandeered Carlson's office to interview her and Trevor.

He took their names and other information down in a notebook. "Okay, Miss Randall, what can you tell me about the men who attacked you?"

Merrideth described the one she thought of as Patriotic Guy, from his smile down to the eagle emblem on the back of his jacket.

"But he wasn't wearing the jacket anymore."

"Then I don't suppose it will be of much help finding him," Sheriff Mitchell said. "What about the others?"

"I don't remember much. I think one had a skull-and-crossbones tattoo on his right—no left—forearm."

He wrote in his notebook.

"Wait," she said. "I'm not sure about that. I may have imagined it. I was thinking about pirates when he grabbed me."

Sheriff Mitchell sighed, and Merrideth could almost read his mind: allowances must be made for hysterical ladies. Again he wrote in his notebook. She would have given a lot of money to know what. After a minute he stopped and looked at her. "You described the first suspect in detail—quite a lot of detail, in fact. How is it that you can describe him and not the others?"

"He stuck with me because I saw him earlier on the street. He offered me a ride on his bike."

"Did you take him up on his offer? Maybe go for a spin around town?"

"Of course not."

"So he had no reason to think you might welcome his

advances?"

Trevor's eyes suddenly blazed. "What do you mean, Sheriff? Are you actually asking her if she wanted to be raped?"

The sheriff glared at him. "Please allow me to conduct my investigation."

Trevor did not respond, although it was clear he wanted to say more. A twitching muscle in his jaw indicated he was clenching his teeth.

Sheriff Mitchell gave him a long look. "You were there. Presumably you can tell me what they look like."

Trevor's face went back to being unreadable. "Miss Randall already gave you a good description of the smiley one. I didn't get a good look at the others. I noticed one had meth-mouth, but that's about all."

"You're not very observant, are you, Mr. Dalton?"

Trevor did not respond to the insult, only calmly said, "I can tell you what kind of bike Smiley rides."

"You do that."

He reeled off a detailed description of the make, year, and model.

The sheriff wrote it all in his notebook and then looked up at Trevor. "What about the license plate?"

"Didn't see it."

"And you don't know his name?"

"I would have told you right off if I did."

"I heard a name," Merrideth said. "I just remembered. One of them was joking and called the other by name."

"Well, what is it?" Sheriff Mitchell asked testily.

"Something like *Elwood* or *Erwin*, maybe. I'm sorry. I'm terrible at remembering names."

Sheriff Mitchell's expression conveyed equal parts exasperation and compassion. "All right, then. Go wait in the lobby, Miss Randall. Somebody get her a chair. She looks like she's about to fall down. You stick around, too," he said, pointing to Trevor. "And try to think of something useful."

Trevor went into the restaurant and came back with a chair for her to sit on. She sank gratefully into it, and he stood a few feet away leaning against the wall.

Shirley came in carrying a cup and saucer. "Here, honey, drink this. Nothing like a cup of Earl Grey to calm your nerves."

"Thanks. That sounds good." It was comforting, the warmth of the cup in her hands as much as the tea it contained.

The office door was not completely closed, and they heard Mitchell's conversation with two of his deputies on his walkie-talkie. He passed on the descriptions of the men and the bike and told them to be on the look-out for them. "I've got a biker here that witnessed the attack. I think he decided his buddies were getting a little out of hand and figured he'd step in and play hero for the lady."

Merrideth darted a look at Trevor, but he remained silent. He had defended her to the sheriff, but apparently he did not feel the need to offer anything in his own defense. He did not react to the sheriff's blatantly biased accusation, just stood there leaning against the wall as if he were resigned to being unfairly condemned.

"Hmmph," Shirley said, glancing at Trevor.

"Those guys were so obviously not Trevor's buddies," Merrideth hurried to assure her. "Anyone could see that. The sheriff wasn't there. He doesn't—"

"No, you were the one there, honey," Shirley said firmly. "So I'm sure you know a lot more about what was what than the sheriff does."

Trevor grunted a small wordless sound that seemed to indicate gratitude for their support. Merrideth smiled to herself.

They continued to listen in on the conversation among the sheriff and his deputies. She soon gathered that the department was always overwhelmed by the extra work associated with the Hellhound Homecoming every year. They were already stretched thin patrolling the streets of Cave-in-Rock and the perimeter of the Hellhound campground. An added mission to go into the camp looking for the would-be rapists would mean even more overtime pay, and the county coffers were nearly drained as it was. One deputy wondered if they even had probable cause to go into "that hell-hole." And the other deputy opined that even being meth-heads, the bikers were surely smart enough to be long gone by now anyway.

"Besides," he added, "you know as well as I do that the charges aren't going to stick even if we can find the devils."

"That is not for you to worry about, Jeff," Sheriff Mitchell said angrily. "You two just get your butts over to the campground. Wait for me, and we'll go in together. And wear your body armor."

The sheriff came out of the office, and Merrideth pushed herself to her feet. Her legs were feeling rubbery again, so she put a hand on the back of the chair to steady herself. Trevor straightened from the wall and looked her way.

The sheriff stood in front of her holding his hat. "I don't suppose you remembered that name?"

"No," Merrideth said. "But never mind, Sheriff. I want you to call it off."

Beside her, Trevor stiffened.

Sheriff Mitchell frowned. "Don't be afraid, Miss Randall."

"It's not that, Sheriff. I'd go through with it if they had succeeded at what they intended to do. But since they didn't—"

"Those men assaulted you," Mitchell said. "Even if they didn't rape you."

"Well, I'm fine and I'm not pressing charges."

Mitchell tugged at his collar. "I suppose you heard what my deputies said, but listen, don't pay any mind to them. We'll go after the sons of—"

"You and your men should get back to your patrols, Sheriff." It was not that she did not want the creeps caught, but it would be a pointless risk for the sheriff and his men to go into that place on a wild goose chase. All she wanted was to get to her room before she fell apart again. Once there, she would crawl under the covers, and not come out for a year or two.

The sheriff stood frowning at her, arms crossed over his chest, for a full minute, but she didn't back down. At last he let out a weary breath and shook his head. "All right, Miss Randall." He pulled out a business card and handed it to her. "My private cell number is on there. Call me if you change your mind."

"Thank you, Sheriff," Merrideth said.

Tipping his hat to the room at large, he went out.

Shirley came out from behind the counter and took the tea cup from Merrideth. "You are not fine. Let's get you to your room."

Shirley tried to usher her along, but Merrideth turned back to look for Trevor. He was halfway out the door. "Wait."

He paused in the doorway and turned her way.

"I never said thanks."

"No need."

"Well, thanks anyway."

A glimmer of a smile passed over his face, and then he went

out, closing the door behind himself.

"What a nice young man." Shirley whistled softly. "And good-looking, I guess! He makes a person rethink the whole tattoo thing, doesn't he?"

"Really?"

Shirley snorted a laugh. "I meant for handsome young fellows, not me."

Merrideth smiled tiredly. "There's really no need to escort me to my room, Shirley."

"It's the least I can do after what happened. I thought you might be a little skittish about going alone. We want you to have a good visit here. And let me apologize again that Mr. Carlson was out of town when this horrible thing happened."

"There's no way he could have prevented the attack."

"Nevertheless, he feels really bad he wasn't here."

Merrideth stopped her. "I get it. You think I'm going to sue."

"Personally, I wouldn't blame you if you did."

"Well, stop worrying about it. I'm not the type."

"Oh, good. Mr. Carlson will be so relieved to hear it."

"When you talk to him, tell him I'm having a great time. Other than just now, I mean. And bright and early tomorrow I'm going to be right back at the cave doing my research. I'm not about to let a bunch of thugs keep me from what I came here to do."

"That's the spirit!"

Once alone in her room, her bravado began to dissipate, especially when she got a look at herself in the bathroom mirror. A bad-hair day had turned out to be the least of her problems. Now, with her white cheeks and tear-smudged mascara she looked a lot more like the Bride of Frankenstein than she did the confident persona she attempted to present to the world: Professor Randall, brave historian and seeker of Truth, Justice, and the American way. The purple boot-shaped bruises forming on the pale skin of her inner forearms proved she was not so invincible after all, and definitely no super hero.

Merrideth showered and put on her oversized sleep T-shirt then sat on the edge of the bed holding her phone. Abby would be expecting her to call. She would worry if she didn't check in, but she would worry even more if she told her what had happened. And there was no way on earth she could keep her voice calm enough to lie. Abby's antennae would pick up on her vibes in a heartbeat and then she would demand to know the details. And John would absolutely freak out. She could text Abby, but what would she say? "Having fun. Wish you were here?"

If she called Brett he would say "I told you so" or at least think it. He had been right about her needing a partner for her cave explorations, just not in the way he meant. He was probably too busy anyway, what with all his Farmer Brown chores. She smiled a little, picturing him beleaguered by Nelda's barnyard animals.

She plugged in her laptop and phone to recharge, turned off the lamp, got in bed, and pulled the sheet over her. She closed her eyes, and immediately Patriotic Guy was there, grinding his boot into her wrist while he smiled down at her. She willed him away, and for a while he complied. But then he was back, and this time he brought his buddies. She suddenly remembered the name she'd heard. Melvin. It was a silly name for a man with meth-rotted teeth who joked about bestiality. At least she hoped he had been joking. She turned over and squeezed her eyes tightly closed, but the men were still there behind her eyelids.

She opened her eyes and sat up in bed.

If she were Abby, she would know how to pray. The woman prayed constantly. About everything. Abby wouldn't feel the least bit like she was bugging God to ask him to make the images in her head go away so she could get a good night's sleep. And God answered *her* prayers. At least she claimed he did.

There was no help for it. She would have to chance calling her. She turned on the lamp, picked up her phone, and punched in her number.

"Merri! I was hoping for an update."

"Is it too late to call?"

"Of course not. You're the early bird, not me. So does *Beautiful Houses* work in the cave?"

"It does. I'm finding all sorts of information. In between interruptions from tourists. And such."

Merrideth filled her in on what she'd seen and learned about the pirate operation at the cave. "I want to get an early start tomorrow to learn more about Mason and the Harpe brothers. Not to mention find out what happened to the Hoffman family. I have a horrible feeling that it's not going to end well for them."

"I hate that you have to experience that alone. Back in the day, when I was rummaging around inside that murderer's head to find out the truth about the Old Dears' ancestor I had John right there with me, and still it was brutal. I had nightmares about that fire for years afterward. Are you going to be able to sleep tonight with visions of pirates dancing in your head?"

"Actually, at the moment it's not the pirates that are messing with my head. I was wondering...if you'd...pray for me. So I can sleep."

"I always pray for you, Merri. But what do you mean? Who's messing with your head?"

"Just some guys. It's nothing. But if you could send a few prayers my way, it might help me sleep."

Abby chuckled. "If you don't mind, I'll send my prayers where they'll do you some good. Now back to the guys you so casually mentioned. What guys? And what happened?"

"I shouldn't have said anything. I knew you'd freak out."

"I'm going to freak out if you don't tell me. Only wait until I get John. I'll put you on speaker phone."

Merrideth told them an abbreviated Cliff Notes version of what had happened in the cave, downplaying the danger and completely leaving out the current condition of her bruised arms. Even so, her friends went completely overboard.

"Okay, pack up, Merri," John said. "I can be there in three hours."

"If I wanted to go home, I could drive myself, John. Besides, you need your sleep if you're going to finish prepping for your case this weekend."

"Then I'll just have to find someone to watch the girls and come down," Abby said.

"No," Merrideth and John said in unison.

"It would only put you at risk, too," he added. "No, Merri should come home. First thing tomorrow morning."

"I'm not leaving until I get what I came for, John. Look, I'm sorry I got you two all riled up. Don't worry about me. I'll be fine. Only, as I said, could you maybe—"

"Pray? Of course we'll pray for you, kiddo," Abby said.

"And for the sheriff to catch those animals," John said.

Merrideth did not mention that she had called off the sheriff's search. There was no since upsetting them more.

***

The sound of motorcycle engines and rock music woke her from a dream in which she had been rowing a small fishing boat down a flooded Chicago street like it was a Venetian canal. It was dark and she should have been scared. But she hadn't been, because as she went along, pairs of street lights came on just ahead of her to show her the way.

She rolled over to see the time. It was nearly two o'clock. Abby and John's prayers must had worked because she had fallen asleep quickly. A few more hours would have been nice, but she wasn't going to complain.

Another motorcycle roared. It sounded much closer. Actually, it sounded like it could be in the lodge parking lot. Adrenalin pumped into her system. She threw off the covers and crept to the sliding glass door. Had she remembered to lock it? Pushing aside the vertical blinds, she saw that of course she had. But would it actually hold against an intruder? Weren't such doors supposed to come with one of those bar things to put in the floor track to prevent them from sliding open?

The deck and the grounds beyond it were well-lit, and the moon was bright overhead, but the building prevented her from seeing the whole parking lot and the bike making the racket. After a moment, the motorcycle went quiet, and a few seconds later a figure came into her line of sight.

Her stomach somersaulted, and she took a step to the side of the glass door. Then she reassured herself that since her room was dark, he would not be able to see her. She looked out again. He was still coming her way. Even through the glass door she heard his boots clicking faintly on the parking lot asphalt. When he reached the yard the grass muffled the sound, not that he was trying to be stealthy. He just kept walking purposefully, like he knew exactly where his destination was.

Which apparently was her deck!

She crept back to the nightstand and felt around until she found her phone, wondering how long it would take Sheriff Mitchell or one of his men to get there.

Phone in hand, she went back to the door and peeked out, afraid she would find herself looking at the smiling face of Patriotic Guy. But whoever the man out there was, he had stopped when he reached her deck and made no attempt to climb over the railing onto it. He just stood there leaning against it looking out into the night. She squinted at the back of his jacket. It was unadorned with American Eagles or any other patriotic emblems. As if he sensed her watching, he turned and the moonlight fell on his face.

Her breath left her lungs in a great whoosh. She opened the door a crack. "Trevor?"

"It's me."

She opened the door a little wider. "What are you doing out there? And how did you know which room—?"

"I watched when you left with Shirley until I saw your light came on. But I'm not stalking you."

"I know."

"Are you all right?"

"I am now that my heart is back in my chest."

"I looked, but I didn't see hide nor hair of them anywhere in the campground. Don't worry. They're probably a state away by now."

"And you came here in the middle of the night to tell me that."

"I thought you'd sleep easier. So go on back to bed now." He turned away and resumed looking out into the night.

"Now what are you doing?"

"Just enjoying a quiet summer night."

Right. He was out there because when he had told her that the rapists were gone he had qualified it with a *probably*.

"Trevor?"

"What?"

"Thank you."

He did not bother to respond, just continued leaning against her deck studying the sky.

She shut the door and relocked it. Knowing he was out there should have made it too weird to sleep. But she began to drift off as soon as her head hit the pillow.

.

CHAPTER 8

Shirley was dusting the glass shelves in the gift shop when Merrideth entered the lobby. She put aside her duster and hurried over to Merrideth. "Well, don't you look perky this morning!"

"I feel pretty perky, all things considered."

"How did you sleep?"

"Like a baby."

Trevor had also been gone when she got up. She didn't know if he had spent the night there or just pretended he was going to so she would feel safe.

She hadn't thought it prudent to mention her guardian angel to Abby when she called first thing to see how she was. Upon learning she had slept well, Abby had burst forth with "Praise the Lord" and "Isn't it wonderful the way God answers prayer?" Whether he actually had or it had been Trevor's vigil, no outlaws, past or present, had made any appearances in her head for the rest of the night.

"But, oh, your arms!" Shirley said.

Grimacing, Merrideth held them out for inspection. "It looks worse than it is."

"Are you going to be able to drive home okay?"

"I'll be fine."

"Mr. Carlson said I was to tell you breakfast is on the house."

"That's not necessary."

"Mr. Carlson insists on it."

"And *I* insist on paying my own way."

"Okay. Suit yourself." Shirley took one of the souvenirs from the shelf beside her and thrust it into her hands. "Well at least let me give you this. So you can remember your stay at the Cave-in-Rock State Park. The good times, not the…incident."

It was a snow globe showing the cave, in front of which three swash-buckling pirates in tri-corn hats and eye patches grinned. Merrideth could almost hear them saying *Arrgh*! "Thanks, Shirley. It's really…cute. I'll keep it on my desk."

"Mr. Carlson said to say that he hopes you'll come back to visit another time so you can see how safe and nice everything is when the Hellhounds and Road Hogs aren't in town."

"I'm sure it is. But you're not getting rid of me yet. I've got more work to do at the cave."

"I thought you were just whistling Dixie last night when you said you were going back in there."

"No, I meant it," Merrideth said.

"Then I'll let Fred know. He can keep an extra sharp eye on the trail head. Make sure no unsavory types go down to the cave while you're working."

"Thanks, Shirley. That would be a relief. But first I need breakfast. And coffee. Lots of coffee."

"The girls will take care of that right quick."

When she got to the restaurant, one of the friendly waitresses who had fussed over her the night before seated her and then went to get her coffee. There were only a handful of other diners, and she wondered how much Hellhound Homecoming cost the lodge in lost sales every year. Merrideth studied the menu. It didn't take long to decide what she wanted. She set the menu back in the table rack and looked up, hoping to see her coffee coming. Instead, she saw that Trevor stood at the doorway scanning the room.

She waved at him, and he started walking her direction.

He was freshly shaven, and his hair was still damp from a shower. He took off his leather jacket and hung it on the back of his chair then sat down across from her.

"I think I'm having a deja vu," she said, handing him a menu.

Ignoring it, he took her arm instead and turned it over to look at the bruises. "I'm sorry I didn't get there sooner."

"You have nothing to be sorry about."

He averted his eyes. "You have no idea how much I have to be sorry about."

"Not as far as I'm concerned, you don't. Order anything you

like. Get steak or something. I'm paying for your breakfast."

"No you're not."

Merrideth laughed. "You sound like me. Shirley tried to pay for my breakfast, and I wouldn't let her."

The waitress came and took their orders. She chose an egg-white omelet. Trevor chose oatmeal and toast.

"If I *were* paying for your breakfast, that would not be much compensation for all you did for me yesterday, not to mention guardian-angel duty last night."

"I happen to like oatmeal."

"But aren't you breaking some big, bad biker rule? Don't you all eat raw meat?"

He didn't smile at her joke, and she wondered if she had offended him. Maybe he just had a serious personality. Maybe he was trying to look cool like James Dean.

"The Road Hogs give bikers a bad name. We're not all bad."

"I think you've already proven that."

He looked curiously at her. "I haven't been able to figure you out. Not vacationing. No one does that alone. And not hiking, even though you're always carrying around that backpack. Or if you are, judging from how you looked yesterday lugging the thing into town, you must not do it often."

"I'm sure I looked a sweaty mess. Thanks for pointing it out."

He seemed distressed. "I didn't mean—did you know in the sun your hair shines like a palomino pony?"

She laughed. "That's the second time this week I've been compared to a horse."

"I'm sorry. I'm no good with compliments."

"It's me. I'm not good at accepting them."

"You should be used to it."

She smiled. "Do you really believe you're no good at compliments?"

He didn't answer. It was becoming apparent that he didn't waste words, especially on rhetorical, self-evident questions. He just sat there looking at her as if waiting for her to say more.

"Why am I here? I'm researching the cave for a paper I want to write. And for my class. I teach history at a small college three hours north of here."

"Well, if you're set on staying around for more research, I hope you believe me now when I tell you the Road Hogs are dangerous.

Sorry. I don't mean that to sound like an *I told you so.*"

"You say that like you're not one of them."

An amused smile bloomed on his face. With a potent weapon like that, it was a good thing he did not smile often. If she'd been standing, she would have tripped over her own feet.

Still smiling, he reached into the pocket of his leather jacket and pulled out a business card. "Here."

According to the card, he was Trevor Dalton from Pittsburgh, a member of the Christian Motorcyclists Association. *We ride for the Son* was printed under the CMA acronym and logo. Funny how a few words on a 2 x 3 ½ inch card could change everything. How had she ever thought he looked dangerous?

When she looked up his smile was gone, and he was back to his usual serious mode. "So what do you do when you're not riding your bike?"

"I'm a structural engineer. I own a firm in Pittsburgh."

She coughed and raised her napkin to cover her mouth. And her surprise. She hoped her stupidity and prejudice were not written all over her face. She had somehow assumed he only had a high school diploma at most, no matter his obvious intelligence.

"It's a small firm. Most of our work is for the city, but we also consult on some high-end home construction."

The waitress brought their breakfast. Merrideth put her napkin in her lap and took a bite of the omelet. It tasted as good as it looked. She realized Trevor wasn't eating and then saw that he was praying. The sight of a big, tattooed man bowing his head did something funny to her chest. After a moment he opened his eyes and trained them back on her.

"I'll say the same thing you did," Merrideth said. "I can't figure you out. An engineer—a Christian—with tattoos. Sorry, I guess I'm guilty of stereotyping."

"They help me remember." He didn't elaborate on what it was he wanted to remember, just extended his arms on the table so she could see better. And this time she didn't feel too inhibited to actually look at them. The tattoos were an intricate intertwining of flowers, leaves, and beautiful script that on his right arm read *Grace—it saved a wretch like me* and on his left, *I once was lost but now am found.*

"The hymn," she said. "*Amazing Grace.* May I see the one on your neck?"

He pulled the neck of his T-shirt down a little.

Of course it was not a swastika, but a cross, an intricate and beautiful one, with a banner and the words John 3:16. It would not be the design of choice for non-religious people who chose to have cross tattoos because they were "pretty" or "cool," not really knowing the symbol's true significance. She was not a fan of body art and would never have a tattoo herself, but she had to give the artist credit for the skillful execution.

"So what's a CMA member doing at Hellhound Homecoming?"

"I'm one of eleven here. We've been coming since 2010. We hand out Bibles, bottled water, and toiletry packs for bikers who forgot to bring toothpaste or soap, things like that."

"Oh, I saw your yellow pavilion down by the ferry."

"There's one inside the campground, too."

"Is it as bad in there as Sheriff Mitchell and his men made it out to be?"

"Pretty much. Like the deputy said, it's a hell-hole. Nudity. Drugs. You can buy whatever your heart desires. Pot, of course, but also crank, ecstasy, coke, and smack."

"I wonder if locals think Sheriff Mitchell and his men are shirking their duty."

"It's not Mitchell's fault. The Hellhounds' campground is privately owned, and they don't let the cops inside without a warrant. They did go in last year, but that was by invitation. A guy died of a heroin overdose. Everyone was too stoned to notice—or care—for over eight hours. When someone finally got around to mentioning the dead guy, they decided it was time to call the cops. But barring anything of that magnitude, I think it makes sense for the sheriff to use his limited manpower for patrolling the town."

"Do you think I was right to call off the search?"

"Your call, but I know it would have stirred up a lot of trouble if they had gone in there. Maybe incited the Hellhounds and Road Hogs to more lawlessness."

"But they let you and your CMA friends in?"

"The event is open to the public. Just not to anyone in a 'pig' uniform."

"Why do you go into a place like that?"

"Someone's got to bring them the Gospel," he said simply.

"Do any of them ever get their acts together enough to convert to Christianity?"

He set down his spoon and looked at her. "No, and I don't expect them to."

"You don't?"

"They're dead men walking. How could they?"

Trevor did not elaborate on his strange statement, just picked up his spoon and went back to eating. Nevertheless, she sensed that he was waiting for her to comment.

She could not think what to say, so she wiped her mouth and set aside her napkin. "Sounds like you've got your work cut out for you. And I need to get back to mine."

"I'm not scheduled to go on duty at the stand for a while. I can keep you company in the cave."

"Oh. That's okay. Fred's on the lookout for *unsavory types*. And this time I'll keep my can of mace right by my side."

They paid at the register and walked out into the humid July morning. "Thanks again for everything," she said, shouldering her backpack.

"I need you to see something."

"What is it?"

"It won't take long, I promise."

"Okay."

She had another deja vu moment when she ended up on the back of his bike, holding his trim middle. He took them the two miles to town and then turned left toward the ferry. He parked in front of the yellow pavilion and turned off his engine. The banner welcoming the Hellhounds and Road Hogs fluttered in the morning breeze, but there were no attendees there to be welcomed. Doubtless they would be sleeping off their drunkenness for some time yet.

Two middle-aged couples manning the courtesy station looked up and smiled. Both the women wore canary yellow T-shirts with the same CMA logo she had seen on Trevor's business card. One man was balding and the other wore collar-length hair and a Fu Manchu mustache. There were bottles of water in ice chests on the grass, and on the counter there were baskets of wrapped hard candies, brochures, and stacks of Bibles. A sign said it was all free to bikers.

One of the women said, "Hey, Trev, who's your friend?"

"Merrideth Randall."

They continued to sit on the bike. Trevor did not offer an

explanation either to her or the two couples, who continued to smile at them. "Would you like a bottle of water?" the other woman asked at last.

"No, thank you," Merrideth said.

The man with the mustache cleared his throat and looked at Trevor expectantly.

"Oh, sorry," Trevor said. "Merrideth, that's Geno Bertinelli and his wife Barb and that's Larry and June Groves."

"Nice to meet you," Merrideth said.

"I thought you were going in," Larry said. "You're not taking Merrideth, surely."

"I've got a little time yet." Trevor kicked the starter and his bike roared to life again. "And no, I'm definitely not taking Merrideth in there."

The bike leaped away, and she grabbed at his waist. It had been a weird three minutes of pointless conversation. Then it came to her. He thought the reason she was reluctant to let him keep her company in the cave was because she still harbored suspicions about him. His only purpose in taking her to the welcome station was to get his mild-mannered, middle-aged friends to vouch for his trustworthiness.

It was not that she mistrusted him. And she certainly was not anxious to go back to the cave alone after what had happened. It would be wonderful to have someone with her, except for the fact that there would be no way to keep what she was doing secret from him.

She had often thought about revealing the program to Brett but had not because she was afraid he would blab. Trevor was the very antithesis of a blabber mouth. But even though she had no trouble entrusting her personal safety to him, entrusting *Beautiful Houses'* safety to him was another whole matter.

Back at the lodge, he parked in the lot, and she got off, prepared to wave him cheerily on his way as if she did not know the purpose of their little excursion to the welcome station. But he turned off the engine and sat there with his face all serious, looking at her as if he knew exactly what she was thinking.

If she asked him to stand guard outside while she went into the cave to do her work, he would probably do it, no questions asked. Her guardian angel. But how could she treat him that way? If she did, he would never believe she thought him a decent, trustworthy man and not one that she lumped together with those other bikers as Sheriff Mitchell had.

After a moment, she said, "I have something to show you, too. At the cave."

A glimmer of satisfaction crossed his face, and then he got off the bike and secured it. He took the backpack from her shoulders and slipped it onto his own. Then, wordlessly he started for the trail.

She put a hand on his forearm to stop him. "You have to promise not to tell anyone."

"You have my word." He put his hand to his heart like a Boy Scout—trustworthy, loyal, and reverent.

"Okay then."

They came across Fred on his hands and knees weeding a bed of petunias next to one of the cabins.

"Hello. Nice morning," Merrideth said.

"It is." Fred smiled at her then sat back on his heels and squinted suspiciously at Trevor. "I take it he's our hero, Miss Randall?"

Trevor gave a little grunt and looked away as if any moment he'd start shuffling his feet and saying "Pshaw, 'tweren't nothin', ma'am."

"This is Trevor Dalton, Fred. I can vouch for him," Merrideth said, grinning.

"All right then. You two go on." Fred unclipped a walkie-talkie from his waistband. "I'll report in to Shirley."

"Thanks, Fred," Merrideth said.

She and Trevor continued down the path. Behind them Fred said, "The package is safe. Repeat. The package is safe. Over."

"Carry on," Shirley answered, her voice crackly over the walkie-talkie. "Over and out."

A tiny smile crossed Trevor's face, and the minute they were out of Fred's hearing, Merrideth laughed out loud. Even without Fred and Shirley's cloak and dagger routine, it would have been difficult not to smile on a morning sweet with the scent of petunias and crepe myrtle and the path sunlit and cheerful.

But when she reached the cave, a rush of sickening fear swamped her system. She saw herself lying helpless and afraid at the hands of the men who intended to rape her, their giant shadows looming on the stone walls. The faces of Samuel Mason and the Harpe brothers also came to her as clearly as if she had actually met them there in person.

It was more difficult to go inside than she had imagined.

"Are you sure you want to do this?" Trevor said.

"I'm sure." She took a breath and walked in. She led him to the stone ledge, took the backpack from him, and got out her laptop.

"You were asking why I lug my backpack around. I don't like to let it out of my sight, because of what's on this computer. I have a program called *Beautiful Houses*. It lets me—" She stopped and took a deep breath. "Never mind. It would take a year to explain it all." She patted the stone ledge. "Sit here and see for yourself."

Fortunately, time had not jumped on her. The scene was paused just as she had left it before she fainted, except that it was no longer in virtual mode.

Trevor leaned in closer and studied the image on the screen. "What am I seeing?"

"It's a man playing Solitaire, only back then they called it Patience."

"In this cave."

"So you figured that out, did you?"

"The mouth of it is exactly the same."

Apparently not much got past Trevor Dalton. Even in the midst of the drama in the cave yesterday, he had noticed what was playing on her laptop. He had not, however, put two and two together yet. It was time to help him do that.

"You've heard about the river pirates of Cave-in-Rock?"

"Yes."

"Well, the man playing cards is Samuel Mason, pirate-in-chief. He's killing time, waiting for morning so he can implement his latest nefarious scheme."

"They've got him looking like a namby-pamby, not a pirate. Maybe if he had a few tats—"

Merrideth laughed. "You still don't get it, do you? How could you?"

"It's a movie, right? Although I'm wondering why we aren't watching it up at the lodge."

"Because that wouldn't be possible. This is not a movie. See the date at the bottom of the screen?"

"October 16, 1797." He looked up at her and then back down at the screen again. "What is it then?"

"When I fast-forward or rewind, we can see Samuel Mason's life unfold. Here, let me show you."

He grabbed her arm to stop her, and she winced. He released it, looking horrified. "I'm sorry. I forgot. Did I hurt you?"

"It's all right. I'm fine. Listen, I know this is a lot to take in, but I've got so much more I want to see before I leave here. So let me—"

"So, it's a documentary, then?"

"No, it's real."

"Real."

"Yes. We're seeing what happened at this very cave over two hundred years ago. I'm trying to discover how the pirates operated. How they managed to lure the settlers in."

"It's a computer program?"

"Yes."

"How does it work, and where on earth did it come from?"

She grinned at the expression on his face. It *was* a miraculous program if it got even Trevor-the-Silent excited enough to start asking questions.

"I have no idea where it came from. It was just there on the computer my dad bought me sixteen years ago. Last year, I copied it to this new laptop. As for how it works, I don't know that either. It sort of rewinds time. It's not a time travel machine. I don't mean to say that."

Most people about then would have expressed disbelief or started asking a million more questions, but Trevor Dalton only sat there, eyes a little wider than usual, waiting for her to finish explaining.

"So it's really useful to me—invaluable really—for historical research. Like for this cave, for example."

"Okay. Make it go."

She laughed. "All right. I'm going to rewind, so you can see the pirates' victims. She rewound it to the point where Mason first stepped onto the Hoffmans' flatboat and then let it play.

"Meet the Hoffman family from Pennsylvania. They're on their way to Kaskaskia and the Illinois Country. Mason has been doing his best to talk them into coming up to the cave to purchase supplies, but the family is not interested. They only stopped to graze their livestock."

"I didn't know they carried animals on their flatboats. I should have realized."

"Yes, this one's a regular Noah's Ark. They have four horses, a bull and cow, and some chickens. And there's Mason, helping the family unload the livestock."

"They look a little suspicious of him."

"They *are* suspicious. The old man especially is nobody's fool. But Mason smiles and chats his way into the family's confidence pretty quickly. And all the while Mason's helping, he's scoping out the Hoffmans' flatboat to see if they have enough valuables to make it worthwhile robbing them. And if so, whether he should relieve them of their belonging right away or let other members of his gang do so when the family gets farther down the river. He's always careful to avoid having settlers connect the robbery to the cave, because he doesn't want word to get out about it to future travelers coming down the Ohio."

"Clever."

"And ruthless. There's no telling how many settlers Mason robbed and left destitute on the wild frontier. But get this, he also has a surprisingly tender heart. See the little girl smiling out the window of the boat cabin? When Mason heard that her doll fell in the river he wished he had one to replace it. He felt genuinely sorry for her."

"So you assume."

"So I know. I was in his head. I also *heard* Mason thinking that the Hoffmans had no idea the pains he took so as not to have to kill them."

"Really?"

"Really. I'll switch to virtual mode, and you'll see what I mean. But I warn you, it's intense."

.

CHAPTER 9

Merrideth paused the program and grinned at Trevor. "And there we are back where we started. Mason is playing his game of Patience, waiting for morning to come. What do you think?"

"You're right. It's intense." Trevor blinked at her and ran a hand through his hair. "I have the most profound sense of guilt." He closed his eyes and swallowed.

She set the laptop aside and leaned her head against the cool stone wall behind her. "I know. My brain feels polluted from being inside Mason's head. But you sort of get used to it when you've time-surfed as much as I have."

He put his knees up and rested his forehead on them. "You wouldn't have agreed to be alone here with me if you knew my past."

"Trevor, don't beat yourself up. Give yourself a couple of minutes, and you'll be able to sort your feelings out."

"You don't get it. I'm an ex-con. I was in prison for over a year."

She turned to look at him. "Is that where you got the tattoos?"

He laughed drily. "That's your first question? Not what I did to end up in prison?"

"No need. Whoever you were then, you're not now."

He blinked in surprise. After a moment he said, "By the way, you're insulting tattoo artists everywhere when you ask if I got these in prison. Prison tattoos are crude jobs made with sewing needles and homemade ink."

"Yours are beautifully done." She remembered the script on his right forearm: *I once was lost, but now I'm found.* "You got them afterwards to remind you."

He didn't answer her unspoken question, so she changed the subject. "Mason is a conundrum, isn't he? You can tell from his vocabulary and thinking that he is intelligent and educated, and yet he chose the life of a pirate."

"He must have fooled lots of people with his fancy gentleman's clothes and posh upper class accent."

"But looks can be deceiving, can't they?"

Trevor looked at her and blinked again, well aware of the subtext of her statement and pleased by it. She was suddenly very glad she had made the decision to show him the software. "All right. I'm going to fast-forward through their night. No sense wasting our time watching them sleep."

After a few false starts, she found the point where Mason left the cave the next morning. She un-paused and they watched him walk down to the river. The Hoffmans were already up and going. It looked like they were getting ready to load up and leave, little knowing what was in store for them at the bend in the river.

At the river bank, Mason greeted Erich Hoffman who was leading the black stallion to the boat, his little girl happily hitching a ride. Under the trees, Lars was rewrapping the lame horse's legs. Martha was milking her cow again. Merrideth hoped Mason would let the old woman keep her beloved Daisy. Mason went to untie another of the Hoffmans' horses.

"Okay, time to go virtual again," Merrideth said, putting her fingers to the touch pad.

✶✶✶

1797

Mason untied the little bay mare, who gratefully blew warm, grassy breath in his face. "Good morning to you, too." She came along docilely up onto the deck, and he tethered her to an iron ring in the floor.

Erich and his little daughter came out of the cabin. "Go stand at the rail, Julianne. Stay out of everyone's way." The girl looked surprised by his sharp tone, and slunk off near tears.

Young Hoffman looked remorseful, and tired. Very tired. "Is everything all right?"

"It's my wife, Anna. She's still sick, worse in fact."

"What ails her? If you'll pardon my forwardness." Mason didn't think it wise to mention that he'd already made the lady's acquaintance and knew her ailment.

"She's got the ague. The doctor in Pittsburgh bled her and gave us Calomel for her. But we ran out of it three days ago."

"Well, you should have said so. We've got plenty up in the store."

"Ma says it's a waste of money."

"Why don't you go on up to the cave. My wife will get you what you need. At no cost to you."

Erich stood taller and his face took on a mulish expression. "I don't take charity, Mr. Wilson."

"Pardon me, sir. I meant no offense."

With a fierce look, Erich turned and ducked back into the cabin. After a moment, Mason heard a low murmuring and then wood scraping on wood. It was a delightful sound to his ears, and it brightened his spirits. After a moment, Erich came out, passed him without comment, and then went down the ramp on a determined course for the cave.

Mason smiled up at Floss, faithfully waiting at the entrance, and then went into the cabin. The outer room looked as neat as the last time, but then he hadn't expected that the noise had come from there. In two strides he reached the gunny sack curtain and pulled it back.

Erich's sickly wife Anna held a silver cup up to the light as if admiring the engravings that covered it. On the floor next to her was a small wooden chest. It held a matching cup and, better yet, a wondrous pile of silver coins.

When she saw him in the doorway she clutched the cup to her chest.

He smiled. "It's beautiful."

"It was my grandmother's. Says *Mutter* on the side...German for *mother.*" She placed the silver cup next to its twin in the chest, then pushed the lid closed. She tried to shove the chest out of sight, but had not the strength of a kitten. After a moment she gave up and drew her pale arms under the counterpane.

He would have liked to examine the cups. No matter. He would get the opportunity soon enough.

"My father gave it to her and Grandfather for Christmas...the year they came to Philadelphia."

Presumably its twin said *Vater*, but she didn't mention it. Perhaps she was hoping he hadn't noticed its existence. He could see now what he had not noticed the day before: the chest was meant to go into the side of the built-in storage box that he had dismissed as nothing but old clothes. There was probably a secret latch mechanism.

"I should have told Erich," she whispered. "I know that now."

"About the cups?"

"I'm in a family way... he never would have gone along with his pa's notion...to go west."

"You just rest up, ma'am. The medicine will be here soon." Although purging a poor woman suffering from diarrhea seemed witless to him.

She didn't answer. Her shivering ceased and she lay so still he thought she had expired. But then he saw the blanket rise with her breathing. He stepped past her pallet and lifted the wooden chest. It was gratifyingly heavy for its size. He smiled happily and set it back on the floor.

The woman groaned in her feverish misery, but did not open her eyes. When he reached the cabin door he saw that Tobias was coming back, leading the chestnut mare. Mason ducked through the door onto the deck and waved cheerily to the boy.

A shot rang out and Tobias dropped at the river's edge.

Then two more shots came in quick succession. The old man fell dead next to his prize gelding. And Martha slid lifelessly off her milking stool. The cow bellowed and jumped, her hide spattered with the woman's blood. The little girl at the rail screamed, but a fourth shot cut her off, and she slumped onto the deck.

"You fools!" Mason went down the ramp, skirting Tobias's body. The mare the boy had been leading shied at the smell of his blood leaking into the river. Mason grabbed at the rope and got it just in time before she tried to run back home to Pennsylvania.

The Harpes came bounding out of the woods, laughing like loons. Frank and Seth followed them less exuberantly, but still looking pleased. Susannah stepped onto the riverbank and gave Mason a defiant toss of her head. Then Hughes and the other men arrived, looking guilty but excited all the same.

"So we've taken to killing children, have we?" Floss shouted angrily from the cave's entrance. The Harpes' other wives appeared at her side, exhibiting neither curiosity nor surprise by the turn of events. No doubt they'd become inured to their husbands' choleric humours.

"What about young Hoffman, Floss?" Mason called.

"I took care of him all right," Floss said, holding up her iron skillet. "Soon as we heard the shots. If you had waited a minute more, he would have bought the blasted Calomel."

"You're a jewel, Floss, that you are." Big Harpe met Mason at the ramp, eager to board the boat. Mason grabbed him by his shirt front. "That wasn't the plan, Harpe."

Harpe shook off Mason's hand and glowered at him. "Susannah wouldn't go. Says she's got the woman thing and wasn't up to being the bait. So—"

Mason shoved at the man's chest and he fell back a step. "That is the flimsiest excuse I've ever heard." As if the brute didn't control the woman's every move.

"Well, it is the truth, Mason. So we came back to get Maria. We was going to go back to the bend. But those people was already up and about to get away." Harpe nodded toward the mare Mason held. "You can see that for yourself."

Mason pushed past him in disgust. Big Harpe and the other men swarmed up on the deck, whooping and hollering in their excitement. Mason led the mare back up the river bank to the grass and tied her to a tree next to the bellowing cow. Martha and Lars Hoffman watched his movements with cold stares. Even in death Martha Hoffman was disapproving.

"There now, Daisy," he said, patting the cow's neck. "Stop your fussing." She calmed and went back to grazing. Mason left her to it and went back to the flatboat.

So far the men had only begun to rifle through the contents of the boxes and supplies on the deck. But then, Big Harpe came grinning triumphantly out of the cabin carrying the small wooden chest. His brother came through the doorway behind him, dragging the sick woman by her hair. Her feeble squeaks were lost in the pandemonium as the other men caught sight of the shiny coins and came rushing up to grab for their share.

Mason took the pistol from his waistband and shot into the air. The men stopped and looked at him in surprise. Into the silence he said, "You'll all get your share. Now put that down, and get to work." The men grumbled but stepped away. Little Harpe still held the woman by her hair and she cried out piteously. "Leave her be, Harpe. I don't countenance rape."

He released the woman and her head hit the deck. She rolled over and crawled back into the cabin.

Sighing at the man's brutish behavior, Mason strode up the ramp. He would have to lay down the law to his men. But he was pragmatic about the situation. It hadn't been his plan, but now it was up to him to make it work. To determine which of the Hoffmans' supplies they could use or sell and which would accompany the family to their watery graves when they sank the boat. The farm equipment was useless to him, but there was always a need for weapons and gun powder.

There was enough food from their last haul to keep them all fed through the winter with plenty more to sell to travelers who happened along. Not everyone packed with such foresight as the Hoffmans. He could make room for the flour. It was hard to come by. And the dried peaches and apples, for sure. He certainly did not intend for them to end up in the river.

A shout came from the high ground above the cave. Frank had come up from his lookout post and stood there, spyglass in hand, watching the activity on the flatboat with interest.

"Another boat, Mr. Mason," he shouted. "Just a puny thing, hardly big enough to fool with."

"How much time do we have?"

"Mebbe fifteen minutes."

Mason waved him away, and he dutifully went back to watch the river.

Big Harpe bent to pick up the wooden treasure chest. "I'll be taking that," Mason said. "You and Little Harpe get your mess cleaned up."

When he only stood there scratching his head, Mason added. "The bodies? The ones littering the riverbank? Get them onboard and out of sight. And then get yourselves out of sight. That goes for everyone except you, Floss."

Big Harpe opened his mouth as if to argue, but Mason stared him down. He handed the chest to Hughes, shoved Big Harpe toward the ramp, and turned back toward the cabin. He sighed. There was that other matter to be dealt with.

The sick woman was not on her pallet. She huddled against the far wall, panting as if she could not find enough air to breathe. Her eyes were huge with fear and the distemper that gnawed at her belly.

"I'm sorry, ma'am. I had it all worked out. Only sometimes things just don't turn out the way you think they will." Mason took the pistol from his waistband and cocked it. He swallowed once then pulled the trigger. It was a clean shot.

.

CHAPTER 10

✢✢✢

THE PRESENT

Merrideth was falling in absolute darkness from a great distance. If she didn't take action to stop it, her head was going to bounce off the flatboat's deck. No, that wasn't right. It would be the cave's rocky floor, which would split her head open like a watermelon.

"Dear God, they wiped out the whole family," she gasped. Her stomach tried to turn itself inside side out, but she swallowed it back down.

She put out a hand to stop her fall, and there was Trevor, steady and solid beside her. It gave her the courage to open her eyes. His face was a carved mask of disgust and outrage, blue-tinged from the monitor's light. He vocalized some incoherent combination of prayer and exclamation, then rose unsteadily to his feet. He didn't seem to know she was beside him. She set the laptop down then followed him as he stumbled outside the cave and stood sucking in great gulps of air.

Merrideth gave up the battle of keeping her stomach where it belonged and turned away to vomit. Trevor pulled her hair back and held it in a ponytail out of the way. Every time she thought she was finished, a bloody image would pop into her head and the heaving would begin again. After a year or two, it stopped. She pulled the neck of her T-shirt up to wipe her mouth.

Even in her own misery, she worried about Trevor. With so little experience at time-surfing, he had to be feeling much worse. His cheeks were pale and his eyes stricken. She reached up tentatively to rub his back as he had done for her the day before. When he did not reject her offer of comfort, her touch became more certain.

"You'd better sit down before you fall off into the river."

He slid down and leaned against the bluff. "The blood," he said. "I could smell it. I thought they were only going to rob that family, but they—"

"I know. It's not so bad when the mind you're inside of is that of an ordinary person, not a murderer."

"I guess I should be glad we weren't inside Big Harpe's head. He was surely an outright psychopath."

She went back inside and got the bottle of water she had brought and took it to Trevor. After he drank what he wanted, she rinsed out her mouth and then took a few cautious sips. She sat down beside him, wishing there was more she could do to help him shake off the after-effects. Too bad guys could not, or would not, vent their emotions with a good cry.

The river went calmly and benevolently by as if nothing horrible had ever happened on its banks. The water was no longer pink-tinged with blood. There were no dead people, staring sightlessly at the scenery. In the distance a barge being piloted upstream by a tugboat came steadily closer. The nearer the barge got, the steadier Trevor's breathing became. The captain sounded the horn when he got nearly even to the cave, and Merrideth waved half-heartedly.

Trevor sighed wearily. "I guess we just got a small glimpse of the evil and corruption God sees every minute of every day."

Merrideth picked up a stone near her knee and heaved it down the slope toward the river. It fell two feet short.

He turned to look at her. "You're angry."

"Yeah, well..." She threw another stone. It missed too. "I always feel so...so.... powerless when I watch tragedy unfolding. I wanted to reach out and stop those men, but I couldn't do one thing about it. Why didn't God smite them or something? He's all-powerful, isn't he?"

"I don't know, Merrideth. I do know all things work together for—"

"For good. Yeah, yeah, I know. My friends always tell me that. Doesn't seem to keep me from being angry. What possible good could happen from the Hoffman family getting murdered on the way to their new farm?"

"I wish I knew, Merrideth." Trevor picked up a stone and sent it skipping across the water.

"Doesn't it bother you that you don't?"

"Lots of times. But that's where the faith comes in."

Merrideth kept her mouth shut. The last thing she wanted to do was insult him, but it never failed to amaze her the way so many people were able to leap blindly off cliffs without any substantiation for their beliefs.

He skipped another stone. Finally it reached the end of its journey and sank out of sight. "I watched a series of documentaries about the earth last week."

Merrideth turned to look at him. If she had been asked to hazard a guess what he would say after her outburst, it sure wouldn't have been that. What possible connection was there to the topic at hand? He glanced at her and then went back to throwing stones. Taking a page from his playbook, she waited to hear what he would say.

"The Sahara Dessert is a vast expanse of barren emptiness, covering 3.6 million square miles of the African continent. Most of the desert gets less than three inches of rain a year. It's a useless wasteland, wouldn't you say?"

"Yes. I guess so."

"And volcanos. They're worse than useless. On any given day there are at least ten of them erupting somewhere on earth, spewing out toxic gases and inundating homes, sometimes whole towns, with molten lava." He looked into her eyes as if willing her to see the point he was getting at.

"The world is full of dangers," she said. "Life is hard, as the Hoffmans found out first-hand."

"The main idea I took away from watching the documentaries is that the earth is a complex, dynamic system, much more so than I realized. Those volcanoes, which rain death and destruction every year, also keep the earth's gases in delicate balance. Without volcanoes no one would be worrying about the greenhouse effect anymore because there wouldn't be enough carbon dioxide in the atmosphere to sustain life. And as for the Sahara Desert, every year winds carry tons of dust across the Atlantic and deposit it on the Amazon rainforest in South America. Turns out the dust contains almost the exact amount of phosphorus the soil loses to flooding each year. Without the Sahara, the rainforest would become depleted of necessary nutrients and eventually die out, taking untold numbers of plant species with the potential for healing man's worst diseases with it."

It was the most she had ever heard him say at one time. "You're telling me to look on the sunny side of life?"

"I'm telling you that the world is more complex than we can possibly understand, and we'd be foolish to make hasty judgments about what's harmful or useless. It makes sense to me that the Creator would have equally complex plans for people, even if we can't perceive them from where we stand. Do you know him, Merrideth?"

"God? How can anyone know God?"

"In the beginning was the Word, and the Word was with God, and the Word was God...And the Word was made flesh and dwelt among us...full of grace and truth."

Trevor didn't say more, as if what he had just said actually answered her question. Knowing him, she had to assume that it did if only she could tease out the meaning. "I take it that's from the Bible?"

"Yes. John 1:1." Trevor threw another stone, and it danced across the water.

Merrideth tried again. This time her stone actually made it to the river where it promptly sank. She turned to study his unreadable face. "The Word is Jesus?"

"Yes."

"It's saying he didn't begin in that manger, then?"

"For by him were all things created, that are in heaven, and that are in earth, visible and invisible...all things were created by him, and for him: And he is before all things, and by him all things consist."

Why had no one ever told her that before? If Jesus were in on creation, it made a profound difference in how a person interpreted everything he did and said in the Gospels. If it were true. How could anyone know which parts of the Bible were to be taken literally and which parts were only metaphors?

If she asked Trevor, he would probably have something wise and Yoda-like to say about that. She rubbed her temples. "I'd like to hear more sometime, but I have a headache coming on. I think it's the mold in the cave." It surely wouldn't count as a lie, because even though she didn't actually have a headache at the moment, she was going to get one if she continued trying to extract the meaning from Trevor's obscure statements.

"It's the answer to your question, you know."

"How we can know God?"

"Yes. Jesus is eternal, the pre-existing One. It is his power that holds the whole universe together. And yet he left Heaven and came to earth in the form of a man to make God knowable to humans."

"Sorry, Trevor. I'm going to have to go up the lodge and get some aspirin. If I don't head this thing off it will turn into the pounding kind, and I'll not be able to get any more work done."

"I'm sorry. I get carried away sometimes."

She could not help but smile at what he deemed *getting carried away*.

He stood and took her hand to help her up. "Anyway, I've got to go relieve Geno and Barb. I'm on duty until late tonight, but I could help you tomorrow."

"I'd love that, but I need to get back home before dark. I'm going with friends to watch the fireworks."

"I'll be watching them with the Hellhounds."

"Something tells me yours will be more exciting than mine."

"You have no idea."

Trevor insisted on walking her all the way back to the lodge reception room. The wire postcard display near the door caught his attention. "I never think to get any of these when I'm here," he said, pulling a card from the rack.

Across the room at the counter, Shirley said, "So how's the research coming, Merrideth? Did you get all the info you need about the cave?"

Merrideth smiled. Shirley's questions had been directed to her, but her curious shoe-button bright eyes were trained on Trevor. "No, I'm heading back for more. As soon as I take some aspirin." Beside her Trevor continued to look at the postcard. From his serious expression, he might have been studying blueprints instead of a photograph of the lodge.

Out of the corner of her eye, Merrideth saw Shirley waving. Apparently at her. The wave changed from one that meant "hey, you" to one that clearly meant "come over here and don't let Trevor know."

Merrideth went to the counter, expecting to get another message relayed from Mr. Carlson. "What is it?" she whispered.

Shirley's eyes twinkled. "Bet it was romantic hanging out in the cave with Mr. Tall, Dark, and Handsome there. Like Tom Sawyer and Becky Thatcher."

"I was working, Shirley. Recording data on my computer. Trevor was just there to lend moral support."

Shirley smiled knowingly. "Right. Are you going to eat lunch together? I can tell the girls to give you two the quiet table by the window."

"I don't think he has time to stay. He has other plans."

"I know I'm old enough to be his mother, but my, my, my." Shirley suddenly looked worried. "I hope you don't mind me looking."

Merrideth grinned. "Be my guest."

"Thanks. I might as well put the eyes God gave me to good use."

Trevor looked up from the postcard display and saw them looking at him. "What?"

"Nothing," Merrideth said quickly.

"We were just discussing the blessing of eyesight," Shirley said with a wink only Merrideth saw.

Trevor put the postcards back and stood there waiting to say goodbye to Merrideth. She went to him, feeling as awkward as a fifteen-year-old at the end of her first date. Should she kiss him goodbye or shake his hand? In one sense, she hardly knew Trevor, and still had no idea what he thought of her. But because of the crucible in which they had found themselves, she had learned a lot about him in a short length of time. And what she did know, she liked quite a lot—his kindness, generosity, and intelligence. But she would probably never see him again.

She decided he was waiting for a cue from her, so at last she held out her hand.

He took it into his. "If you're ever in Pittsburgh, look me up."

"I will. If ever."

"Do you still have my card?"

"I do." He didn't ask for her phone number. But was that because he considered leaving the ball in her court the gentlemanly thing to do or because he did he not feel the same connection with her that she felt with him?

"Thanks for everything," she said. "I'll never forget it."

"Me neither." He took her arm and turned her away from Shirley's blatant stare. And then he leaned in and kissed her temple.

Behind her, the door to the lodge whooshed open. Trevor looked over her shoulder at whoever had just come in. His face remained impassive, but when she turned, she saw that Brett Garrison stood just inside the doorway, looking anything but.

At the counter Shirley said, "Well butter my buns and call me a biscuit! Here's another one."

The emotions playing over Brett's face ran the gamut, but then he smiled and said pleasantly, "Am I interrupting something, Merri?"

"Uh-oh, the fat's in the fire now," Shirley said.

"Hi, Brett." Merrideth refused to move away from Trevor as if she were a girlfriend caught cheating on her boyfriend. She and Brett were not dating, no matter what he thought. And thus she certainly wasn't obligated to explain Trevor to him. She could hang out with whomever she chose. Kiss him if she felt like it. Brett had not shown much of a jealous streak before, but it was definitely there now, just beneath the civilized mask he had donned. Even Shirley had read it in his face the moment he came through the door wearing a fake smile.

And Trevor apparently had the same talent for picking up on people's emotions, which was amazing for a person who showed so few himself. Still carefully watching Brett, Trevor took two steps away from Merrideth as if required by some male code of honor to turn the little woman back over to her rightful owner.

She wanted to smack both men. Instead she put on a mask of her own. "What a surprise, Brett. What are you doing here?" As if she didn't already know that Abby and John had sent him to drag her home like she was a recalcitrant child. It was probably killing John that he could not come down himself and go all big-brother with her.

"Aunt Nelda released me from her never-ending to-do list—temporarily, at least. All work and no play and all that. So here I am, ready for a little recreational spelunking."

"Aren't you the lucky one, Merrideth?" Shirley said, looking first at Trevor and then Brett. "Just as one handsome fellow leaves, another one arrives ready to play guardian angel for you."

"I have no need for that. I'm not afraid."

"No one's disputing your courage," Trevor said. "But since your friend is here now—well, it would sure be better if you had someone with you. No one should have to do what you do alone."

"I agree," Brett said. "As I told Merri, spelunking is best done with partners."

"It's all well and good to get back on the horse that threw you, honey," Shirley chirped. "But you should have a cowboy by your side. I like your nickname, by the way. Is that spelled with a *Y* or an I?"

"*I*," Merrideth said. "But Brett knows he's not supposed to call me that. And *I* know why he came, and it wasn't to go spelunking. Go on back and tell Abby and John to stop being such worry warts. I'll be home before nightfall."

Brett barked a laugh. "You think they sent me? Not likely John would ever willingly send me your way. I came because I happened to be worried about you being down here alone."

"I told you the cave was safe. And I can't believe you left Aunt Nelda when she's sick. You should go home."

"Listen, Merrideth," Trevor said, "If he has to leave I could get someone to take my place at the stand if you need me here."

"Thanks, but she won't need you," Brett growled. "I'll be here."

"Fine, just so long as someone is with her." He lowered his voice so Shirley wouldn't hear. "If another one of them decides to explore the cave while she's time-surfing, she'll be too out of it to protect herself."

Brett's eyebrows rose. "I don't have the slightest idea what you're talking about."

"You don't know about—?" Trevor's face registered a rare show of emotion. "I'm sorry, Merrideth. I just assumed—"

"That's all right, Trevor. You'd better go relieve Geno and Barb."

He gave her a long look. "Okay. Goodbye, then. Stay safe."

"You, too."

Trevor nodded at Shirley and Brett and then left.

"Know about what, Merri?" Brett said. "What happened at the cave?"

"Show him the boot treads," Shirley said.

"Let's step outside," Merrideth said, pulling Brett by the arm.

She looked up to gauge his face. "So Abby and John really didn't send you?"

"No, why would they?"

She held out her arms and turned them for him to see. "Because of these." The perimeters of the bruises were beginning to turn lime green. It was a pretty contrast to the dark purple.

After a stunned moment, he pulled her into his arms. "Honey, what happened?"

"I was working alone in the cave, and four guys came, and…and they—"

He pulled away so he could look at her face. "Are you all right? They didn't—"

"No, no. Not that they didn't want to. But then Trevor came."

"Did he call the police?"

"Yes, and the sheriff came, but it was too late to catch them. Trevor looked, but the campground is a zoo, and he never found them."

"Trevor? What about the cops?"

"I told them not to."

"What?"

"Don't yell at me."

"I'm not. Okay, I am. Sorry. I'm a jerk."

"He's the one you were a jerk to," she said nodding toward the parking lot.

Trevor had just reached his bike. He mounted it and kicked the starter. The engine came to life, and he rode slowly out of the lot. When he reached the road, he picked up speed. And then he was out of sight.

"You're right. I should apologize to him," Brett said. "I think I was having trouble seeing past the leather and tattoos."

"A lot of people do that. Actually, you have more in common with Trevor than you might think. He's here in town with a Christian biker club. They come to preach to the Road Hogs and Hellhounds."

"Hellhounds? Like Cerberus the three-headed dog?"

"Very good, Professor. And mythology is not even your field."

"Let's go. I want to see the cave."

Since he had come all that way, there was no way around it. She had to show him the cave. But then, somehow, she would have to get him to run along home. "Okay, as soon as I gargle. I'm sure I have vomit breath."

"Why do you have—? Never mind. You can explain everything on the way to your infamous cave."

☆☆☆

"So this is it," Brett said.

They stood near the center of the cave, and sunlight speared in from above, gilding their faces and clothes.

"I was over there when the four bikers came in and cornered me," Merrideth said. Hopefully, he would not ask too many questions. It would be difficult to explain why she had fainted and was lying vulnerably on the floor of the cave when they got there. "I can still see the one who smiled at me while he—"

"Shh," Brett said, drawing her into his arms. "Don't think about it anymore. I won't let you." And then he lowered his head and put his lips on hers. As a technique for dispelling the Road Hogs from her brain it was quite effective. Excellent, actually. His kiss grew more insistent, and every other thought was pushed out as well. Except for Brett. He was all she could think of. His scent. His arms around her. His hands tenderly rubbing her back. His friendship and unquenchable good spirits, so different from her own jaundiced outlook on life.

Friends. That's what they were. And she cherished that. She turned her face away from his kiss and rested it against his chest. His heart was pounding. She should put space between them, but at the moment she could not make herself do it.

He stroked her hair. "Here we are—Tom Sawyer and Becky Thatcher."

Merrideth smiled into his shirt at the thought. It was good that he did not know Shirley had said the same thing not twenty minute before, only about Trevor and her. Happy-go-lucky Brett was more the type to play Tom Sawyer than Trevor. And if Shirley knew her better, she would never cast her as the sweet Becky. Huck Finn with his broken, dysfunctional family was more Merrideth's speed.

"I should have been here, Merri. Why didn't you at least call me afterward?"

"And have you say *I told you so?*"

"You're right. I probably would have."

He turned her face up to the light and studied it. "Now about that other thing. What your friend Trevor said back at the lodge."

"What other thing?"

"Shall I quote? 'If another one of them decides to explore the cave while she's time-surfing, she'll be too out of it to protect herself.' I believe that's fairly close."

"I believe it's verbatim." She had been hoping that with all the turmoil he had not caught Trevor's slip. But she was not surprised that he had. Brett had the ability to remember crazy-huge amounts of detailed data, and he had an above normal—a far above normal—degree of curiosity.

"So are you going to explain? Or don't I rate?"

"Of course you rate. It's just that..." What should she say? That she had told Trevor because he had come to her rescue? That she felt sure that Trevor would keep quiet about *Beautiful Houses* but was not sure she could trust Brett to? And then like one of the beams of sunlight streaming in on them, the realization came that of course she could trust Brett. How had she ever thought she could not?

She laughed with the relief of it. "Come on. Let's sit on that ledge over there. You're going to love this."

"What?"

When they were seated with her laptop in front of them she said, "Abby and I found a software program on my computer. The computer my dad bought for me, not this laptop. It was sixteen years ago, the summer Abby came to tutor me. We only got the chance to use it for a few weeks before it stopped working. But when I spent the night at John and Abby's house last Halloween, it started working again."

"What does it do?"

She paused and took a deep breath. "I know when I tell you, you're going to get all sciency and tell me it isn't possible, but try to keep an open mind, okay?"

Brett spluttered. "I have a very open mind."

"I know you do," she hurried to assure him. "But you're going to start throwing around the Second Law of Thermodynamics and all that. Or is it the Third Law? Whatever, I think the laws of physics don't apply here because it's only virtual."

"What is?"

"Time travel."

"Time travel."

"Right. Only as I said, it's only virtual. I call it time-surfing."

"Virtual time travel."

"I want you to know that I appreciate the fact that you're not laughing."

"As I said, I'm very open-minded," he said virtuously. "I'm willing to hear how your program manages to circumvent the laws of physics. You were right the first time. It is the Second Law that applies here. "

"John and Abby and I all agree that it wouldn't be possible to physically go back in time or it would alter the course of history. John says it's ridiculous to even think humans could change God's sovereign plan."

"It's a huge argument against the concept."

"But what if you were only rewinding time, not changing it? What if you could see all the people and events that happened in the house you happened to be in on your computer screen?"

"That may remove any theological issues. But in terms of physics—the first problem that comes to mind is the fact that time is not symmetrical."

"What does that mean?"

"Think of a video. If time were symmetrical, you could play the video forwards or backwards and it would make sense and seem realistic either way. But a video of real events looks silly played backward. People do not walk backward. A water balloon dropped from a third floor window doesn't fly back into the hand of the person who dropped it. In other words, time is not reversible."

"I get what you're saying, Science Man. But this isn't like that."

"I could give you another analogy if that would help."

"You're going to tell me about the Arrow of Time, aren't you?"

"Well, it does handily illustrate increasing entropy and—"

"Or I could just show you." Grinning, Merrideth opened her laptop and started *Beautiful Houses*. After a moment, the home screen with the banner popped up, and then the latest selection of houses began scrolling by.

"So what do you do? Select one of the houses, and bam! You're in the past?"

"No, if I selected one of these houses, we'd get a very nice little tour of all the rooms inside it. It's really fun, but not what I'm talking about. Just wait a second for the program to pick up the vibes from the cave."

"Vibes? Does this involve magic cave crystals?"

Merrideth rolled her eyes and ignored him. After a moment more, the images on the monitor scrambled and re-sorted themselves into the cave they sat in. It was still paused at the horrible point where she had stopped the action right after the pirates murdered the Hoffmans. "Wait. I don't want you to see this part," she said, turning away to shield the scene from his sight.

"Why not?" he said, trying to see over the top of the screen.

"Because it's a little too much for your first time-surfing experience. But how would you like to meet some early settlers who knew your ancestor James Garretson?"

"Sure. Why not?"

Merrideth shrugged off the tinge of sarcasm in Brett's voice. It was a lot to take in, and he *was* being amazingly open-minded about the whole thing. But he would be a true believer before the hour was out. Smiling, she set the date and un-paused the software. After a moment Captain Piggot and his group of tired travelers were once more inside the cave cooking their supper over the campfires.

"It's this cave," Brett said. "The mouth is exactly the same."

"It's definitely this cave. In order to work properly, the program has to be set up in an old house, but this cave was used for human habitation so it runs here, too. I rewound the time to the year 1780. Cool, huh? And we're not even in virtual mode."

"What's that?"

"It's difficult to describe. The best way is for you to experience it for yourself. Guess who that man is?"

"I don't know. Daniel Boone?"

"Captain James Piggot."

"As in the builder of Fort Piggot."

"As in. He and his party are on their way to the Illinois country."

"So this is a documentary about James Piggot?"

"That's exactly what Trevor said. But it's not." As soon as the words were out of her mouth, she wished she could delete them. Brett didn't show any further signs of jealousy, but he had to be hurt that in the year she had known him she had never shown the program to him, but had shown it to Trevor after knowing him for only one day.

"Okay. I'm going to switch to virtual now. You'll understand it works once we get inside Piggot's head."

"That sounds painful for everyone concerned."

"You'll stop smirking soon enough, Professor Garrison. This software program is not like anything you've ever experienced. It's certainly not a documentary video."

"Okay. Prove it."

She grinned. "Oh, I will."

CHAPTER 11

✷✷✷

THE PRESENT

Merrideth switched off virtual mode, but Brett continued to stare at James Piggot's life playing out on the screen. She shook his shoulder, but still he sat watching the monitor. "Hey, snap out of it."

Finally he turned to stare at her. "Feel free to say *I told you so*. I will never smirk in your presence again, Merri. What is this thing? I just heard Piggot thinking about how he planned to build the fort. He was worried their supplies wouldn't hold out until they could harvest their first crops."

"Amazing, isn't it?"

"It's astonishing. Miraculous. Stupendous." He blinked several times. "So all this time while I've been blathering on about how time travel isn't possible—"

"Because of the Second Law of Thermodynamics. Oh, and the famous Arrow of Time."

"Yes, that. All this time you knew. You had this…this… miracle software that takes you back in time."

"Only virtually."

"Only?"

"I know. It's amazing. I wanted to tell you about it. I was going

114

to."

"Not just because your friend Trevor let it slip?"

"No, that's not why." At least not the only reason, not the main reason. "I wanted to tell you right from the beginning, but even your own aunt said you couldn't keep a secret."

Brett expelled a disgusted breath. "All because of that blasted second-grade birthday party you still think I'm not trustworthy?"

She put a hand on his arm. "I'm sorry. I know you're trustworthy, Brett. Now. If you choose to keep the secret you will, it's just that —"

"You think I don't realize the world-wide implications of this technology? Of course it must be kept secret. Give me some credit, Merri."

"I figured you'd feel compelled to tell the science world."

"No, I'm not saying a word about this. At least until I can think of a safe way to make it known to a select few trusted scientists."

"Not even if I tell you that *Beautiful Houses* proves the theory of time warp?"

"How?" For a couple of seconds he stared into the distance—or more likely into the recesses of his own ginormous brain. "Oh, of course. You noticed a discrepancy between your own real time and the passing of time for the subjects in the past."

"Exactly. It's only apparent if you time-surf for long periods."

"Awesome! But all the more reason to keep the software under wraps. How many people know about it?"

"Well, Abby and John, of course. And Abby's college roommate Kate and her ex-boyfriend Ryan. Kate's not Abby's. But we don't have to worry about Kate and Ryan because as far as they know the software program went bonkers and never started working again. Same for Patty Frailey, another friend. And now there's you. And Trevor."

"A biker you met during Hellhound Homecoming."

"You're implying he's a Road Hog, but he's not."

"And you have some super power that allows you to judge him trustworthy."

"I just know. Somehow."

"All right. I'll trust your judgement on that. Even though it was faulty when it came to me."

"I said I was sorry."

"Okay. Apology accepted. So, how does this thing work?"

"I have no idea. I'm hoping you can figure it out. And there's more you should know." She gestured to the monitor before them. "About Captain Piggot here. It was Fort Jefferson he was thinking about building just now. He doesn't get to the Illinois Country for a couple more years—where he will build Fort Piggot a few miles north of the Garretson family's blockhouse fort."

She waited, watching his face, to see how long it would take him to make the mental leap.

After only a fraction of a second, his eyes bugged out and he grabbed her arms. "You saw him! James Garretson!"

"Oh, Brett, wait until you meet him! You look almost exactly like him. Same hair. Same eyes. Same manly jaw. You don't have to worry. You're a true Garrison."

"I have a manly jaw?"

Merrideth rolled her eyes. "As if you didn't know. Let's get back to the discussion at hand, which is that you're definitely a descendant of the heroic James Garretson."

"I wish. But how *can* I be?"

"Well, first the daddy and the mommy kiss, and then—"

"Stop it," he said, laughing. "I was referring to the fact that my alleged dad wasn't home at the appropriate time for me to be conceived."

"I don't know, Brett. Maybe you should just ask Aunt Nelda."

"No. Whatever secrets she's been keeping all these years must be bad if she felt the need to deceive me."

"I agree there's something fishy about her altering your family scrapbook, but that was when you were a boy. Tell her you're old enough to know the truth now."

"Maybe I'm not. What if my father was an ax murderer and my mother conceived me during a conjugal visit at his prison?"

"That's ridiculous."

"Well, whatever it is, I don't think I want to know."

"Okay. Do you think you're ready to know about the pirates of Cave-in-Rock?"

"Sure. Let's go."

"Don't be too sure. Being inside Samuel Mason's head is a lot different from being inside Captain Piggot's."

"I can take it if you can."

"Okay, if you insist. In the interest of time, is it all right if we begin where I left off?"

"I suppose so. But won't I need to see what happened before to make sense of the present?"

"It would be helpful, sure, but then you'd have to experience the pirates slaughtering a whole family of settlers."

Brett's face registered his distaste. "No, that's quite all right. I don't feel the need to witness a murder. Maybe you could just give me a summary to set the scene."

"Good choice. Because if we're going to make it home in time for the fireworks tonight, I'd better get back to my research."

She described the situation and gave him a concise explanation of Samuel Mason's plan for robbing the Hoffmans and how it had gone horribly wrong when the Harpe brothers took matters into their own hands.

"So are you sure you want to see this, Brett? You could wait outside the cave and make sure no one's coming while I carry on. No sense in both of us having to see what Mason does next."

Brett bent and kissed her. "No way I'd let you face that alone, Merri."

She was relieved she would not have to. But she would have to have a long talk with him about the kissing thing. Soon.

***

1797

The men were celebrating. Loudly. The noise was bouncing off the cave's walls and then bouncing again inside his skull. Perhaps his head had turned into a cave. It felt like it. A cave full of rowdy men watching chickens fight to the death. Mason laughed. He must be drunker than he thought. He took another sip of whiskey and concentrated on putting the red ten on the black jack. He squinted. Or was that a queen?

Tommy wouldn't stop with his infernal fiddling, although thank the saints, he had switched to a new song. Each time the man capered by Mason's table, the screech of his bow on the strings nearly burst his skull open.

Frank held up his victorious rooster, its spurs dripping blood on the fool's shirt, and the men roared, some in victory the others in disappointment. Mason held his head to keep it intact. Charles Fleming picked up his dead rooster by its bloody feet and carried it out to throw it in the river. Money changed hands in a complicated manner too confusing for Mason to work out. Money that had only two hours earlier been safely locked away in a wooden chest on the Hoffmans' flatboat.

Big Harpe expressed his disappointment over the outcome of the fight by back-handing Susannah who had the misfortune of standing within his reach. The other wives were a cautious distance away holding their babies. Maria's baby commenced crying, either from hunger or all the commotion, and Big Harpe glared at her. "I told you I didn't want no crying around me. Keep your brat quiet or I'll—" He stopped before completing his threat, perhaps inhibited by the looks some of the men were giving him. Not waiting to hear him complete the thought, Maria took the baby into the back room, and after a minute the crying stopped.

Sarah continued rocking her own child. How the wee lad could sleep in all the noise Mason did not know. Every so often Sarah darted a look his way. He was not so drunk that he could not perceive that the woman had something weighing on her mind. Well, if she knew what was good for her she had best not let Little Harpe see her looking at other men.

Mason belched and looked down at the last scion of the Hoffman family who lay unconscious at his feet. Young Hoffman had been so intent on procuring Calomel for his puny wife. Now, she would never have to take the foul-tasting stuff again. If the woman had had the presence of mind to speak before he blew her brains out, she might have thanked him for putting her out of her misery.

"What are you going to do with him?"

Mason looked up, surprised to find Floss there.

"Throw him to the alligators. What else?"

"Sure you are."

"I am. As soon as my head stops feeling like there's a hatchet in it."

Floss knelt and began going through the man's pockets. "Here," she said after a minute. "I'd hate to see this go to the alligators."

She laid the man's belongings down on the table. There wasn't much, just a folding knife, which Mason tucked away into his own pocket; a ragged handkerchief, which he flung away in disgust; and a slim leather purse, which contained two coins. For the Calomel, no doubt. He added the coins to his pocket to keep company with the knife. There was nothing else of interest, just two folded papers, which he handed to Floss. "I am sure my aching eyes will not allow me to read these. What do they say?"

"This one is a bill of sale for the flatboat." She snorted. "They paid fifty pounds for that boat. That's robbery, sure and certain."

Mason grinned. "Your sentiment denotes a good heart, dear, though you're being a trifle ironic, don't you think?"

She sniffed. "I'm sure I don't know what that means."

He patted her arm. "Never mind."

"It says Lars Hoffman. Do you suppose that's him?" she said, nudging the unconscious man with the toe of her boot. "Or the old one?"

"I forget. If he wakes up, you can ask him."

Floss unfolded the other paper. "Must be religious. He's got Psalm 23 wrote out."

Mason drained the whiskey in his tankard. "How does that go?" he said slyly. "Yea, though I float down the river of death, I will fear no evil."

Floss laughed and slapped his shoulder, nearly taking the top of his skull off. "He should have feared, eh?"

He handed his empty cup to her. "Get me more whiskey, will you?"

"I don't think so, Samuel."

"You're a cruel woman, Floss." He put the tankard back down on the table and laid his head next to it. "If I ever get the notion to carry around a scripture in my pocket it will be from Revelation, not the Psalms," he mumbled to the table. "*And the sea gave up the dead which were in it. Then death and Hades were thrown in the lake of fire. And if anyone's name was not found written in the Book of Life, he was thrown into the lake of fire.*"

Floss sighed. "No use thinking about that yet, Samuel. You should sleep."

Perhaps he should. Just for a short while. Then he would decide what to do with young Hoffman. He shut his eyes. There came a groaning sound. He was fairly certain it had not come from his own throat, although he felt like groaning. He shifted his eyes and saw that the unconscious man had sat up and was holding his bloody head.

"I know just how you feel," Mason said.

Hoffman groaned again.

"Well, look what we have," Big Harpe said. "He's not dead after all."

Little Harpe looked over and a matching smile lit his equally ugly face. He hurried over like a vulture on a sick rabbit.

"You want me to take care of it?" Hughes said.

"I'll do it," Big Harpe said gleefully.

Mason hauled himself upright and looked at the man at his feet. "I beg your pardon, Mr. Hoffman. My mother warned me of the dangers of hard liquor. If I hadn't been in my cups, I would have taken care of the matter while you slept."

The Harpes each took one of the man's arms and hauled him to his feet. Hoffman, squinting as if the light hurt his eyes, seemed to be having trouble taking in the scene before him.

Mason waved them away. "Be quick about it."

Big Harpe's laugh boomed out like thunder in the cave. "We'll see it's quick. I promise."

They dragged the half-conscious man between them out of the cave. Mason put his head back down on the table. But sleep would not come, even though the noise had stopped crashing around inside his skull. The men were getting tired of celebrating. Even Tommy's fiddling had ceased. The only sounds left were a soft rumbling of voices and the occasional scrape of boots on the stony floor.

"Mr. Mason?"

He opened an eye and saw that Sarah knelt beside his table.

"Did you finally rustle up enough gumption to speak?"

Holding her baby on her knee, she pulled a folded paper from the folds of her skirt. After a worried look at the cave entrance, she shoved it into his hand where it lay on the table beside his face.

"What is this, woman?"

"It's a letter. Please, sir, can you send it for me?"

"A letter." Her face wavered in and out of focus, but there was no mistaking the pleading in her eyes.

"To my pa."

He closed his eyes. "Go away and let me sleep."

"Please, Mr. Mason. I need your help. Me and my babe." She closed her fingers around his so he would grip the paper. "Just keep this safe and think on it."

A man's scream came from outside, and Mason bolted upright from the table, nearly overturning it in the process. "By all that's holy, what was that?"

Sarah didn't answer, just scurried to the back of the cave and hid behind the log wall. His men rose from their various positions and ran to the entrance. Before Mason could get himself up from the table, another scream came, joined a moment later with the neighing of a terrified horse, then wild laughing and a voice that called out. "Yee haw!"

Mason stumbled toward the cave's mouth. When he was barely a yard shy of reaching it, a horse dropped from the sky, furiously working all four legs as if galloping on air. It was blessedly blindfolded and could not see its death fast approaching. Erich Hoffman, tied naked to the horse, was not blindfolded. He shrieked the whole way down. He and his mount hit the rocky ground in front of the cave with a loud thud. There was a moment of stunned silence, and then the wild laughter came again from above the cave.

Together with his men, he stared in shock at the old man's beautiful gelding and its naked rider, shattered and bleeding in front of them. It had happened in an instant, but he had seen young Hoffman's eyes, wide with terror, as he fell to his ignominious end.

The Harpe brothers came down from the bluff, laughing and congratulating each other until they saw that no one else was joining in.

"What in Hades have you done?" Mason roared.

"What bee's in your bonnet?" Big Harpe said, grinning.

"It was lame anyway," Little Harpe whined. "You saw that."

"That's the last time I'll put up with your fiendish ways. You're devils!" Mason screamed. "Leave!" He hated to lose his temper, and the thought that the brutish Harpes had caused him to do so made him even angrier.

Big Harpe's ugly face turned uglier still, and, placing his hand on his dagger he took a step toward Mason. Little Harpe growled like the cur that he was and came to stand at his brother's side. Mason's men drew their guns and knives and stood ready to prevent the Harpes from coming into the cave. Floss came, too, brandishing a hatchet from the Hoffmans' boat.

In the red haze of his anger, he had nearly forgotten the women and children. When he saw that poor witless Mabel was cowering with the Harpes' wives, he reined in his temper and lowered his voice. "Tell your pathetic women to gather their squalling brats and every bit of filth you brought into my cave and get out."

Big Harpe stood his ground for a moment, then jerked his chin at the women. They scurried to obey his wordless order. He turned back to Mason. "We'll leave," he spat out. "But you'll give us what we have coming."

"I'll give you what you have coming."

Floss put a restraining hand on his coat sleeve. "You might want to reconsider, Samuel."

After a moment, he huffed, then reached into his pocket and pulled out the small cloth bag that held his own share of the Hoffman's hoard. He threw it to Big Harpe. It clinked when he caught it. Then the brothers stepped back to wait for their women.

After several minutes they came forward lugging their snotty babies and the few things they owned. When they got to the front of the cave, the Harpes, gallant knights that they were, started down the trail, leaving the women to carry it all as best they could.

Sarah was the last to go. She stared at Mason. At first he assumed her look was meant to convey hatred for being thrust from the safety of the cave. She did not plead with him to let her and the babe stay. She just looked him up and down, as if taking his measure.

"Floss!"

"No need to shout. I'm right here."

"Let the woman have the milk Mrs. Hoffman sold you."

"I was going to give it to Mabel," Floss said petulantly. "For a special treat."

"Just get it."

Floss brought the corked jug and thrust it at Sarah. "Here, I suppose the babes need it more than Mabel does."

Sarah took the jug, but still she stood there, her baby riding her hip, silently assessing him. At last she hurried to catch up with the others.

"Hughes, take some of the men and follow them a ways to make sure they don't take any horses that don't belong to them. Then set up extra guards in case the snakes decide to come slithering back."

"We'll watch for them."

The men left and Mason turned to Mabel, still standing timidly in the back. "Come on, dear. No need to worry your pretty little head."

"What do you have there?" Floss said.

Mason looked down and realized he still held the paper Sarah had thrust into his hand. He unfolded it. After he read it, he gave it to Floss. The anger was draining away. He went to the bar and poured three whiskeys. "I'm feeling hopeful, ladies. Almost cheerful, I think." He handed a cup to Mabel and then one to Floss. "Here, drink with me."

Floss looked up from Sarah's letter. "She wants you to get this to her pa?"

"Yes."

"Then, I don't know what you have to be cheerful about, Samuel. Her father will likely bring the Regulators with him. Right to our doorstep."

He sighed. "We'll be long gone by then, as much as it pains me to leave my cave."

"Then why do it?"

"Because it'll prove I'm not such a bad fellow, not nearly as bad as those Harpes. The Almighty will surely let me into heaven, when he weighs our deeds on Judgment Day."

***

THE PRESENT

Merrideth came back to the present when Brett clutched her arm, nearly causing the laptop to slither off her lap. She caught it in time and then turned to assess his condition. Judging from the look on his face, he was either really, really blasé about what they had just witnessed or he was completely shell-shocked.

"Brett?" she said, rubbing his arm. "Are you all right?"

"No, not really. I'm telling myself that what I just saw happened too long ago to matter. Of course, that's not true, but let me think it for a while, okay?"

"Sorry you had to see that. I thought the Harpe brothers were done murdering for the day."

Brett rubbed his eyes. "I suppose they'd be labeled sociopaths today. If I believed in the death penalty, they'd be on my short list for the electric chair."

"They'd be on my list for Hell, if I believed in that. Mason? I'm not sure. He wasn't as evil as the Harpes. A complicated man, wasn't he? Goes to show you can't pigeon-hole people. But—"

"Hold on a minute. You don't believe in Hell?"

"The Bible says God is love, doesn't it? And if he's a loving God—although sometimes I have my doubts—he wouldn't create a place like Hell, much less send people there."

"I've always figured that if you believe in Heaven you have to believe in Hell."

"Why?"

"Because Jesus spent as much time talking about Hell as he did Heaven. Because in addition to being loving, God is just. How could he let such evil go unpunished? That scenario we just saw gives me a new appreciation for what God experiences. How does he stand seeing mankind's wickedness day in and day out? Actually, it's much worse than seeing it as it happens. That's our finite perception of time, not God's. He sees, and has always seen, all of human sin, including mine, throughout all history, all at the same time."

Maybe Brett was right about Hell, but where was the cutoff? At what point did God determine that a person was just too bad to allow into Heaven? "If there is a Hell, I agree that the Harpe brothers deserved to go there. As for Mason, all along I've thought that he was an odd mixture of evil and…and… honor, for lack of a better word. Wasn't it weird hearing Bible verses coming out of his drunken mouth?"

Brett smiled tiredly. "Even Satan can quote the scriptures. And Hitler was said to like puppies. I just made that last part up, but you know what I mean. There's some good mixed in there, I suppose."

"Even the Harpes? And the Road Hogs?" Merrideth shuddered as she pictured them holding her down only inches from where she now sat.

Brett took the laptop and set it beside him on the ledge. And then he drew her close and wrapped his arms tightly around her. "There's nothing we can do to stop Samuel Mason and the Harpe brothers from preying on innocent travelers, but we can do something about modern-day brutes who attack helpless women."

"I'm not helpless."

He kissed her temple but didn't speak.

"What? You might as well say what you're thinking, Brett."

"All right, I'm thinking you're acting like one of those women who let rapists go scot-free because they're too scaredy-cat to prosecute. Or at least too ashamed, like it was their fault."

"I am not a scaredy-cat. And I'm under no misapprehension about whose fault it was."

"Then why did you tell the sheriff not to go after them? You don't want those creeps to go on attacking other women, do you?"

"Of course not. You don't understand, Brett. The Hellhounds don't let the cops inside." She explained what Trevor had told her.

"But surely Sheriff Mitchell had probable cause?"

"His deputies didn't seem to think so. Trevor and I couldn't give him much in the way of description anyway, so it seemed pointless to have him and his men go in there when they didn't know who they were looking for. The sheriff doesn't have enough resources to patrol the area as it is."

"Okay, I get it. Why don't we go get lunch, and then you can rest in your room while I go hunting. Too bad I didn't think to bring Duke. Did you know he's an excellent ratter?"

"You're kidding."

"No, you should see him go after them in the barn."

"You know very well what I meant, Brett Garrison. You cannot possibly mean to go in there looking for those guys."

"Surely it's not too dangerous during the day."

"Probably not in the daytime or Trevor and his friends wouldn't be in there. But why take a chance? Those guys are long gone by now. Probably."

"What if they're not? What if they're lolling around in a drunken stupor just waiting to be collared? Unlike Samuel Mason, most criminals are pretty stupid."

"You don't know what they look like any more than the sheriff did."

"Tell me what you remember. I'm good with things like that."

"I know, but there's no way I can describe them well enough to do you any good. I'd have to see them." So, if you insist on going in there, I'm going, too."

"I take it back, Merri. You're not a scaredy-cat, and you don't have anything to prove. Really."

"I'm not trying to prove anything."

"Good. You just relax, take a nap, while I handle it."

Merrideth snorted. "Right."

CHAPTER 12

They took Brett's Jeep. It was the second time she had ever been in it. Fortunately, he did not offer to put the top down. He had done so the time they had driven to Nelda's, and she had found that having the wind and sun on their faces made a trip together feel more date-like than was good for her peace of mind. Added to that uneasiness was a low-grade worry about her laptop. She had left her backpack under the bed in her room, figuring it was safer there than at the Hellhound Homecoming. Now she was experiencing separation anxiety like a kindergartener on the first day of school. She willed the feeling away and concentrated on the two bikers they were following.

Not knowing precisely where the campground was, they had decided to follow a pair of bikers wearing Road Hog jackets heading in the right general direction. One of the men on the chrome-encrusted Harleys in front of them had long blond hair, which blew wildly behind him like a flag flapping in the wind. Like the vast majority of the bikers she had seen go through town, he wore no helmet. His buddy, however, wore a spiked Nazi-style helmet. Merrideth and Brett debated whether it was out of concern for his brain or a political statement.

Two and a half miles outside of town, the Harleys' brake lights came on and a second later, their right turn signals. Merrideth was just about to ask Brett if he thought the bikers were luring them into an ambush when she saw a sign that indicated the Hellhound Homecoming was just ahead.

The sign was small and nondescript, as if it were pointing the way to some private family gathering. If she had not already looked it up online to verify that Trevor was right about it being a public event—the Hellhounds had their own Facebook page, for crying out loud—she would have stopped Brett from following the bikers beyond that point. But according to their page, the Homecoming was open to anyone over the age of twenty-one who wanted to party hard.

After a glance her way, Brett turned down the gravel road after the Harleys. One dusty mile later they came to a fork. The Harleys went left toward the campsites, and Brett turned right into the parking lot, or rather the parking *field*. Row after row of cars and motorcycles of all kinds were parked on the bedraggled, July-dry grass, and it took a while for Brett to find an open spot. Finally, he parked between a motorcycle and a trailer for hauling one. The latter was papered over with dust-coated bumper stickers. The bike had only one on its windshield that bragged "I rode mine."

The minute they got out of the Jeep, the afternoon sun beat down on their heads, and blaring music assaulted their ears.

"Holy moly, it's hot!" Brett said.

They went to join a line of people waiting to pass through a gate in a tall chain-link fence. Two burly men were taking money and handing out black wrist bands and programs.

"I think we're entering Hades," Merrideth whispered.

"It's hot enough for it. Maybe it'll be like Dante's Divine Comedy—which I didn't find the least bit funny, by the way. If it is, we can cool off at the frozen lake at the ninth circle of Hell."

Merrideth laughed. "I was referring to Cerberus, not the heat." She pointed to the Hellhounds' namesake artfully depicted on a vinyl sign above the gate. The monster had three heads, a serpent's tail, a mane of snakes, and a lion's claws. Each of its three mouths snarled down at those who dared enter its domain. Next to it was a smaller sign, declaring that it was Ladies' Day.

Two laughing women at the head of the line lifted their T-shirts, flashing the ticket takers. The men grinned, put bead necklaces over their heads, and then shooed them through the gate.

Brett nudged Merrideth's side and smiled slyly. "Looks like we picked a good day to come. I'll get a discount on your ticket."

She glared at him. "You wouldn't be the one getting the discount, because you're not paying for my ticket. And do not think for one second I'm going to pay anything but full price."

"Hey, you're my old lady for the day, and I provide for what's mine."

She gouged his ribs with her elbow, and he grunted out a laugh. "Just kidding about that. But when we get in there, stick close, okay?"

"I will make like a barnacle. And don't forget. If we spot them we'll—"

"I know. I know."

"I mean it, Brett. You promised not go all Rambo and try to take on those guys. We'll just call Sheriff Mitchell and let him handle it."

"If he gets here in time."

"Don't worry about that. If we can get pictures of them, Sheriff Mitchell can hunt them down at his leisure."

"Good idea. I'll keep my phone handy."

Once past Cerberus, the Hellhound's venue was surprisingly benign. All along the main thoroughfare, vendors under brightly colored awnings were selling hotdogs, barbecue, and beer. Other stands featured things like hats and sunscreen. To the right was a row of porta-potties. The whole atmosphere looked like an ordinary summer festival or maybe a county fair, except for the throbbing music coming from somewhere beyond the last row of vendors. And there were no squealing children eating cotton candy and begging to ride the Ferris wheel or jump in the bouncy ball room.

Otherwise, the attendees were of all ages. Most were young, but plenty were middle-aged or older. Were they trying to recapture the rebellious glory of their youth, or had they never grown up in the first place?

"Okay, what am I looking for?" Brett shouted over the music.

"I thought I'd be able to spot the one guy by the American eagle emblem he wore. Stupid, huh?"

"Why is that stupid?"

"The eagle was on the back of his leather jacket. And no one's wearing leather on a day like this."

Brett smiled grimly. "I suppose even tough guys get hot."

Some people wore ordinary shorts and T-shirts much like what she and Brett had on. But most had dressed in a variety of alarming counter-culture styles very different from what she was used to. Whatever everyone wore, weird or normal, they had all dressed for the brutal heat. She would have to rely on recognizing their faces.

"What color of hair and eyes?" Brett said.

"They all had brownish hair. Pretty much. I didn't notice their eyes, except for Patriotic Guy. His were an icy blue."

"What about hair length?"

"It varied. One had a pony-tail. He's the one with the skull-and-crossbones tattoo on his right forearm. Patriotic Guy wore a haircut worthy of a Wall Street tycoon. So don't look for your stereotypical biker dude. What I remember most about him was his white teeth and Hollywood smile."

"All right. I'll be on the lookout. We should be systematic about it. Let's start here and work our way through all the aisles."

"Wait, there's the CMA pavilion. We should check in with Trevor first. Maybe he's seen them."

"Good idea."

They hurried as fast as they were able through the milling people. When they got closer Merrideth saw that Trevor stood outside the pavilion, offering bottled water to passersby. Like everyone else, he had forgone leather for cooler clothes, in his case a blue pocket T-shirt and worn-thin jeans. When he saw them approach, his eyes widened and then he frowned first at Merrideth and then at Brett.

"Somehow I don't think he's thrilled to see us," Brett said.

It was confirmed when the first thing out of his mouth was, "You shouldn't be in here, Merrideth."

"Hey, good to see you, too," Brett muttered.

Trevor's middle-aged friends Larry and June rose from lawn chairs and came forward to greet them. "Don't be rude, Trev. Hi again, Merrideth." June's smile was not nearly as whole-hearted as it had been when they had first met at the stand near the ferry. In spite of her friendly words, she obviously shared Trevor's concern with their presence there.

"Who's your friend?" Larry said.

"This is Brett Garrison."

Brett reached over the table of Bibles and other goods and shook his hand.

"Glad to meet you."

June looked at them curiously. "If you don't mind my asking, why on earth are you two in here?"

So Trevor had not told them about the attack in the cave.

"We're looking for the guys who..." Somehow the words would not come out of Merrideth's mouth. She shot a look at Brett, and he took over, telling Larry and June what had happened.

June gasped. "Are you all right?"

"I'm fine," Merrideth hurried to assure her. "Trevor came in time."

"I can understand how you'd want to track down the snakes," Larry said, scratching his bald head. "But you need to be very careful while you're in here."

"It doesn't seem too dangerous," Merrideth said.

"It's early," June said. "The camp is just waking up."

"At three o'clock in the afternoon?" Brett said.

"That's because most everyone was up all night," Larry said. "To be considered a full-fledged Hellhound you have to. The real party begins after the bands on the main stage quit about two o'clock."

"That makes it sound like more of a club than a rock festival," Merrideth said.

"Almost a cult," June said. "Hellhound Homecoming has a following of faithfuls who come here every year. It grew out of Insane Clown Posse's annual festival here and—I see by your faces you aren't familiar with the band."

"No, can't say I've ever heard of them," Merrideth said.

"Me either," Brett added.

"It's a punk rock band with rap overtones," June explained. "Back in the day, they put on a huge production that drew 10,000 fans who converged on Cave-in-Rock every year. But the violence and drugs got out of hand, and so the producers moved the festival to Ohio some years ago."

Larry slapped at a mosquito on his arm. "About the time citizens and the sheriff's office were sighing in relief, musicians from several of the regional back-up bands reformed into a new band they called Hellhound. And then they came up with their own festival. I'm no judge, but their fans think they're wonderful. In addition, smaller rock bands from all over the Midwest perform here. Hellhound Homecoming doesn't get as large a crowd as the original festival, but they're growing and have the same kind of loyal following."

"And the same drugs and violence," June said. "They advertise that they have all the insanity and mayhem of the original, only without the rap."

"So how did the Road Hogs end up a part of it?" Merrideth said.

"They happened to be passing through town on a run one summer during Hellhound Homecoming and took a fancy to it. They've come to Cave-in-Rock every summer since. Then other unaffiliated bikers started showing up along with assorted bad-boy wannabes. It gets interesting."

"What does Hellhound think about them glomming onto their festival?" Brett asked.

"Oh, they like it," June said. "Adds to the ambience."

Merrideth shook her head in amazement. "Sounds like a three-way cross between Woodstock, a biker rally, and an insane asylum outing."

"It's no Sunday School picnic, that's for sure," Larry said.

"Not even your parents' rock festival," June added. "So don't let the calmness now fool you. As I said, they're just waking up."

"Then I say we go position ourselves to see who comes crawling out of the tents ready for the next round of depravity," Brett said.

"Makes sense," Larry said. "The campsites are over that way."

Trevor had remained silent throughout, content to let his friends do all the explaining. But as Merrideth and Brett started to leave he finally said, "I'll continue to keep my eyes open here."

Merrideth dug in her purse and pulled out one of her business cards. "Call me if you see anything," she said, handing it to him.

Something like surprise showed briefly in Trevor's eyes. Then he tucked the card into his shirt pocket and watched them leave.

Brett took her hand. It seemed perfectly normal to let him. But it was another thing she would have to put a stop to. As soon as they were out of this place.

The shortest way there took them down the row of vendors. She had not paid much attention the first time because they had been anxious to get to Trevor. Now, she saw that not only junk food favorites and the usual kitschy souvenirs were being sold. There was also merchandise definitely not found at county fairs: motorcycle parts and chrome adornments, condoms in assorted colors, and a plethora of drug-related supplies, including glass pipes, bongs, and other paraphernalia the purpose of which she only vaguely understood.

Merrideth was trying to get over the shock of that when she saw that an enterprising young woman was hawking the actual drugs that went along with the paraphernalia. She held a sign, consisting of Magic Marker words scrawled on a torn slab of corrugated cardboard, announcing that a special Hellhound Homecoming sale was now going on over on "The Bridge." Beneath that headline she had helpfully listed her stock:

Acid: $10 per dose. $15 for two.
Trazadone (if you can't sleep) $5.
Opium: $25 for 1 gram. $40 for two.

"Toto," Merrideth said, "we're definitely not in Kansas anymore."

"I was saving my money for a snow cone," Brett said, "but it's hard to resist such a bargain."

"I'm sure you'll manage."

The crowd was growing by the minute, making it more difficult to study each face before it passed out of view. A couple crossed in front of them. The male had a long, *Duck Dynasty* type beard halfway down his chest and a red bandana on his head. He wore camo cargo shorts and a white undershirt that strained across his pudgy stomach. But it was the woman with him who caught the eye. She wore only a black string-bikini bottom and sandals. Her long, frizzy red hair and several strands of beads were all that covered her breasts. Sort of. Brett politely averted his eyes even though that was presumably the opposite response the woman intended. Merrideth tried not to gawk.

They threaded through the attendees, trying to look nonchalant when another topless woman passed them, this one nursing an infant.

"Think of what that's doing to the poor baby's hearing," Merrideth said.

"What?" Brett said.

"I said, think of what—" She stopped when she realized he was joking. "Ha ha."

Brett stopped and pulled her to the side. "I think it's pointless now to go to the campsite. From the way the crowd has swelled, the Hellhounds have obviously awakened and come out of their kennels."

"What should we do?" Merrideth said. "I'm sure I'm not getting a look at everyone passing by us."

"I suggest we go where the people are congregating—and not moving."

"You mean one of the shows. I get it. They'll be so distracted by the performance they won't notice us sleuths scoping out the crowd."

"Exactly. Do you still have that program they gave you at the gate?"

She dug in her purse and found it. Cerberus' three growling faces were on the front. Inside was a welcome message and general explanation into which the writer had worked the F-word more times than she had ever seen in one paragraph. But the Hellhounds did apparently have their moral standards, because below the profanity-studded paragraph were the words in bold print: *No stealing allowed!* After the warning was the schedule of events.

"There's a bunch of stuff about the various bands playing," she said. "According to this, Twisted Corpse is playing on the main stage, even as we speak."

"So that's what that noise is. Is there anything else going on?"

"Apparently the biggest attractions are the motorcycle customization and burn-out contests, but those are tomorrow. As for today's schedule, we just missed the tattoo contest, sponsored by *Ingrid's Ink Slinging.* Ooh! Here's another contest that sounds promising. But it's not until five."

"Anything sooner?"

"In fact there is. Now showing in the Den of the Damned is *Bloody Mania,*" she said, using air quotes. "In case you didn't guess, that's a wrestling match. It's almost over, so we'd better go there first."

"Wait, Nancy Drew. If we're going to be successful sleuths, you should do something about the way you look, or you're going to stick out like a whore in Sunday School."

"Thank you, Brett. Lovely analogy. And what's wrong with the way I look?"

"You look too much like the wholesome young thing you are." He studied her outfit. Not much we can do unless you jettisoned your scruples about going—"

Merrideth yelped. "I'm not going topless!"

Brett grinned. "I was going to say braless, but I didn't figure you would. Ah, but there's this." He unfastened her tortoise shell clip, and her hair tumbled around her shoulders. "Don't you have some kind of goo for it?" he said, scrunching her hair. "Something to make it stick up? And more gunk for your eyes."

"Mascara?"

"Yeah, that."

"No, Brett, I don't. And what about you, Mr. GQ?"

"Ah! Fortunately, *I* have no scruples about going topless." He pulled his T-shirt off and stuck the tail of it into the rear pocket of his shorts. "Does this help?"

"Humph. I thought we were trying to blend in, not attract a pack of she-hounds. I wonder if they call them—you know, that word that rhymes with *riches*."

"I wonder. But forget that. Professor Randall, I do believe you just complimented me."

How about that. She had. "Come on, Hardy Boy, before your head gets so large you can't put your shirt back on."

To reach the Den of the Damned they had to get past the main stage, so they decided they might as well take a quick look there. Twisted Corpse was performing *Highway to Hell*. Some music lovers sat in lawn chairs or sprawled haphazardly on blankets. Others danced, or stood in place moving to the beat. Sort of. A haze of pot smoke hovered over the sea of people.

"I can't see anyone's faces all that well, can you?" Brett said, peering at the crowd.

"No," Merrideth said. "We should hurry while the wrestling is still going on. Besides, we'll get high if we stay here much longer."

"That would never do. We'd forget the guys we're looking for and start hunting for the nearest family-sized bag of Cheetos to munch on."

Merrideth looked at him in surprise.

"So I hear," he quickly added. "Trust me, I've never had a desire to mess up my brain."

"Me neither. Not when I saw what it did to my dad."

Brett took her hand and led her through a gap in the audience. There was a commotion to Merrideth's right. People started hooting and whistling. She thought it very rude until she realized they were not directing their cat-calls toward the performers on the stage, but rather toward a young couple in the audience. They lay on a quilt. Or rather, the man did. The woman straddled him and wore a full skirt, so nothing actually showed, but it was obvious they were going at it to the delight of those nearby. In public. In broad daylight. In a crowd of hundreds, no less.

Shaking his head in amazement at the couple's lewdness, Brett led her on. Merrideth was relieved to get past all that. But then the sound of another excited audience came to her, and she wondered what new shock was in store for them.

They got to the Den of the Damned just as a man carrying a microphone stepped into the roped-off area that served as an arena. He was apparently the event's announcer, although he had the bulging muscles to be a contestant. His shaved head was covered in tattoos that inched down his neck and disappeared into a T-shirt with the sleeves cut off. He announced that the final bout of the day was between the Tasmanian Devil and Cujo.

When the former came into the ring, the crowd showed its appreciation by clapping and calling out loud X-rated comments. But when Cujo entered, they went totally berserk. A man beside Merrideth whistled so piercingly next to her ear that she was afraid her eardrum had burst. It took a moment to register that Cujo had only one leg and had come into the ring with the aid of a cane carved to look like a serpent.

The people began to chant "I-Hop, I-Hop," and Cujo grinned and bowed. The Tasmanian Devil also postured for the crowd, puffing his massive chest and glaring at his opponent.

"Weirdest match-up I've ever seen," Brett shouted. "Equivalent of pitting a gladiator against an unarmed Christian. And something tells me this isn't going to be a choreographed and scripted contest. I don't see any referees either. It's going to be painful to watch."

"We're not here to watch them. Watch the crowd."

It wasn't easy. No one stood conveniently still to allow Merrideth to study their faces. And in their blood lust, everyone had expressions similar to what her attackers had worn as they looked down at her helplessly struggling on the cave floor.

Brett nudged her arm. "There," he said pointing to their left. "What about Smiley at ten o'clock?"

"No. Our guy is better looking. I mean really good-looking. I'm talking Ashton Kutcher only with blue eyes instead of brown."

"Okay, a pretty-boy, then."

Grinning, Merrideth looked him up and down. "Yes. Like that."

A few men in the audience wore the same hellish clown paint

she had seen as the bikers came into town the first night. The heat had caused the paint to drip, making them appear all the more fiendish. But unless the paint dripped completely off their faces she would not be able to identify those who wore it.

The crowd oohed, and Merrideth's eyes were drawn to the arena. Cujo was on his back, struggling to get up. The Tasmanian Devil pranced around the perimeter, gloating as if taking down a crippled man was a great coup. But he made the mistake of getting too close to Cujo, who hooked his ankle with his cane and brought him down. Then Cujo scooted to the ropes and pulled himself up, all the while beating the other man with his cane.

"Hence the expression *no holds barred*," Brett said near her ear.

The crowd resumed its chant of "I-Hop," and she and Brett resumed scanning faces.

"What about him?" Brett said. "He has a nice smile."

She could tell by his voice that he was kidding and laughed when she saw who he was referring to. A huge man near the front had turned to laugh at a friend behind him. He was ugly as sin, and he wore gold caps on his front teeth.

"That's one solution to meth-mouth, I suppose," Merrideth said. "Stylish, isn't it?"

"I was thinking he probably lost his teeth from scurvy. All he needs is an eye-patch to play the part of Captain Hook. Arrrgh!"

Merrideth laughed, appreciating the touch of levity, and continued studying the crowd to her right. And suddenly there was Patriotic Guy in the very back, smiling at Cujo's antics in the arena.

CHAPTER 13

He had left off his leather jacket with its distinctive Eagle emblem. But ever the patriotic American, he now wore a white T-shirt emblazoned with the Stars and Stripes. She grabbed Brett's arm, and he turned to look.

Once he understood, Brett unclasped her hand from its death grip on his arm and took out his phone. "He's too far away for a clear photo." He started pushing his way through the people standing behind them. He did not bother to be polite or ask for pardon. She followed in his wake the best she could, wishing for the millionth time she was not such a pygmy. At least he was tall enough that she could track him in the press of people.

A camera flash went off in Merrideth's face, making her too blind to go farther. The light continued flashing behind her eyelids. After a moment, she risked a look and saw a woman wearing a press badge. She was not aiming her camera at her but rather at the girl beside her who was holding up her shirt to bare a naked breast with one hand while giving the world a middle-finger salute with the other. Her belligerent expression dared anyone to say one word against her shameless vulgarity.

Merrideth shook her head in disgust. Oh great. Her face was going to show up in the newspaper next to the Hellhound girl's. Her mother would be so proud. And President Peterson, too. She finally spotted Brett and shoved her way through until she reached where he stood glaring at the crowd.

"He slipped away before I could get a photo," Brett said. "I have no idea where he went."

"I do. The main stage."

"Why?"

"Did you notice the alleged music stopped?"

"You're right," Brett said, putting his hands to his ears in wonderment.

"That means the contest is starting."

"What contest?"

"I'll give you a clue. All the contestants are women and the scoring involves the size and perkiness of a certain part of female anatomy."

"Sounds like something right up the alley of Smiley and the gang."

"I agree, even though personally I am really getting tired of looking at boobs."

She figured Brett would jokingly leer at her and make some funny comment about how he sure wasn't. Instead his face grew serious. "It's no wonder, with the attitude everyone here seems to have toward women, that those men didn't see anything wrong with rape." He took her hand again. "I think we should check this out, but I promise that I'll be watching the audience, not the stage."

Merrideth smiled to herself as Brett tugged her along to the main stage. Back when Abby and John first started dating, Abby had invented an imaginary chart for him. Whenever Abby thought John did something swoon-worthy she had awarded him an imaginary gold star. Merrideth did not know what category Brett's attitude fell under—chivalry, maybe? But if she had a chart for *him*, he would be getting a star about now.

The contest was every bit as raunchy as they expected. The Hellhounds, both audience and performers, acted as if they actually did belong to the canine species, the women flaunting their attributes and gyrating as if they were in heat, and the men howling out their approval with blatant invitations to mate, expressed in the crudest terms imaginable. There were a surprising number of women in the audience egging on the contestants to further debase themselves.

True to his word, Brett kept his face turned away and together they searched the crowd as inconspicuously as they could. Only a few men wore white T-shirts, and they stood out among the dark clothes favored by most Hellhounds and Road Hogs. Merrideth and Brett wound their way through the exuberant spectators, systematically approaching each beacon of white until they could get close enough to see the face of the wearer. None of them looked remotely like Ashton Kutcher. They saw one white shirt with a flag, but on closer inspection it was a satiric, decidedly unpatriotic version that startled Merrideth with its vitriolic attitude.

As they did their sleuthing, Merrideth tried to keep an eye out for skull-and-crossbones tattoos, too. Lots of the men sported ink, but they were waving their arms around so excitedly that it was hard to make out what the designs were.

Merrideth sighed. "This is hopeless. Maybe we should leave." She saw a flash of white from the corner of her eye and turned toward the stage. It was a white T-shirt, but it was not worn by a man. It belonged to a smiling woman who was whipping it off as she approached the stage to a crescendo of catcalls all around her.

"Don't look now," Merrideth said. "But contestant number twelve is Casey."

"A friend of yours I should know?"

No, it had been Trevor, not Brett who had met her. "She's a store clerk at Casey's."

"Did they name—?"

"The store after her? No, and she doesn't own it either. She was so nice to me. Wow, I had no idea she had such large—and there's a tattoo on one of them."

"How nice for her," Brett said. "I'm glad you're enjoying the show."

Merrideth turned back to him. "Oh, sorry. I was surprised, that's all."

"Let's go find out if your friend Trevor has seen any of them."

"I wish you'd stop referring to him as my friend Trevor."

He laughed with just a hint of scorn. "I don't. He's *your* friend."

She felt her phone vibrate in her pocket and pulled it out. "Speaking of *my* friend Trevor, I just got a text from him." She grabbed Brett's hand. "Come on. Patriotic Guy's at the CMA stand. We've got to hurry if we want to get him."

Trevor's text had said to meet him across from the CMA stand at the Porta-potties so as not to spook the guy. The whole way there she chanted to herself, "Be there, you patriotic scumbag. Be there."

He was. When they turned the corner into the aisle, his white shirt was the first thing she saw. Amazingly, he stood at the CMA table reading a Bible. Across the aisle, Trevor secretly watched him, partially hidden by a Porta-potty.

She and Brett detoured out of the guy's line of sight and came up to Trevor from behind the toilets.

"Is it him, Merrideth?" Trevor said. "You saw him better than I did."

"It's him all right."

Brett took out his phone and snapped a picture of Patriotic Guy. "It's no good. He's still too far away to see clearly."

"Let me see," Merrideth said. He handed his phone to her and she saw that he was right. The man's face was a small blur that would only get worse when enlarged. She tried with her own phone but the results were no better.

Trevor nodded toward the CMA stand. "Look. There they go into action."

June handed the man a bottled water. He said something and gave her his Hollywood smile. He took the cap off and swilled down a long gulp of the water. Then he wiped his mouth with the back of his hand and went back to reading the Bible.

"He's thirsty," Trevor said softly. "Eventually everyone comes to the realization that booze just isn't going to quench their thirst."

"A cold drink sounds wonderful," Merrideth said. "And afterward a nice long shower to wash the contamination of this lawless place away."

"They're not completely lawless," Trevor said. "The Hellhounds have a code of sorts and mete out their brand of justice where needed. Two years ago I watched them go totally feral and destroy some guy's Grand Am because he stole stuff from several festival goers."

"*Do not steal,*" Merrideth said, remembering the flyer.

Larry approached the table and said something to Patriotic Guy.

Trevor smiled. "He's telling him the story of the Samaritan woman and Christ's offer of living water. If he seems open, Larry will show him where a few key verses are in that New Testament he's holding."

Merrideth expected him to sneer and leave. Instead, he seemed to be seriously considering what Larry was telling him.

"I never expected to see a Road Hog reading a Bible," Brett said. "Actually, I'm surprised Hellhound even lets CMA in."

"They're surprised we want to come in," Trevor said. "But

they're usually genuinely grateful for what we do to minister to them."

"Isn't it hopeless, Trevor?" Merrideth said. "I mean look at them."

Brett answered before Trevor could. "It's never hopeless. Jesus came to seek and to save the lost." He cleared his throat, and Merrideth saw with astonishment that he looked remorseful. "I've been thinking about this wrong all day. The whole time I've been anxious to get my hands on them and make them pay for what they did to Merrideth." He swallowed. "Revenge instead of redemption."

Trevor's eyebrows rose in surprise.

Merrideth was about to say, *hey, what about justice?* when Trevor said, "I'll be praying for this guy's redemption, but that doesn't mean he shouldn't pay for his crime."

"I'll call Sheriff Mitchell." Merrideth dug in her purse for the business card he had given her. "I've got his number in here somewhere." She stopped digging. "No I don't. It's in my backpack."

"Surely you remember *that* number without looking it up. It's only three digits."

"Very funny, Brett. Sheriff Mitchell said to call his personal cell phone number."

Trevor looked out over the crowd. "I figure the Hellhounds and Road Hogs are ripe for salvation, because they've reached the first step of recognizing they're sinners. They all know they're going to hell. Sometimes they'll laugh and say they want to go there where they'll be in friendly company. But that's just bluster."

Patriotic Guy paused to swig more water and then said something to Larry, who smiled kindly and said more. The man looked back down at the Bible, and Larry shot a smile across the way to Trevor. His expression conveyed an excitement that reminded Merrideth of a car salesman about to clinch a deal.

Patriotic Guy looked up and turned to see who Larry was smiling at. Trevor ducked behind the Porta-Potty, and Brett tried to pull Merrideth back behind him, but it was too late. The man stiffened and then darted away like a gold-medal sprinter.

Trevor took off after him. Brett turned to her and shouted, "Stay here!" then followed him. All three men quickly disappeared into the crowd.

So much for Brett's promise not to go Rambo. Even if his goal was only to get a photo of Patriotic Guy, he was not going to stand still waiting for Brett to snap his picture. He and Trevor would have to wrestle him to the ground to get it. And how would any nearby Road Hogs react when they saw one of their brothers under attack?

There was no point in trying to follow Brett and Trevor. Even if she spotted them, with her short stature she would never be able to keep up with their long strides. That did not mean she had to remain standing by an odorous toilet waiting for them to get back.

She threaded her way through the people meandering around in the aisle and went to the CMA stand. Larry and June were staring at the path the men had taken and did not notice her.

"He sure was in a hurry," Larry said. "At least he took the Bible with him."

"Praise the Lord! His Word will not return unto him void." June turned and saw her. "Oh, Merrideth. I'm glad you came over. It's not safe for you to be alone out there. Did Trevor say why he had a notion to light out like that?"

"They're following that guy. He's one of the men who attacked me."

"You're talking about that young man with the nice smile?" Larry said.

"That's the one."

"Well, I'll be."

"Would you like a water?" June said.

"Yes, thank you." Merrideth wondered if she would be served a sermon to go along with it. Her fear turned out to be groundless. Instead, they offered her one of the lawn chairs, and she took it gladly, even though it was weird to find herself in the company of radical evangelists hawking salvation experiences to hell-bound Hellhound groupies and biker dudes.

Larry and June took turns standing in the thoroughfare offering bottled water to people walking by. While one worked the crowd, the other sat to rest feet, tired and swollen from the heat. Merrideth felt guilty, like she should take a turn and let them rest. But that would send the weirdness completely off the chart.

A few festival-goers stopped briefly at the table, one man for a bar of soap, which he desperately needed, and another because he had heard they might have needles. When he was told they did not, he mumbled his thanks and went on. Merrideth wondered what nefarious use he had planned for them. But then again, maybe he just needed one to remove a splinter or sew on a button.

In between customers, Larry and June regaled her with some of their experiences during the years they had been coming to the Hellhound Homecoming. Some stories were hair-raising and others heart-warming. It didn't sound like they had made many conversions, but both assured her that the main thing was that the seed had been sown.

After an hour, Merrideth edged past the table and peered the way Brett and Trevor had gone. There was no sign of them. Soon after that, another CMA worker came, bringing hot barbecue sandwiches and a zippered bag of carrot strips.

"You should eat Trevor's sandwich," June said. "We can get him and your friend Brett more when they get back."

If they got back. What if Patriotic Guy had lured Brett and Trevor away so that Skull-and-Crossbones and their other thug buddies could ambush them? What if they were lying bleeding and unconscious somewhere with tread marks of their own, only on their faces instead of their arms? She could call 9-1-1, of course. But should she do it without knowing whether Brett had managed to get photos of any of her attackers? Would Sheriff Mitchell even come if she did call? Or would he say she had missed her chance to press charges?

Her stomach growled, and she decided she might as well eat while she worried.

At seven-thirty, there was a disturbance in the thoroughfare as two fierce-looking, leather-clad bikers came bulldozing their way through the crowd, dragging a slumping man between them. The man briefly lifted his head. It was Brett! His face was covered in blood, and some had dripped down his neck and onto his bare chest.

Stumbling over her lawn chair in her haste, Merrideth rushed out of the pavilion and into the aisle, pulling her phone from her pocket as she went. She parked herself pugnaciously in front of the two hulks and glared up at them. "You let him go right this minute or I'm calling Sheriff Mitchell."

The bikers had full, bushy red beards that gave them the appearance of Vikings. They were similar in build and coloring, and she spared a moment to wonder if they were brothers. They only glared at her and kept coming, forcing her to step aside or be trampled.

"Lady, instead of yipping at our heels like a poodle," one of them growled as they passed her, "how about you get him a chair?" His voice was gravelly as if he had smoked a dozen cartons of Marlboros that day.

Brett looked up and grinned, actually grinned at her. "Put your phone away, Merri. These men came to my rescue."

Merrideth felt her face heat. "Oh. Sorry." With terror no longer clogging her brain, she saw that they were not dragging Brett, but supporting him as he hopped along on one foot.

"Over here." Larry shoved the display table aside to allow more room, and the men brought Brett under the pavilion and helped him into the lawn chair she had just vacated.

"It's not as bad as it looks," Brett said. "You know how scalp wounds bleed."

"What about your foot?"

"I think it's just a sprain." Brett looked beyond her and smiled. "Ah, just in time."

Trevor slipped around the Vikings and handed Merrideth a plastic bag. "I stopped off at the first-aid station for a few things. I hope I got the right stuff."

"Thanks. Now can somebody tell me what happened?" Merrideth said.

As usual, Trevor-the-Silent didn't waste words, and the Vikings offered nothing, just stood there taking up most of the space under the pavilion. And Brett's efforts to explain were hampered by a swollen lip and her ministrations to his sore scalp and swollen ankle. But eventually she pieced together what had happened.

Brett and Trevor had followed Patriotic Guy, trying—they said—only to get a photo, which of course was impossible at the speed they were moving. He led them on a merry chase down the thoroughfares and then through the audience watching the musicians on the main stage. When the drummer got a panicked expression and suddenly left in the middle of the song, Brett deduced that he was one of the attackers and that PG, as he decided to call him, had come that way to warn him. With difficulty, Brett and Trevor had tracked the two Road Hogs through the crowd of stoned spectators and then on to the campsites where they lost the trail among the tents and popup trailers. Figuring the two had somehow slipped past them, they decided to go to the parking lot and watch for anyone leaving in a hurry. At that point Brett and Trevor had separated, each keeping an eye on a different section of the lot.

A few minutes later, someone bashed Brett over the head with what he later learned was a beer bottle. He got a glimpse of a skull-and-crossbones tattoo before he fell. As he went down, his foot tangled in a Harley and it came with him. He blacked out for a short while, although he remembered hearing the roar of motorcycles. When he came around, two angry bikers were screaming at him. He did a little screaming of his own when they jerked him up and he landed on his right foot.

At that point in the narrative, one of the Vikings sheepishly mumbled, "Sorry about that. We saw those guys leave but didn't think anything of it. All we had on our minds was that you were trying to jack my Harley *Fat Boy*."

Brett only laughed. "This is where my silver Irish tongue was put to good use. I had to do a lot of fast talking to convince these two not to finish the job PG and his buddy had begun."

"Meanwhile, I was wasting time on a wild goose chase," Trevor said. "I never did see either of them."

"Sorry, Merri," Brett said. "I never did get a photo of him. And they're surely gone now."

"I'm just glad you made it back okay. Relatively okay." She had cleaned the blood from his face and bandaged his sprained ankle, but he still looked a mess. "At least you won't need stitches."

"Here," June said. "Put your foot up on this chair. I've made you an icepack."

"I can get you Percocet, Vicodin—anything you want," one of the Vikings growled.

Easing his foot onto the chair, Brett cleared his throat. "That won't be necessary, Gary. It's just a minor sprain, I'm sure. But thanks anyway. Thanks for everything, you guys."

The Vikings started to go, but then the one named Gary turned and said to Merrideth, "We'll keep our eyes open for the...losers that hurt you, Miss. I doubt they'll ever come to another Homecoming, but if they do, when we get done with them, they'll never think about rape again."

"Thanks," she said weakly, hoping she would not have to go on trial as an accessory to murder. When they were gone she added, "I guess that means they have a second rule: No raping."

"Ironic," Trevor said.

"Why?" Merrideth said.

"They both had '1%' tattoos."

When he did not say more, June explained, "Ninety-nine percent of all bikers are law-abiding citizens. Mostly, anyway. Leaving one percent who are actually outlaw gang members."

"So those two were bragging," Merrideth said.

"In a subtle way," Larry said. "Sometimes they wear patches on their jackets."

"Actually, the percentage here might be a little higher," Brett said. "I counted four one- percenters, and taking into consideration the attendance at the Homecoming…but I digress."

Larry turned to Merrideth. "And here's another irony. That smiley guy has been by our stand several times over the weekend. He seemed really interested in what we had to say. Had good questions, too."

"I never saw him," Trevor said.

Larry scratched his head. "Come to think of it, he always seemed to come when you were gone. Do you think he watched and waited for you to leave?"

"Maybe." Then Trevor smiled. "Or maybe his stops were ordained for just the right time."

"I hope he took the Bible with him," June said.

"He still had it in his hand the last time I saw him," Brett said.

"It will be getting dark soon," Trevor said. "You two should leave."

"He's right," Larry said. "If you thought it was wild in here before, it's nothing to what happens after nightfall."

"Are you staying over?" June asked.

"We had planned on going home, but now, I don't know," Merrideth said, looking at Brett's bedraggled appearance.

"Well if you decide to stay, you're invited to our chapel service tomorrow," June said.

"Here?" Merrideth said.

"No, we hold it down by the ferry dock," Larry said. "Just for the CMA workers. It's our traditional send-off."

"Thanks. I'd like that," Brett said.

"We'll have to see how you're doing in the morning." Merrideth would have helped Brett up from the lawn chair, but Trevor stepped in to do it before she could.

"Thanks," Brett said, putting his arm around Trevor's neck.

Chasing Road Hogs had apparently been a male-bonding experience. Brett was no longer bristling at Trevor and actually looked happy for his help. Merrideth followed the two men as they did a three-legged walk to the parking lot.

✢ ✢ ✢

Carrying the two ice packs she had made from plastic bags the night clerk had rustled up for her, Merrideth snagged the extra pillow from her bed and went out onto her little deck. "Did I miss any good ones?"

Brett looked up from where he sat propping his injured ankle on her small suitcase and smiled tiredly. "There was a pretty orange glow in the trees just now. I thought at first someone had set the woods on fire. But I haven't heard sirens, so my guess is one of the Roman Candles malfunctioned. I shudder to think what condition the guys in charge of igniting them are in."

"Someone should add a new rule to the Hellhound flyer about not being drunk while on fireworks duty."

Brett grinned. "I can see it now: *No blasting while blasted.* Or maybe *No lighting while you're lit.*"

"Forget fire truck sirens. I keep expecting to hear ambulances. Trevor said a few years ago someone blew off a hand. And speaking of appendages, lift your foot a little." She eased the pillow under his ankle and the ice pack over it. "How's that?"

"Thanks, Merri." He smiled sweetly up at her and she wanted to kiss his poor battered face and make it all better. Instead, she gave him the smaller ice pack. "Here, you can decide where you want this one."

"Thanks. I've got lots of places to choose from."

A burst of red, white, and blue stars popped in the black sky and then fell in a shower to the ground. As before, only a small portion of the fireworks display could actually be seen from her deck because of the trees. But they oohed and ahhed, Brett adding an *ouch* when he opened his mouth too wide. He decided to put the ice pack to his lip first.

Merrideth cringed at his obvious discomfort. "I'm sorry. Just think, you could be watching real fireworks with Bill and Kevin and the gang. The only ice would be in your Coke."

"Don't worry. I'm happy right where I am. This pyrotechnic wonder is the perfect ending to a really, really strange day."

"That it was." Merrideth settled onto the deck bannister and waited to see what would appear in the sky next. So much had happened that it was difficult to know what to think about first. No telling what kind of dreams she would have as her brain processed it all. Then she remembered that she had not told him what she had found out.

"They got away."

"I know. I'm sorry, Merri. It doesn't look like you're going to get justice. Or closure. If only your friend Trevor and I had—"

"That's all right. You certainly went above the call of duty. But I wasn't talking about the bikers. I meant Sarah and the other wives. Well, not real wives, even though they called them that."

"Did I miss another time-surfing adventure?"

"No, a good old-fashioned Google adventure. I did a little follow-up research while I was waiting for you to finish your shower. I found another article about the Harpe brothers in a history journal."

"So Samuel Mason came through for them with the letter?"

"Presumably. The author didn't say who, only that someone smuggled a letter out to Sarah's father. He caught up to them and brought her home. It didn't say what Little Harpe thought about that. The other women weren't free of Big Harpe until the loathsome brothers were killed. I'm going to have to read more about that. The author hinted at a gruesome end to their lives."

"I wonder if Susannah mourned for Big Harpe. Was it just me, or did you sense a little Stockholm syndrome going on there?"

"I couldn't tell if it was that, or she genuinely admired her husband. Anyway, Sarah went on to marry a decent man. They lived in Knoxville and had other children. By all accounts they were happy."

"Except maybe once in a while when Sarah looked at her first-born son and saw Little Harpe's eyes looking back at her."

It was a terrifying thought. Did a mother's love ever entirely overcome the revulsion of a child fathered by a rapist? How much worse when he was a serial killer.

Suddenly she was tired. Not only physically, but also tired of contemplating so much evil. How did homicide detectives manage to stay sane? Did they all take Prozac? All the filth and corruption she had seen over the past few days had undoubtedly messed with her brain chemistry. And now what she thought of as the Brown Cloud had come for one of its sporadic visits. It had been steadily building, starting even before she saw the Hoffmans' bloody end. It was time to think happy thoughts. That was the thing to do. Especially if she hoped to get any sleep that night.

She pasted on a smile. "Speaking of eyes, you'd better give your right eye equal time with that ice pack. You've got a shiner coming, Professor Garrison. On second thought, maybe not. Your groupies would think a black eye only adds to your rakish, Indiana Jones charm."

He chuckled, then groaned and said from behind the icepack, "Ouch! It's not nice to make a man with a busted lip laugh."

She grinned. "Oops. My bad."

"Indy would have had at least a dozen bad guys to show for a black eye. And he never would have tripped over his own feet and sprained an ankle. That's just plain wimpy."

A barrage of snapping and popping sounds filled the air, leaving the sky smoke-filled without anything to show for it. It gave her an excuse to change the subject just as she had been about to blurt out that he was *her* hero. "I wonder if that was supposed to be the grand finale?"

"I bet you're right."

"Did you call home?"

"I apologized for not making it home, but Aunt Nelda told me not to worry about it. 'Just have a good time,' she says. I told her I had already had about as much fun as I could stand for one weekend. My ears are still buzzing from the music. Did you know that just during the time we were there, the bands played twenty-seven songs either about hell or with mentions of it?"

"No, I did not. What else have you been counting today, Number Boy?"

"You would find it boring."

"How many Road Hogs were at the Homecoming?"

"I estimate the total number, including those that only stayed for a short time, to be two thousand four hundred and fifty. Approximately. I sort of lost count when we were stumbling over stoned music lovers in the grass."

Merrideth laughed. "That skill must come in handy."

"At one time I thought about going into market research. Take motorcycles. I noticed there was a surprising diversity of brands in the parking lot. Road Hogs tend to favor Harley-Davidson, but not by as large a margin as you might think. Yamaha and Kawasaki were the next most popular with—"

"Stop! You're right. It's boring. I'd say you were an idiot savant but you're missing half the prerequisites."

Brett chuckled. "That's what Aunt Nelda says."

"I feel terrible that you're not there with her."

"It's not your fault. By the way, she said to tell you hello. So hello."

"Abby said *hello* to you, too." Abby had also laughingly told her to give Brett a kiss for her, but she saw no need to mention that fact to him. "Is Aunt Nelda okay?"

"When I asked her how she was, she said she was fine and for me to stop fussing over her like she was an old lady. I reminded her that she was an old lady. She laughed. But then she said she was going to bed as soon as we hung up."

"You're worried."

"It isn't like her. She's normally such a night owl." He turned to look at her. "But you, Merri, are an early-bird, so I'll leave and let you turn in. That is if you'll help me get my pathetic, crippled self back to my room."

"All right, but let me turn on the light. I wouldn't want you to trip. Again."

"Ha, ha. Very funny."

Grinning, she reached inside the room and found the switch for the deck light.

He was rather pathetic, looking up at her with his cuts and bruises. She should not have teased him. He obviously felt like he had come up short in the hero department. And then, without knowing she was going to do it, she bent and kissed his cheek below the eye that was turning purple. When she pulled back in surprise, she saw that he did not look pathetic any more. His green eyes glowed like backlit emeralds that might start emitting smoke any minute.

"Well, didn't that just make this day worthwhile?" He added one of his killer smiles, his teeth white in his tanned face.

"Just a sympathy kiss, Dr. Garrison. That's all."

He laughed, but she paid him no mind, just turned her attention to the practical matter of getting him up out of the chair and down the hall to his own room before either of them did something even stupider than a sympathy kiss.

CHAPTER 14

Half way through her bedtime routine, Merrideth realized that she was far too revved to even think about sleeping. Normally, by nine-thirty, she was yawning and having trouble keeping her eyes open. But it was already nearly ten o'clock, and she was not at all sleepy. Like a pilot whose plane was approaching the runway too fast, she needed to throttle back. She checked the patio door, even though she knew full well that she had locked it when she and Brett came inside. Yes, it was still locked. As was the hall door. And the little coffee pot in the bathroom was still unplugged.

She pulled back the bedspread, got into bed, and switched off the lamp. The numbers on the clock glowed red, and a strip of moonlight sneaked in where the drapes met in the center of the window. The pulsing dot coming from her laptop where it was charging on the desk was tiny, but she supposed it had to be counted as a light source too. Still, the room was dark enough for good sleeping. The air-conditioner hummed nicely. That would help, too. She manufactured a yawn and shut her eyes.

On the movie screen of her eyelids, the young Hoffman woman stared up at her from the flatboat's deck with dull, sightless eyes. On her pale brow, a neat round hole oozed a little blood, and beneath her head a red tidal wave of it gushed onto the rough planks. The reverberations from Samuel Mason's pistol still hung in the air along with the cloud of acrid gun smoke.

Gasping, Merrideth sat up in bed. What the heck!

The flashback had been almost as real as when she had first seen the murder in virtual mode in the cave. Did she have posttraumatic stress disorder? What other horrors would she see if she closed her eyes again? She scooted back and leaned against the headboard.

Mrs. Hoffman had seemed to look accusingly at both Mason and *her*. It was a foolish notion, of course. The poor woman was not sending her post-mortem messages of condemnation. She could not possibly blame *her* for the pirates' murderous schemes. It was not *her* fault the woman had died so young—and pregnant. If Merrideth had known a way to intervene she would have, but unfortunately *Beautiful Houses* did not work that way.

The Hoffmans had probably thought they'd die of old age working their new farm. But before they could even get there, they had been cut down in the space of only seconds. Their relatives back in Pennsylvania had no doubt waited eagerly for a letter describing the adventurous journey and the rich land on the frontier. How long had it taken before they started worrying? How long before they gave up ever hearing from them again? They probably blamed Indians, never knowing it had been "civilized" white men who killed them, greedy for their meager possessions. Had they prayed that some kind soul came along to bury them properly?

She had not been able to stop the murders, but she could make sure the family's experiences were not forgotten. Lars and Martha's line had died out, but other branches of the family tree back in Pennsylvania had presumably gone on. She would hunt down one or more of their descendants and contact them. Just like any other genealogy job, only she would do it gratis. She would let them know what had happened, and they could add a footnote to their tree.

And then she would be able to rest, knowing that she had done what she could to help the family. Now it was time to get the literal kind of rest. She slid back down under the sheet and turned onto her side, then closed her eyes cautiously. Good. No more gruesome flashbacks. She ordered herself to relax, to not think about what needed to be done tomorrow. There would be time enough to begin the search when she got home. Now was the time to sleep. Past time to sleep. To think about sleepy thoughts like puffy clouds and soothing ocean waves. Clouds and waves. Clouds and waves.

The boat rocked pleasantly and beautiful cumulus clouds sailed overhead, almost cartoon-like in their perfection. But in an instant, one low cloud went from white to shades of angry gray that blocked out the sunlight over the boat. The wind kicked up, turning the canvas sun awning into a flapping sail. But there was no sound. Someone must have turned the speakers down too low.

The boat strained to break away from its mooring. Water washed over the deck, foaming pink when it reached the woman lying there. It was the young Hoffman woman. Why didn't she wake up and get that awning down? If the rope snapped, the boat would take her down the river alone without her family. No, wait! They were already on board. And they were sleeping, too, only in a pile, their arms and legs tangled together, like the girls' sometimes got when they slept together in their Cinderella tent. Why didn't one of the men get up and do something before it was too late?

Some of the pink water splashed over Mrs. Hoffman's face and at last she opened her eyes. But still she made no move to do anything, just lay there serenely. Couldn't she see the danger she was in? The boat began to rock back and forth. Mrs. Hoffman rocked with it, like a rag doll with no ability to control its own movement. Except for her eyes, which began to dart to the right and then the left as she anxiously looked for something or someone. Her lips moved, too. She was saying something, but what? Someone should turn up the sound!. Another gush of water poured over the deck, lifting Mrs. Hoffman's limp arm above her head in a parody of a wave. She continued to speak, her words going unheard.

Merrideth's eyes flew open, and she flung herself onto her back, struggling to drag in enough air to inflate her lungs. Then relief poured through her, and she could breathe again. It was a dream! Only a dream! First a flashback and now a nightmare. Was she doomed to see Mrs. Hoffman every time she closed her eyes?

It wasn't difficult to interpret the dream. Her overactive sense of responsibility was telling her that she needed to help the poor woman. It didn't seem fair to have a nightmare about it, seeing as she had drifted off to sleep planning how she *would* help her.

Mrs. Hoffman. She did not know her first name. She and Trevor had not been able to remember it when she wrote down the names of the other family members. Her blasted memory! Brett with his super brain would remember it if he had been there for that part, but he hadn't.

Was that what the dream was about? Was her brain trying to tell her not to leave Cave-in-Rock without learning her name?

It probably was not crucial to her search. But what if she left not knowing it, and then could not get a hit on the right Hoffman family? Even if she came back to the cave someday, after so much time there was no guarantee that she would ever find the precise moment when Erich Hoffman said his wife's name. *Beautiful Houses* was quirky that way. There was nothing to do but go back in the morning and time-surf until she heard it. And, if she locked onto one of the Hoffmans, she could retrace their journey back to Pennsylvania and find lots more names to add to her list. The more she had, the more likely it was that she would be able to find a contemporary Hoffman relative.

It would take a lot of time to go that far back, not to mention the time it would take to snoop around once she got to Pennsylvania. She would have to hustle to finish time-surfing before the chapel service. And after that, they needed to get home pronto. Nelda had not expected Brett to be away overnight and probably needed him. And Merrideth would leave when he did and follow him home. He would need help or he'd damage his ankle even more. She would make him keep his foot up while she took care of things around Nelda's place.

Across the room on the little desk a neon blue light poured from her laptop into the black room. A "Blue-Light Special!" *Beautiful Houses* had not given her one since the night in Abby and John's attic last year. But it was giving her one now, beckoning her to get to work. Now, not in the morning.

She got out of bed and went over to look at it, stubbing her toe on the desk chair in the process. Yes, she was definitely awake and not dreaming it. In the past, each time the blue light had awakened her and Abby in the night, they had learned something of tremendous significance from their subsequent time-surfing— something *Beautiful Houses* seemed to want them to know.

But time-surfing at ten-thirty at night—in a cave—was insane! Sure, she had spent hours sitting alone in the dark in Nelda Garrison's woods time-surfing just fine. With illumination from her powerful flashlight, it had not seemed any scarier than being there during the daytime. But then there had been no creepy Hellhounds or Road Hogs lurking about, only Odious Ogle, and he was more weird than scary.

Brett was in no condition to go with her to the cave, and she had no idea where Trevor was. But there was little likelihood that any Road Hogs would show up. They were occupied with their drunken shenanigans down at the camp. And lightening never struck twice in the same spot, or so they said.

Still, it would be crazy to go to the cave alone. But apparently she was supposed to. First she'd had the flashback and then the dream in which Mrs. Hoffman had cried out for her help. She would have chalked those up to sensory overload after a busy day. But that didn't explain the "Blue-Light Special."

No matter what time it was, it was time to see what *Beautiful Houses* wanted her to know. She turned on the lamp and got up. After she dressed, she got out her flashlight and checked to see that it worked. Satisfied that it had plenty of juice left, she put it and her laptop back into her backpack. Then, checking to make sure she had her room key, she stepped into the quiet hall.

No light showed under Brett's door. Hopefully, he would get a good night's sleep and his ankle would be better in the morning. Anyway, she had begun the project without a man's help, and it would be nice to end it the same way.

The lights were dimmed in the lobby, and the night clerk slept with his head on the counter. She did not wake him. He was sure to think she was insane if she told him what she was up to.

The door whooshed quietly shut behind her and she stepped out onto the portico. Dew sparkled on the grass in orbits around each street light, and the yellow glow of lamps came from the windows of the first cabin. A new family had taken the place of the little cowboy's.

Even though it was hot and humid, the windows were open, and a baby's vociferous cries filled the night. Apparently the air conditioner was not working. Or maybe they were into nature and intended to "rough it." The other cabins were dark, so hopefully there were no annoyed neighbors to hear the noise and tell the parents to stop already and turn on their air-conditioner, for crying out loud.

But at least one other cabin was inhabited. She might have peed her pants if the red glow of a cigarette had not warned her in time that someone was sitting on the porch of the fourth one like Boo Radley.

"Nice night," a faceless woman said softly as Merrideth passed by.

"It is, isn't it?" she agreed and went on.

A few yards past the last cabin, the light from yard lamps and windows gave out, and Merrideth turned on her flashlight. Crickets and tree frogs made a comforting accompaniment as she continued on, the mosquitos not so much. When she came to the end of the bark path, she stopped and shone her light down the concrete steps. Who knew what nocturnal critters were lurking about? Did she really want to go down there? Her child self answered, "No! Don't go! There are wolves, bears, vampires—maybe even Bigfoot— in that cave!" But her adult self sighed in disgust and said, "Don't be such a mouse. Take the blue-light special, Professor Randall. For the sake of history."

"Okay," she whispered. "Let's rock and roll."

After slapping at a mosquito on her neck, she started cautiously down the steps, conscious of where she placed her feet. The last thing she wanted was to trip and kill herself. No, worse would be to break a leg and spend the rest of the night lying in the dark waiting for help to come.

If Brett were there, he would know at any given moment how many steps she had already traversed and how many were left to go. Also, even crippled himself, he would be willing to manfully deal with any snakes that might come slithering across the steps. Or to heroically defeat the various monsters waiting to pounce on her in the cave.

She was congratulating herself on making it halfway down the steps unscathed when a light shone from above her, and a gruff male voice said, "Stop right there."

Or policemen. She hadn't thought of that.

Nearly dropping her own flashlight, Merrideth stopped in her tracks, wondering if a standard issue Smith and Wesson were aimed at her back.

"Now put your hands up and turn around."

She complied, except she automatically used one hand to shelter her eyes from the glare. Hopefully, he wouldn't deem it resisting arrest and blow a hole through her. The light bobbed as whoever held it descended the steps. She couldn't see his face, but finally the voice registered.

"Fred?"

"Is that you, Merrideth?"

"Yes, could you maybe—?"

"Oh, sorry," he said, pointing his flashlight away. He continued slowly down the steps until he was on the one above her. "I saw the light and figured it was kids up to no good."

"Surely, you're not still working this late?"

"No, I live here. In one of the cabins. But *you* must be working late, huh?"

"Yes. I'm leaving tomorrow and thought of something else I needed to check on before I go." While she waited for him to ask what on earth she could possibly check in the dark, she tried to come up with something remotely plausible. Photos of the graffiti? Mold readings? Measurements of the rocky protrusions?

"Well, then I'll keep you company while you work," he said with a smile.

"I couldn't possibly impose. You work hard enough as it is without doing overtime."

"And *I* couldn't possibly let a young lady like yourself go unescorted. Shirley would skin me alive."

"It may take me quite a while."

"I don't mind in the least, Merrideth."

Maybe he was another guardian angel sent by God. If he were, she couldn't very well reject his offer of help. But she couldn't have him hanging over her shoulder either. Then it came to her.

"Then, if it's no bother," she said, "I'd like it if you watched the river for me, Fred. Make sure it doesn't start to rise while I'm in the cave."

"I'd be happy to." Grinning, he pulled the ever-present earbuds out of his pocket. "I'm listening to Huck Finn. Watching the river go by will make me think I'm right there on the raft with Huck and Tom."

"Thanks, Fred." She was grateful for the comfort of having him there and even more grateful that she hadn't had to tell him a cock-and-bull story. They continued together down the steps, their twin flashlight beams illuminating the way.

He sat down on one of the boulders in front of the cave and switched off his flashlight. "You go on and do your work, Merrideth. I'll be right here."

"Good. I'll try to hurry." She paused at the entrance of the cave, shuddering at the images flooding her brain. If Fred realized that her courage had shriveled into a small, pitiful thing, he would insist on coming in with her. So she took a deep breath and forced herself to walk inside.

She trained her flashlight over every part of the cave to reassure herself that Bigfoot really didn't lie in wait for her. There was no sign of monster activity of any sort. Actually, the cave looked sort of cheerful. Minerals in the walls, which had not been apparent during daylight hours, now sparkled gaily. She smiled, remembering Brett asking about magic cave crystals. The idea didn't seem so far-fetched at the moment. It was as if she were inside the snow globe Shirley had given her, where only pretend pirates lived and nothing bad ever happened.

She laughed softly at her fancifulness. No matter how pretty the light made the cave, she couldn't keep her flashlight on. If a barge happened to go by on the river and its pilot saw the mouth of the cave lit up, he might start entertaining the idea of ghosts. Or call the authorities and have someone check it out. And the next investigator might be more inquisitive than Fred was. So once she got herself settled on the rock ledge and the program launched, she turned off her light. Once her eyes adjusted to the dark, there would be plenty of light from her computer monitor.

Before Fred's arrival she had been considering which of the Hoffmans to lock onto. The easiest would be Erich. All she had to do was find the point where he came into the cave to buy medicine for his sick wife, then she could easily rewind to the time where he mentioned her name. But to do so would mean running time back and forth, and thus she would risk having to see his horrible death all over again. And anyway, for the trip back to Pennsylvania, it might be better to be inside either Lars' or Martha's head. It would give her a greater chance of learning the names of more Hoffmans, including those from earlier generations.

But the safest way to avoid seeing any more bloody scenes was to lock onto Samuel Mason as he went down to the river to greet the Hoffmans that first day—before any of the violence occurred—and then switching the lock on the fly from him to one of Hoffmans. It was an added challenge, but she hadn't encountered any problems doing it in the past.

Flicking on her flashlight again, Merrideth consulted her notes for the approximate date and time of the Hoffmans' arrival. Using those coordinates, she was able to zero in on it in less than a minute. She followed Mason from the cave down to the riverbank where he stood out of sight assessing what goodies the flatboat might have on it. Then he came out of hiding and smiled warmly at the Hoffmans.

Mason was being relentlessly helpful, Lars was being taciturn and suspicious, and Martha was scurrying around on deck, preparing to disembark. It was a good place to go virtual and make the switch from Mason to one of them.

CHAPTER 15

***

1797

The little girl came out of the cabin and peeked at Mason through the rails. "Betsy falled in the river," she said solemnly. "She drowneded."

Mason tipped his hat. "I'm sorry for your loss, folks. The river is treacherous, indeed."

The old man lost his frown and chuckled, and the girl's father grinned and said, "Julianne's meaning her doll baby."

"I am quite relieved to hear that it wasn't a little sister." Covering a smile, Mason gave a little bow to Julianne. "Still, a tragedy to be sure."

"Don't you dare buy her that doll, Erich. Julianne needs to learn her lesson," the woman said. "I told her not to hang it over the rail. And besides, you oughtn't go up to that place. I know the kind of entertainment they have."

Neither Erich or his father paid her any heed. "Let's get the stock to shore, boys," the old man said.

✿✿✿

THE PRESENT

"I choose you, Martha Hoffman," Merrideth said to herself. "You're a cranky old thing, but you have lots of opinions to share." She figured she would have to try several times, but she successfully locked onto her on her first attempt. And then she took a breath and prepared herself to see what was on the woman's mind.

✿✿✿

1797

Lord have mercy, the man was slow as molasses. By now wouldn't you think he'd be faster getting them landed? "Do hurry, Lars," Martha said. "I've got to milk Daisy."

"And you will, Martha, in due time."

Erich and Tobias had caught on to a boatman's skills quick as lightening, but then they took after her side of the family. She watched with pride as they helped their father get the flatboat hitched to the dock. When she was sure the boat was secure, she untied Daisy's lead rope. Tobias came and took it from her. He was a smart lad, and she knew she wouldn't have to remind him to be careful with a cow frantic to be milked.

Erich was a good son, too, but he wasn't much help with that wife of his all sickly. As usual, instead of helping his mother, he was in the cabin mooning over her. He had spent nearly the whole journey catering to her whims. Erich was spoiling her, that's what he was doing. Julianne, too. He needed to be firmer with the girl. She had tried to warn him, but he didn't listen to his mother anymore. Well, he'd come to rue his indulgence one day.

Mr. Wilson seemed like a nice fellow. He was offering to help Lars with the horses, but the stubborn old coot was snubbing his generosity. She was about to remind Lars of his manners, but then he gave in and let Mr. Wilson come up the plank onto the boat. He tipped his hat when he passed her, and she smiled to show her appreciation for his help, even if her husband didn't. Mr. Wilson untied the chestnut's rope and led her down onto the dock. Poor horses were as anxious to reach good dry land as she and Daisy were.

Lars was fiddling around with his precious gelding's rope, frowning at the world.

She shook her head at him. "It wouldn't hurt you to say thanks when someone lends you a hand."

"I don't like this place," he whispered. "Something odd goin' on here."

Martha kept her opinion to herself, though it took effort, because she was a good wife. But he was the odd thing. She took her milking stool and pail down from their hooks and, after a deep breath, started down the plank. It was the trickiest part of the whole process, but she managed to keep her balance. She stepped onto the dock and sighed in relief.

When she made it up the riverbank, Tobias had already tied Daisy to a tree and was talking with Mr. Wilson like a grown gentleman instead of a farm boy. At least she had raised her sons to be polite.

"Where do you hail from, Mr. Hoffman?" Mr. Wilson said. "We're always on the lookout for folks coming down the river with news from home."

"Monongahela Valley," Tobias said. "Pennsylvania."

Martha set her stool and bucket down beside Daisy. "Don't just stand there jawing, boy. Go get my stove a-going. I reckon you do want supper?"

"Yes, Ma."

Martha sat down alongside the cow, now happily grazing on the grass under the tree. "Don't think because of Daisy's fussing she's a bad cow."

"No, ma'am," Mr. Wilson said, rubbing Daisy's flank.

"She doesn't have much milk now," she added. "But it's rich. I'll have butter to sell you, Mr. Wilson, if you're interested."

"My wife and I would like that. Haven't had any in quite some time."

"She'll have her calf in the spring. Then you'll have lots of milk, won't you, Daisy?" Martha got her rhythm going, and a stream of fresh, warm milk began spraying into the bucket.

"Where do you plan to settle, ma'am?"
"We're aiming for the Illinois Country north of Kaskaskia. Heard the land is good."
"Then you're only ten days away from your new home."
"None too soon, Mr. Wilson. None too soon. We intend to claim four hundred acres and get a cabin up before first snowfall."

✻✻✻

THE PRESENT

When it occurred to Merrideth that she was wasting time watching a woman milking a cow, she paused the program and stretched her back. How different that little slice of life was when seen from Martha's perspective instead of Mason's! She must have been a terror of a mother-in-law to Erich's poor wife. Merrideth still didn't know her name, but she took out her notebook and jotted down *Monongahela Valley*. It would help narrow her search. Now she had better get busy getting them back to Pennsylvania before Fred got tired of watching the river.

She set the program to rewind and watched Martha retrace her steps back onto the flatboat and then watched as the boat began to travel upstream. She smiled, thinking of Brett's reaction to the feat. She turned the speed up, and the images on her screen became an unrecognizable blur. At last she was tired and turned her eyes away from the rushing colors on the screen before she hypnotized herself.

After five minutes, she turned back to her laptop and set the scene to run forward in real time. Martha was sitting in a chair on deck sewing. Everyone else was out of sight, either on the other side of the cabin or inside it. It was a peaceful sight, with the trees, lush and green with their summer foliage, passing by on both sides of the river. The sounds via the laptop's crummy speakers were garbled of course, but she thought she heard the cow's moos and the lap of water against the boat.

If Merrideth were the one sitting there sewing, she would not have been able to stay awake. But Martha continued to energetically stab her needle into the cloth.

Another, not so peaceful sound came, and Martha sprang up, hastily putting her sewing on her chair, and stormed off down the boat. When she got past the cabin, Merrideth saw that Tobias and Julianne were squabbling about something. The teenage boy wore an angry expression clearly tinged with guilt. Little Julianne cried with her eyes tightly closed and mouth open wide in a look of complete despair. It was only some little childish drama, but Merrideth couldn't resist hearing what was going on.

She clicked on *Virtual*.

***

1797

"Julianne, stop your caterwauling this very instant," Martha said. "You're giving everyone a headache." The girl sank down onto the deck in a pout, but at least the wailing stopped.

"Now tell me what on earth is wrong with her, Tobias."

"I tried to stop her from holding her doll over the edge, like you're always telling her, Ma. But she wouldn't listen to me."

"That's because she's a willful little girl." *Brat* was the word that came to mind. She took Julianne by her arm and pulled her to her feet. "Come here, girl, and I'll give you something to cry about."

Lars turned from where he was fishing from the side of the boat. "Tobias was teasing her for the doll, Martha."

"I was just trying to make her mind, Ma. I couldn't help it her doll fell in the river"

"Guess you learned the hard way, didn't you, Julianne?" Martha said. "Tobias, go get your pa's strap."

"Leave her be, Martha."

"It's time I taught her to mind her elders."

"Don't you think it's enough punishment that her doll fell in the river?"

"I don't appreciate you shouting at me, Lars Hoffman." She looked down at her sniveling granddaughter. "But I suppose you're right." For once.

THE PRESENT

Pausing the scene, Merrideth blew a breath out of her pursed lips. Wow, some grandmother Martha was, the old witch! No better at that than she was at being a mother-in-law. She was vain, dismissive of her husband, and defensive of her son Tobias at the expense of her granddaughter. And completely blind to her faults.

None of the Hoffmans were showing their good sides now that they were alone on the boat. Tobias, the fine son Martha was so proud of, was entirely too old to be teasing his little niece that way and then telling on her to his mommy. But Julianne was no angel, either. Frozen on the screen, she stuck her tongue out at Tobias behind her grandmother's back.

And Lars! What a wimp! Perhaps Martha would not have been riding roughshod over the family if he had grown a pair and acted like the man of the family. Merrideth snorted a laugh, amazed that she had thought such a thing. But come on!

A man should not lord it over his wife, but that didn't mean he should be a pushover either. She would never tolerate a "head of the house" type of husband, even a benign one like Ward Cleaver, but neither would she want a weakling like Lars. She would want someone who saw her as his partner. Someone like Brett, for example. He would treat a wife equally, but he would never allow one to disrespect him or emotionally abuse his children or grandchildren. The thought of that had her smiling. Grandpa Brett. Time went by so fast, even when you were not rewinding it with magical software. He would probably be a grandfather eventually. In only a few years, relatively speaking. It was a sobering thought.

And it was sobering to watch the Hoffmans. She had idealized the family in her mind and seen them as the pirates' innocent victims. And they were. But they had their faults same as any other family, not that they deserved to die at the hands of pirates.

Merrideth switched back to rewind and upped the speed to the maximum. Then she set the laptop on the ledge beside her and leaned back to wait. Maybe the next time she checked they would be docked at Pittsburgh, or better yet, already back at their farm in the Monongahela Valley. She closed her eyes. It would not hurt to rest them for a short while.

After ten minutes, she checked again. Several days had gone by, but the Hoffmans were still on their little ark going down the Ohio River, cow mooing, chickens clucking, and people talking. In her own time there would be buildings and signs along the river, or even recognizable city skylines. But in the Hoffmans' day there was nothing from the surrounding landscape to give her a clue about exactly where they were.

Lars stood at the rail fishing even though a fine rain came down. They had rigged up a canvas. Under it, Martha was cooking on her little cast iron stove, which surprised Merrideth. Apparently, they had some way to keep it from catching the deck on fire, a sand pit under it maybe. That meant the Hoffmans did not always have to go ashore to cook their meals, which meant that if Lars' horse hadn't gone lame, they probably would not have even stopped at Cave-in-Rock.

The stove also provided at least a little heat, and the rest of the family, except for Erich's sick wife, crowded around it. For once, he was not inside the cabin with her, but sat under the tarp holding Julianne on his lap. The girl was crying again and clutching her doll like it was her only friend. They all looked so miserable.

Merrideth was starting to feel miserable, too. Her eyes were grainy from lack of sleep, and her neck had a crick in it. And nagging in the back of her mind was the thought of Fred sitting out there patiently waiting for her to finish.

She couldn't in good conscience keep him from his bed much longer while she made the journey with the Hoffmans. Who knew when someone would get around to mentioning the poor woman's name? Or how much longer it would take for them to get home? If Brett were there, he would estimate the boat's speed, factor in the distance between Pittsburgh and Cave-in-Rock via river—which he would probably remember from an encyclopedia he memorized in kindergarten—and be able to tell her within seconds how long and how fast she needed to run in reverse to get back to Pennsylvania. Without his computer brain, she had no idea, only that it would take a while even on fast speed. And then, when she got there, it would take time to sort through Martha's life to find the names she wanted to know.

The old witch sent a stern look Julianne's way. Erich said something, and Tobias got up and went into the cabin. A moment later he came back carrying a parcel wrapped in leather. Merrideth thought at first it was the treasure chest, but when the boy unwrapped it she saw that a thick book was inside. It looked like a Bible.

He handed it to his older brother. Erich opened it in Julianne's lap and leaned over her head to read from it.

Merrideth knew that a Bible was the only book many pioneer families brought along on the journey. They used it, and maybe a McGuffey Reader if they were lucky enough to have one, to teach their children to read and for informal family church services in their cabins. So it was not a surprise that they would have a religious service on their flatboat.

Whatever Julianne's father was reading from the Bible seemed to cheer her. She stopped crying and wiped her eyes on her sleeves. In fact, everyone looked a little happier. Lars turned from his fishing and smiled, and even Martha's dour expression softened.

It was nice, but it was not getting Merrideth anywhere. The clock on her computer told her it was getting close to midnight, and she just could not let Fred stay out there a minute longer. Maybe she would go to him and insist that he go home. But remembering his gallantry before, she doubted he would go.

She heaved a sigh and started to close her laptop. She gave the family one last look. They had not been as perfect and wonderful as she had first thought, but they still had not deserved to die the way they had.

"I'll do my best," she whispered. "With what I have. I promise."

Erich was still reading from the Bible. Julianne looked up at him and said something. He pointed at the page.

The first page. No, the inside cover itself!

Merrideth stabbed at the touch pad, which did nothing, of course. She forced her fingers to relax and at last managed to rewind the scene to when Erich first opened the Bible. Then she switched to virtual mode.

✢✢✢

1797

"You shouldn't bring it out here in the rain, Erich," Martha said.

"I'll be careful, Ma."

Land sakes alive, it wasn't even Sunday! Not for two more days. Maybe three. She had lost track. But she supposed it would do them all good. "Read Psalm twenty-three, why don't you? It's my favorite."

"I know, Ma," he said. But he wasn't turning to the middle of the Bible where he knew good and well the Psalms were. Instead he had it open to the family tree inside the front cover.

Martha sniffed at his selfishness and went back to stirring the stew. Well, see if she gave him seconds tonight.

"I know you're sad, Julianne," Erich said. "We're all sad to leave Grandma and Grandpa Schneider back in Pennsylvania."

Martha snorted softly to herself. "Not all of us are," she muttered under her breath. Anna's folks were unbearably sanctimonious and difficult to stand for more than a minute at a time. Always *praise the Lord this* and *Hallelujah that.*

"And Aunt Frieda and Cousin Herte," Julianne said. "And Uncle Johann and—"

"I know, punkin pie. I know," Erich said.

"I never thought I'd say it," Lars said. "But I'm even going to miss Cousin Otto."

"But look, Julianne," Erich said. "We're sort of bringing all of them with us. On this side of the tree's your Grandpa and Grandma Schneider and all your—"

"That ain't a tree, Pa," Julianne said. "It's just words and lines."

"Don't sass your pa," Martha said. "And you shouldn't have that doll of yours out here in the rain either."

Clutching the filthy thing under her arm, Julianne buried her face in Erich's shirt. He whispered something to her that Martha didn't catch, and then he pointed at the page. "This is not a real tree, punkin, but it's a way to keep track of all our kinfolk. So like I was explaining, over here is for your ma's side of the family, and this side is for mine."

"There's me," Tobias said, reaching in to point. "And there's you, Julianne."

"Where's Betsy?" Julianne said.

"Dolls can't be in there," Tobias said. "Don't you know that?"

"Maybe we'll find a place for her name," Erich said, hiding a smile. "Anyway, I wrote everyone's names in here so we won't ever forget anyone no matter what."

"But we ain't never going to see them again," Tobias said.

Julianne started blubbering again, and Erich hugged her close. "Thank you, little brother," he said over his daughter's head. "That helped greatly."

"Well, Tobias has the right of it," Martha said. "So she might as well get used to it."

Anna came through the curtain, pale and puny-looking as always, and sat on a crate like there wasn't work to be done getting supper ready.

"You should rest, Anna," Erich said. "Stay out of the damp."

"Let me hold Julianne."

He gave her a look then transferred the girl to her lap. She clung to her ma like an ugly little possum.

"Don't cry, sweetheart," Anna said. "Pay no mind to what your uncle Tobias said. He was forgetting that we'll see Grandma and Grandpa again—all of them—someday. Don't you worry on that for one minute. It might not be for a long time, honey, but we'll see them, that's for sure. In glory, if not on this earth."

"Meanwhile," Erich said. "We'll write letters to them, and they'll write letters to us."

"But... Grandpa...and Grandma, they don't...know...where we are," Julianne blubbered.

Erich stroked the girl's hair. "Even if they don't. God does. We'll never get so far from home that he loses track of where we are. He's watching out for us right now."

✾✾✾

THE PRESENT

Merrideth pulled herself to the present. A drop fell on the back of her hand as she reached for the touch pad to pause the action, and she realized that she was crying. Watching over them, was he? And yet God would do nothing to stop the massacre when they reached Cave-in-Rock.

Spending the additional time with the Hoffmans, seeing more of their faults and foibles, had made them so real to her. Knowing what would happen to the family, her heart literally ached with sorrow. Did God feel the same way, or did he not care?

Poor little Julianne had grieved so. That was the downside to having a close family. When you lost one of them to death or, in this case, to a move across the country, it broke your heart. Maybe it was better that Merrideth knew her own relatives only slightly. Both her parents had been estranged from their families ever since she could remember. The little she knew about her extended family was from occasional second-hand comments her mother or father had made about their parents and siblings.

Growing up, she had not gotten to sit on grandparents' laps for stories or play with cousins in an aunt and uncle's backyard. But Julianne undoubtedly had back in Pennsylvania.

Tears burned in Merrideth's throat. But she would grieve for the family later. She swiped an arm across her face and went to work writing down what she had just learned.

Now she knew the sick woman's full name, Anna Schneider. She did not know how to plug in the names of the aunts, uncles, and cousins she had heard, or whether the family tree in Erich's Bible went back beyond his parents Lars and Martha Hoffman.

But she knew how to find out.

She un-paused the family's journey toward their doom and rewound a little to the point where Erich opened to the front of his Bible. Then, using *Beautiful House's* perspective tool, she shifted the point of view until she could see what he was looking at—the family tree he had recorded there. She froze the scene and zoomed in as far as she could. Thankfully, Erich had written the names in a neat and legible print and not in the flowering cursive typical of most nineteen-century documents.

And there they were. The Hoffmans on the left and the Schneiders on the right, just as he had described to Julianne. She got her notebook and pen and recorded the names as neatly as *she* could, given that her hand was trembling with exhaustion and her eyes were almost too dry to blink.

In a short while, the pirates would throw Erich's Bible into the Ohio River, and it would gradually dissolve into a pulp and be carried downstream. Or perhaps the sodden pages would be eaten by curious catfish and carp nosing around the riverbed. But now she had the priceless genealogical information the Bible contained, and she would use it, come Hell or high water, to find the surviving Hoffmans.

After a last look at the family, she closed her laptop and went to find poor Fred.

CHAPTER 16

"Good morning," Shirley said when Merrideth entered the lobby with Brett leaning on her shoulder. The button du jour on her smock was neon green and said, "Give Peas a Chance."

"You both look pretty good, considering. Especially you, Mr. Garrison. Floyd said last night you looked like something the cats had drug up."

"Thanks," Brett said with a grin. "Nothing like a good night's sleep and a little *peas* and quiet to charge your batteries. And please, call me *Brett*."

Shirley laughed uproariously at his pun. Merrideth wondered who was winning in the woman's estimation, Trevor or Brett?

Merrideth had only gotten half a night's sleep, but it was good to know she was not showing the effects.

"Are you going to have breakfast?"

"We sure are," Brett said. "Merrideth says your biscuits and gravy are to die for."

Shirley grinned. "It's our ploy to keep you'ns coming back to see us. I'll tell them to give you the table by the window." Fortunately, she did not mention that it was the same preferential table she had given her and Trevor the day before.

"Come on then," Merrideth said. "Let's get you in there."

"While you're eating, I'll go rustle up a pair of crutches for you. I still have mine here from when I had my knee surgery."

"You don't need to go to the bother, Shirley," Merrideth said. "We're leaving after breakfast anyway."

"We are?" Brett said. "I thought we were going to your friend

Trevor's chapel service."

"Wow," Shirley said. "That would be a sight. Both of them escorting you to church at the same time."

Merrideth gave her a repressive look and then turned to Brett. "I'm worrying about how you're going to drive home, much less do any extensive walking."

"My ankle is much better this morning. Nearly cured, actually. All due to your expert nursing care."

"Then why are you leaning on me, you big lug?"

Brett grinned. "Carpe diem, Merri. Carpe diem."

"Go ahead and get those crutches, Shirley. I'm going to hit him over the head with them."

Shirley chuckled. "You two enjoy your breakfast."

"I know I will," Brett said. "But Merrideth is planning on ordering cereal and fruit. Says she's too much of a blimp for biscuits and gravy. Sad that she's such a fatty, isn't it?"

Shirley harrumphed. "Wish I was a blimp like her."

Merrideth smiled at their teasing. Sometimes she forgot that she was no longer the overweight adolescent she had once been. It was nice to be reminded, but still, she would not be eating biscuits and gravy a second time in one weekend. She had no intention of ever being a blimp again.

Brett put his hand on her shoulder, and she pushed it off. "Come on, you big faker. You're getting to the restaurant on your own steam."

Laughing, Brett transferred his hand to the small of her back, and they started for the doorway that led to the restaurant. He still limped a little, so he obviously was not as cured as he had let on.

Sunlight reflected off the glass fronts of the display cases on the wall. Merrideth changed her course and went to the one with cave artifacts. "How could I be so stupid?"

"Is that a trick question?"

"The cup, Brett. Look." Merrideth turned back to Shirley. "Would it be all right if we took it out?"

"I don't suppose Mr. Carlson would mind. But I'll have to find the key." She went back behind the counter and began opening drawers. "It's around here somewhere. The case hasn't been opened in years."

"It's nice and all," Brett said. "But could we go eat before we look at it?"

Merrideth ignored him. "Where were the artifacts found, Shirley? Do you know?"

"Different places. Different times. You'd have to talk to someone from the Hardin County Historical Society. They put that display together." She straightened and came up smiling. "Here it is." She brought the key, inserted it into the brass lock, and paused maddeningly. "But I know the cup came from the river."

"It did? How?"

"Divers brought it up. Every once in a while someone will come along with diving equipment and go treasure hunting in our stretch of the river. They've found several cool things. The Society tries to get its hands on what they can. They've got lots of nice pieces in their museum downtown. I would have mentioned it earlier, but they're closed for renovation. You'll have to come visit again."

At last Shirley turned the key and took out the silver cup. "Not too tarnished, considering how long it's been in there, but I might as well give it a good polishing while I have it out." She started to walk away.

Merrideth grabbed her arm. "May I have a quick look first?"

"Oh, sure," she said, handing the cup to her.

"May I remind you that I am a cripple in need of sustenance?" Brett said. "It's a well-known fact that biscuits and gravy have restorative powers."

"The silver cup, Brett. Don't you remember?"

"No."

"Oh, sorry. That must have been Trevor."

The cup had a dent and in some places the silver plating had worn away revealing the copper beneath. On the bottom, the silversmith had engraved *Philadelphia* as the place of origin. Below that was his identifying mark. It was too worn to make out, but whoever he was, he had been a talented artisan. The engraving and bas relief were wonderfully detailed. The engraved word *Vater* showed clearly on the belly of the cup.

"It's German," Merrideth said happily. "It means—"

"*Father*," Brett said, looking over her shoulder.

She took a few steps away from Shirley as if she wanted to see the cup in better light. "It looks like one the Hoffmans' had," she whispered. "But I'd have to see it closer to be sure."

"You want to go now, don't you?"

"Yes."

"I'm not getting my biscuits and gravy, am I?"

She patted his arm. "Go on and eat your breakfast. It won't take me long to find out."

"That's not how this works, Merri."

She tipped her head up and looked at him curiously. "How what works?"

"Friendship. Friends don't let friends…" After a glance at Shirley, he added, "let them surf in dangerous waters."

"I don't mind."

"Well, I do." He handed the cup back to Shirley. "Thanks for getting it out for us. I'll wait here while you go get your laptop, Merri. Then we'll mosey on down to take a look."

"At what?" Shirley said, perplexed.

Merrideth left, pretending she had not heard the question. Brett was the one with the silver Irish tongue. Let him come up with a suitable reply.

When she got back with the laptop, Shirley was holding the door for him as he stepped out onto the portico with the assistance of a pair of ancient wooden crutches. "Thanks, Shirley," he said with one of his mind-numbing smiles. "I admit, these will be a big help getting down to the cave."

Merrideth hurried out the door while Shirley was still too befuddled to ask any uncomfortable questions about what they planned to look at. She was not sure if Brett was sincere or still faking. By the time they made it to the cave she had decided it was probably a mixture of the two. He had not thrown away the crutches once they were out of Shirley's sight, but neither had he seemed overly dependent on them.

Brett led the way into the cave. The angle of the sunlight coming in through the mouth and pouring down from the *chimney* made the carvings on the walls stand out in sharp relief and gave the interior an even happier feel than the crystals had. Still, the beauty and mystery were cancelled out by the evil associated with the cave, and she had no desire to spend any more time there than necessary. There wasn't much time until the chapel service anyway.

Comforting herself that it would only take a minute or two to learn what she needed to know, she ran the program back to the point where Samuel Mason stood over the bloody corpse of Anna Hoffman, his pistol still smoking.

She closed her eyes for a moment and swallowed, glad that she had not eaten breakfast. "It's nauseating, isn't it?"

"And we're not even in virtual mode."

Taking a deep breath, she un-paused the scene. Samuel Mason put his gun back into his waistband and went out onto the deck. He commanded the Harpes to get rid of the evidence before the people on the approaching flatboat got close enough to see their deadly handiwork. Mason pointed and shouted, and other members of the gang joined the effort, hurrying to drag the bodies on the river bank onto the boat. They flung Lars, Martha, and Tobias carelessly on top of Anna like they were stacking logs. Then Mason came from the other side of the cabin carrying Julianne's little limp body in his arms. He laid her carefully on top of her family. Then one of the men pulled down the Hoffmans' rainy-day tarp and covered the pile of corpses with it.

He barely got the tarp back in place before the newcomers' flatboat came into view. If they had arrived only a few minutes earlier, Mason and his gang would surely have killed everyone on board to keep them from spreading the word about the murders. The boatmen would not have griped about not getting any of "Wilson's" liquor if they had only known how close they came to dying that day.

Merrideth paused the scene. Would the pirates throw the bodies into the river or set fire to the flatboat and let it float on down the river with them on it like a Viking funeral ship? She did not have the stomach to watch long enough to find out where their bodies ended up. She and Brett did not speak, just sat there staring at the cave walls so they would not see the tarp-covered funeral mound on the deck of the Hoffmans' flatboat.

After a couple of minutes, when Merrideth was certain her stomach was going to stay right side out, she took a deep breath and turned back to do what she had come to do. "Okay, I'm going to rewind to the part where Big Harpe brings the wooden chest out. But it's sometimes difficult to find a particular point in time, so I can't guarantee we won't have to run through more bloody scenes again. I'd turn away, if I were you."

Brett gave her a sour look. "I'm not letting you go there alone, Merri."

"Your call." It took a few stops but at last she found it. After a glance at him, she let it play. "Keep your eyes peeled. It was about now that I saw the silver cup."

The men rushed madly to the treasure chest Big Harpe held. The first man there scooped up a handful of coins.

And then another hand from behind Big Harpe stretched forward and snatched something.

"There," Brett said. "He's got the cup."

Merrideth paused it. "I couldn't see it clearly. Could you tell whose hand that was?"

"No. Run it again in slo-mo."

Again, the pirates scrabbled to get the treasure. Again the hand, whose she still could not tell, grabbed the silver cup. Big Harpe lifted the chest out of the other men's reach. At the edge of the screen Mason raised his pistol to the air. A puff of smoke came out. The cup slipped from the hand that held it and fell in a flash of silver light. Merrideth paused the action while it hung in mid-air.

Beside her, Brett leaned in and studied the screen. "It looks like the same cup. Can you zoom in more?"

"Sure."

Then he smiled, and she grinned back at him. The cup was shiny and untarnished, its scrollwork and engraving brilliant, and exactly alike in every detail as the cup in the display case, except that the word *Mutter* stood out in fine detail. It was the mate to the cup they had just handled in the lobby.

She un-paused and the cup fell in slow motion to the deck, then rolled under the railing and into the river.

Merrideth laughed. A moment later, she realized tears were leaking out of her eyes. Again. How many tears had she shed in the past three days? "Remember when I said I didn't believe in Hell? Well, I do now."

Brett looked at her with surprise. He stood and pulled her to her feet and against him, crutches and all. She buried her face in his shirt and sobbed.

"Try not to think about it, Merri, or it'll make you crazy."

Had he somehow detected the Brown Cloud and was trying to steer her clear of it?

Brett whipped around, bringing her with him, and Merrideth saw a figure backlit in the cave's entrance. Her heart did a free fall in her chest before she realized it was Trevor, doing a reprise of his avenging-angel role. He came quickly toward them but then stopped short and put his hands in his pockets. "Are you all right,

Merrideth?"

"Not really," she said and buried her face on Brett's chest again. "I can't stop blubbering like a baby."

"You know the Hoffman family? Yes, well it didn't end well for them," Brett explained, stroking Merrideth's hair.

"We already knew that," Trevor said.

She lifted her head and looked at him. "It got worse, Trevor. The pirates piled all their bodies in a stack like...like...trash. And what the Harpes did to Erich Hoffman.... I'm glad you didn't have to see it."

"I wish *you* hadn't," Brett said. "I never should have let you wade through anymore of that filth and ugliness just now. And If I'd known how bad it was going to be—make that, if I'd known about the existence of the software—I would have been here with you from day one."

"I agree," Trevor said. "She should never time-surf alone. No one should."

Merrideth pulled away from Brett and narrowed her eyes at the pair of men standing in front of her. "Ha! I have managed just fine for quite some time without either of you, thank you very much! And I've seen plenty of horrific stuff, almost as bad as what happened to the Hoffmans. I know I'm crying like a baby now, but I have never once fainted into a girlish puddle and required smelling salts. Granted, I felt awful for weeks after I witnessed the Cherokee landing at Golconda. And I expect to feel awful for a long time after this. But you can rest assured that—"

"You actually saw that?" Brett said. "When you said you were writing about the Trail of Tears—"

"Yes. It was amazing, Brett. And horrible all at the same time."

"Well, thanks for letting me know."

Merrideth huffed. "What with chasing Road Hogs and patching you up, I haven't exactly had the right moment."

He put up a conciliatory hand. "Sorry. I get it."

Merrideth sniffed. "Anyway, I rewound back to 1838. Abby and John were with me. We saw the Trail of Tears—a small part of it, anyway." Just the thought of what the Cherokee suffered made her start crying again. Brett pulled her close and patted her back.

Through her tear-flooded eyes, Merrideth saw Trevor pacing angrily back and forth. It dawned on her that he wanted to say something but was waiting for her to stop crying. Or, startling thought, he paced out of frustration because he could not be the one to hold her while she cried. Maybe he cared more about her than he had let on. Or maybe it was another example of overblown male protective instinct like John had.

Merrideth pulled away from the comfort of Brett's arms and dug in her backpack for a tissue. "So as I was saying, I don't need you two hovering over me like I was a two-year-old. Do I have mascara running down my face?"

"No," both men answered.

Brett frowned and Trevor turned away, ostensibly to study the graffiti on the cave wall.

"I mean it would have been nice to have had one of you along last night, but I managed just fine by myself. And now I have—"

"What are you saying?" Brett said.

"I needed more names, that's all."

"You came here last night? After I went to bed? By yourself?"

Trevor stopped looking at the graffiti and came to frown at her.

"How was I supposed to know you were faking about your ankle? I thought you were a poor cripple. And I had no idea where you were, Trevor."

Merrideth wiped her eyes and smothered a tired laugh at the expressions on their faces. They looked like twin brothers horrified to discover that their baby sister had been swimming in the deep end of the pool without her floaties on. "Don't get yourself in a lather. I was perfectly fine. Fred kept me company, and it didn't take long to get the names I needed."

"Who's Fred?" Brett asked exasperatedly.

"The groundskeeper here," Merrideth said. "He's really nice."

"He's also about one hundred and eighty years old," Trevor said, shaking his head. "Anyway, come see what I found."

He pointed high on the cave wall. "Look. It says *Charles Fleming, 1797.* Wasn't he one of them?"

"Yes. We just saw him," Brett said. "Fleming was the one taking down the tarp—and the one with the losing chicken in the cockfight."

"You have a good memory," Trevor said.

"You have no idea." Merrideth contemplated the engraved signature on the wall. "Visitors to the cave probably ooh and aah when they see that name, marveling at the date and wondering who he was. Which is why I wade through all the filth, Brett. Historians have to in order to find and preserve the past. History books can't—or at least shouldn't—read like the whitewashed Hollywood tales of singing, dancing pirates quipping jokes. They have to tell what really happened, no matter how ugly it was."

"The Bible says to dwell on things above," Brett said. "To let your mind be on Christ."

"It also says to be wise as serpents," Trevor said. "If we don't study the past, how will we learn from our mistakes?"

"There's a lot to learn from." Merrideth sighed wearily and sat down on a rocky shelf. "The history of mankind is one selfish, greedy action after another in one long, never-ending chain reaction of evil. And yet you say, Trevor, that God brings good out of bad things. Supposedly even volcanoes and deserts. But that still doesn't answer the question of why he lets it happen in the first place. Why the Hoffmans had to die the way they did."

"I'm not wise enough to know the answer to that question," Trevor said. "But I do know this, Merrideth. God knows what happened to the Hoffmans—and every other family lost at this cursed cave. He'll raise them up from their graves on the last day."

Trevor sent a telling look toward Brett who returned one of his own.

Then Brett squatted on his haunches in front of her. When she tried to turn away, he tipped her chin up and looked into her eyes. "Trevor's right, Merri. Let God take care of things." He smiled sadly. "You're not nearly big enough to carry all that around on your shoulders. No one is."

She wiped her eyes. "Maybe I should think about something else for a while."

"You didn't tell Trevor about the cup."

"Yes," Trevor said. "Tell me about the cup. What cup?"

"I'm sorry. I forgot to tell you." She explained about the silver cup they had discovered in the display case.

"The one the sick woman had," Trevor said.

"No, the mate to it," Brett said. "Hers may still be buried in the mud at the bottom of the river."

"If no one's found it by now it's probably long gone," Merrideth said morosely.

"You never know," Brett said. "Now that we know to look for it, maybe someone will find it."

"It would be nice if they could be reunited," she said.

"What time is it?" Trevor said.

Brett glanced at his watch. "Oh, shoot, it's almost ten. We're going to be late."

"No you won't," Trevor said. "The service is going to be here in the cave. That's what I came to tell you. Shirley said you were down here."

Just as he said it, Larry and June Groves came in wearing matching CMA T-shirts and holding hands. "Hi, you guys. Great idea about the cave, Trevor."

"I hope everyone thinks so," Trevor said, sending a look to Merrideth that she could not interpret.

"I, for one, heartily approve," Geno said, coming in behind the Groveses. Next to him, Barb said, "Me, too, Trevor. Bill and Deanna may be a little late, Larry. They're bringing goodies."

Brett nudged Merrideth in warning, and she hurried to shut her laptop and put it away. Gradually, half a dozen or so of Trevor's friends she had not yet met came trickling in.

Some of them looked like Sunday School teachers, while others looked more like the Hellhounds and Road Hogs they ministered to—only their eyes were bright with healthy living and good humor and not glazed over from drugs and alcohol.

Everyone introduced themselves to her and Brett in a way that indicated they already knew who they were. She wondered if Larry and June had spread the word. She could not imagine Trevor doing so. He and Brett had probably been lying through their teeth about her mascara. But even if not, she knew her eyes had to be puffy and red. However, no one was rude enough to mention the fact. And they did not say anything about the attack in the cave either, although she had a feeling everyone knew about it.

A couple, presumably Bill and Deanna, came in carrying a white pastry box and a tray of lidded cups. "I have donuts for anyone who wants them," she said.

"And I have coffee for whoever is most desperate. Sorry, I spilled half of it on the way here," he said sheepishly.

Everyone burst out laughing. "It's an old joke," June explained to her and Brett.

"A very old joke," Bill muttered good-naturedly.

The bond of friendship that connected the group was strong, as if they had known each other forever, and yet they happily welcomed her and Brett into their conversations. Trevor was the only unattached member of the group, and although he did not do much of the talking, it was obvious he cared deeply for each of them, and they for him.

A man named Bryan, wearing a leather vest from which an assortment of tattoos showed, engaged Brett in a discussion about the merits of various types of motorcycle carburetors. His wife Joyce, who had long blond hair and dressed more mainstream than her husband, asked Merrideth what she and Brett rode.

"Only four-wheeled vehicles, I'm afraid," Merrideth answered with a smile, and Joyce laughed.

Then John told a funny story about his elderly dad taking his dog to the vet for the first time. He had everyone near him laughing, until his wife Jackie shushed him. "The service is about to start."

Larry got everyone's attention and the cave grew quiet. He prayed, and then a youngish woman named Jean, a girl really, brought out a flute and skillfully played a tune Merrideth did not recognize. Afterward, her husband, whom everyone jokingly called *Beef*, passed out photocopied song sheets for a hymn called *There Is a Fountain Filled with Blood*. No one but her seemed to be put off by the disgusting title, and everyone sang with gusto, including Trevor on her left side and Brett on her right. Both had rich, mellow voices that resonated pleasantly in her ears. She would have liked to see their faces, but contented herself watching those of the others across the circle from her.

Everyone looked so happy. The harmony welled up and filled the space. Earlier she had thought the cave magical, but now *spiritual* seemed a better word.

When the hymn was over, Larry called Trevor to the front, and Trevor-the-Silent became Trevor-the-Eloquent. "I love that hymn," he said. "But there's another I like better, and it's fitting for this setting. *Amazing Grace*. Did you know it was written by a sailor? I've been thinking a lot lately about those who sailed down this river in the olden days." His eyes came to rest on Merrideth for a moment.

"Some of the people on this river and in this very cave were pirates. Some of them were innocent settlers on their way to new lives. Hard-working, productive citizens. Good people. God-fearing in most cases."

The type who carried Psalm 23 written out on paper in their

pockets, Merrideth thought. The type that trusted God to watch over them.

"And the pirates preyed on them, did unspeakable evil to them," Trevor continued. "The closest I've come to that kind of evil was when I was in Albion Prison. There were some really bad men in there. I won't kid you. It was a horrible time for me."

Merrideth sensed Brett's surprise. She wondered what he thought of "her" friend Trevor now.

"But three good things happened while I was in prison," Trevor said. "I kicked the cocaine addiction that had landed me there. I stopped hating my wife for divorcing me. And I met a goofy little guy named Dave Markel who wasn't afraid to go into Hell itself if it meant he could talk to someone about Jesus.

"Dave told me that I had it all wrong. That I was measuring myself against the wrong yardstick. He said, 'Hey, Dalton, try comparing yourself to Jesus, why don't you?' He told me that instead of pointing at the speck of sawdust in the other guy's eye, I should be worrying about the log in my own.

"It was the worst possible thing to say to a man just trying to survive in prison. I was furious. I had expected Dave to praise me for my victory over cocaine. I had expected him to say I was basically a good man, so much better than the foul criminals around me. That my sin was a puny thing compared to theirs. But Dave wouldn't let me off the hook. He just kept hammering me about how we're all wretched sinners in God's eyes. What kind of preacher was he to come into prison and mess with a guy's head like that? I unleashed all my pent-up rage on him, but Dave didn't even flinch.

"After that, I fell into a deep depression. And Dave just let me stew in my misery for a while. Then one day he asked me if I'd ever heard of John Newton. Newton, he said, was a really bad dude. So bad he made a living off human trafficking." Trevor smiled ironically. "I thought at first he was warning me about a new inmate. Then he explained that John Newton was the captain of a British slave ship back in 1773. He was also the author of *Amazing Grace*." Trevor held out his arms to show the words of the hymn tattooed there.

"*Amazing grace, how sweet the sound that saved a wretch like me.* I'd heard it plenty of times. Who hasn't? But when squirrely little Dave sang it to me that day, I finally really listened to the words. Newton wasn't exaggerating when he described himself as a 'wretch.' But Dave helped me understand that I was no less a wretch than he. That was the bad news. The good news was that if God could save a slave trader, then he could save me. And he did that day, with Dave looking on, grinning like a donkey. And that's how I know God can save those wretches over at the Hellhound Homecoming. And that's why I come every year," he said, glancing at Merrideth.

Then he began to sing the words of the hymn:

Amazing grace! How sweet the sound

That saved a wretch like me!

I once was lost, but now am found;

Was blind, but now I see.

'Twas grace that taught my heart to fear,

And grace my fears relieved;

How precious did that grace appear

The hour I first believed.

Through many dangers, toils and snares,

I have already come;

'Tis grace hath brought me safe thus far,

And grace will lead me home.

The Lord has promised good to me,

His Word my hope secures;

He will my Shield and Portion be,

As long as life endures.

Yea, when this flesh and heart shall fail,

And mortal life shall cease,

I shall possess, within the veil,

A life of joy and peace.

The earth shall soon dissolve like snow,

The sun forbear to shine;

But God, who called me here below,

Will be forever mine.

When we've been there ten thousand years,

Bright shining as the sun,

We've no less days to sing God's praise

Than when we'd first begun.

The song ended and the last of Trevor's words finished reverberating off the cave walls. He had spoken of the wretches down at the Hellhound festival, but he had no doubt also been thinking of the wretched river pirates, too. As the hymn had filled the space, it seemed as if Trevor were staking a claim on the cave and casting out its demons once and for all. And several times he had looked her way as if to tell her he was also exorcizing the evil she had experienced at the cave as well.

She would never forget what had happened to her, but now Trevor's singing would overlay the other dark memories. The Brown Cloud in her head seemed far away.

After that, Larry went back to the front. He spent a few minutes discussing the next CMA rally scheduled for Seattle in the fall, and then he said, "Let's pray before we go our separate ways. For safety on the road. And for the Hellhounds—that the seeds we planted this weekend will bear fruit."

Merrideth bowed her head and waited for Larry to pray. But he didn't. Instead, across the circle Joyce prayed, and then next to her Beef boomed out a short prayer. And then Jean. Merrideth's stomach fluttered. Wasn't one prayer enough? Did they really intend to go around the whole circle? What would she do when it was her turn? But then the pattern broke when Jackie across the way piped up with a prayer. Maybe it was just random after all. Maybe every last one of them would not pray. Maybe she would not find herself standing there with a giant spotlight shining on her as they waited for her to pray.

But, no, the prayer marathon continued, bouncing from one person to another. Several people said short prayers, and then eventually it was down to four. Larry, Trevor, Brett—and her. The cave went silent, and her nerves calmed. That was it then. She breathed a sigh of relief and opened her eyes. Everyone still stood with their heads reverently bowed, so she closed her eyes again.

After a long moment, Larry said a one-sentence prayer. And then Trevor began to pray. "Thank you, Jesus, for leaving Heaven to come to our miserable, fallen world. You said that you came to seek and to save the lost. To prove it, you ate with unclean sinners and hung out with the worst of the worst—whores, tax collectors, thieves, and adulterers. Truly you are the Light of the World! Thanks for giving us the opportunity to hang out with the Hellhounds this weekend. May they see your love in us. Shine your light into their wretched hearts as you did in mine. Amen."

When his prayer ended, the fluttering in Merrideth's stomach grew into a veritable swarm of butterflies. But a new thought brought her hope. Maybe they were only expecting CMA members to pray, and outsiders like her and Brett would be off the hook.

But then, beside her Brett began to speak, drat him. She could barely hear what he was saying for the blood thundering in her head. He would not pray long. None of them had. He would finish any moment, and then she would stand there like a dodo bird, mute and stupid, or she would blurt out something idiotic and juvenile. The only thing that came to mind was *God is great and God is good; now we thank Him for our food.* The Old Dears had taught it to her when she was eleven, and even then she had been far too old for such a baby prayer. Other than the spontaneous cry for help when she was attacked, she had not prayed in a very long time, probably since the Old Dears died. And then it certainly had not been out loud. She was a firm believer that faith should be a private thing, between the person and God.

She had never learned to pray the way Trevor and his friends did. But one thing was certain, if she did come up with a prayer, she would not call herself a wretch. No, she had too much of a problem with low self-esteem as it was. She refused to put herself down any longer for anyone, not even God. She sure would not grovel.

Trevor's talk had brought her father to mind, and she had pictured him in the Joliet visitor's room, sitting across the table from her in his orange jumpsuit. In all the years, he had never mentioned anyone coming to the prison to preach to the inmates. Maybe they did, and her father declined to go to the services and be called a sinner. But if anyone deserved to be called a wretch, it was him. He was the one who had cooked meth in their back yard, risking the lives of his family. He was the one who sold meth to anyone who wanted it, including school kids in their very neighborhood. Probably even to her own classmates. He had even branched out into gun sales, and God only knew where those had ended up and what crimes had been committed with them.

And the men who had attacked her, they were wretches. She was the victim, and it was stupid for victims to blame themselves. Trevor and Brett had both said so themselves. Were they all expecting her to turn the other cheek, waiting to hear her pray for those bikers—even though they had stood in the cave arguing about who would rape her first?

Brett ended his prayer with the ever-popular "in Jesus' name," and once again the cave fell silent. When the silence drew out to the point of being unbearable, Merrideth opened her mouth. But she could not think of what to say, so she shut it again. Maybe she would just repeat some of the things the others had said. *Dear God, bless everyone as they travel home.* She opened her mouth to get it out, but then Larry said "amen," and the others echoed it back to him. It was too late.

When she opened her eyes, everyone was smiling and hugging each other. Had they thought her shy and decided not to pressure her? Or had they somehow sensed she was not truly one of them?

Trevor had asked her if she knew Jesus, and she had shut him down with the excuse of having a headache, because she had been too uncomfortable with the question. No, she did not know Jesus. Not the way these people seemed to. Like they were on a first-name basis with him, like he was just another person in their circle of friends.

But no one was looking at her with disappointment or disgust. They were not looking at her at all, just chatting among themselves and saying their goodbyes. Trevor and Brett were across the way talking and looked her way. Were they talking about her?

Larry and June came over. "It was nice to meet you, Merrideth," June said, hugging her. "God bless and keep you."

"Thanks. Have a safe ride home," Merrideth said.

The others told her goodbye and wished her well. And then they left to go take down the pavilions. She followed Trevor out of the cave and up the trail. Brett came last, hobbling along on his crutches.

Walking single file, sandwiched between the two men, it was impossible to talk, which was fortunate because she did not know what to say anyway. When they reached the top of the trail Trevor waved his friends on, telling them he would be there soon to help. The three of them stood there watching the others go to the parking lot for their motorcycles.

She was struck again by how similar the two men were. Both were over six feet tall with dark hair and light eyes. But they were as different as night and day in personality. Brett exuded friendliness and good humor. Trevor was quiet and reserved. Even so, they had forged some sort of bond over the weekend.

Brett extended his hand to Trevor. "I should have told you before, but thanks for coming to Merrideth's rescue."

"Thank God, not me," he said, shaking Brett's hand.

Trevor turned to her.

It was their second goodbye, but this time a kiss didn't seem in order at all. And not just because Brett was standing right there. He probably wouldn't even be jealous, now that he and Trevor were blood brothers, or whatever it was they were. Before, she had thought that kissing Trevor would be a surefire way of finally getting a read on what he thought of her. A chance to see if there was anything between them—or could be anything between them. She had told herself that maybe he would call her when he got home. Maybe they would think of a way to overcome the distance.

But now a kiss was no longer necessary, because she already knew she was not going to pursue a relationship with him. The realization had been growing all weekend, but seeing the two men standing there, it was suddenly a settled conclusion. Even though Trevor would probably understand her scarred soul and dysfunctional background in a way Brett never could, and even though he was a really nice man, a hero who had come along just when she needed one, he was not Brett.

If she kissed anyone, it should be him.

So instead of kissing Trevor, she smiled and shook his hand. "Thank you for everything."

He smiled. "Any time." Then he gave Brett a meaningful look

and said, "Good luck."

"I don't believe in luck," he said, grinning.

"Me neither."

Interesting. She wondered again what they had discussed back at the cave.

Trevor walked across the parking lot to his bike, put on his helmet, and started the engine. He looked their way briefly. She and Brett waved. And then he roared away.

When he was out of sight, Brett said, "He's a nice guy."

"Yes, he is. How's your ankle?"

"You mean cankle?"

"Brett! You should have said something. It's really swollen."

"I'll ice it for a while. And then if you wouldn't mind wrapping it again before we head for home, I'd appreciate it."

"Sorry. I guess you weren't faking after all."

He grinned. "I was at the time. But I'm being paid back now. This hurts like a bear paw in a trap."

"Come on. Nurse Merri will patch you up. Then let's tell Shirley and Fred goodbye and get out of here."

CHAPTER 17

Merrideth followed Brett as he turned into Nelda's long driveway. Both their cars were dirty from sitting all weekend in the Hellhounds' parking field. Her poor beat up Subaru was a faded, dull blue on the best of days. But now Brett's Jeep, normally so shiny and red, looked almost as bad. The white gravel dust billowing up from the driveway was sure to give both vehicles another layer of grime. She slowed until she was out of his cloud enough to see where she was going. Duke was around there somewhere, and she wanted plenty of notice if he came bounding out to greet them.

Even watching carefully, she nearly clipped a white chicken as it ran, wings flapping, across the driveway in front of her. Getting hit by a car had to be one of the major downsides to being a free-range chicken. And why *did* the chicken cross the road anyway? Its friends seemed perfectly content to stay on the other side of the drive pecking and scratching in the grass.

She wanted to see the rest of Nelda's menagerie, but Brett continued on toward the house. She did get a glimpse of the goats' new patio.

He parked in front of Nelda's garage, and Merrideth pulled in behind him. She hurried to help him before he decided to go all macho and walk unassisted on his injured foot.

He opened his door and frowned at her. "You didn't have to do this. I'm perfectly able to—"

"Shut up and take it like a man, Brett."

Rolling his eyes, he eased himself out of the Jeep and slung his right arm around her neck. "Well, don't come crying to me if we land in a heap."

"If we land in a heap, both us will be crying."

His only response was a grunt. Together they awkwardly made their way down the sidewalk to Nelda's back door.

Duke exploded out of his doggy door and danced around them, whining his excitement. He meant well, but it was not helping the situation at all. She maneuvered Brett into the mudroom and through to the kitchen with Duke following closely behind them sniffing curiously at Brett's bandaged foot.

"I hope your Aunt Nelda isn't trying to take a Sunday afternoon nap. We weren't exactly quiet."

"It's late for a nap. But she must be sleeping or she'd be out here by now." Brett lowered himself into a chair at the kitchen table and heaved a deep breath. "Thanks, Merri. I guess I did need a little help."

From the looks of it, the aspirin she had given him was not doing much for the pain. And driving for nearly three hours had given him an elephant-sized ankle. For all his attempted stoicism, he looked so pitiful that the urge to kiss him came on strong again. Maybe she would allow herself another quick comforting peck on his forehead. As she leaned in, his eyes widened and then he turned his face away.

To refuse that, he must be in more pain than she realized. "With Aunt Nelda being sick and you lame, you're going to need more than just a little help. Who's going to feed the animals?"

"I'll be fine once I get my crutches."

"Not until you get the swelling in your ankle down." Merrideth dragged one of the other chairs in front of him. "Here, put your foot up."

"There's a bag of frozen peas in the freezer, if you'd be so kind, Nurse Merri."

"Frozen peas aren't going to make a dent through your elastic bandage. I need to make you another ice pack."

"If you insist on going to the trouble you'll find all the plastic bags you'll ever need under the sink."

He was right about that. A large canvas tote was stuffed to the brim with Walmart bags. Fortunately, Nelda's ice bin was likewise full. When the ice pack was ready, she laid it gently over his ankle. "Let's give this a good twenty minutes or so, and then we'll see whether you're fit for duty. Meanwhile, where are those crutches?"

"Hanging on the garage wall. On the left side."

"That sounds easy enough."

"Wait until you see what's between you and them. Don't trip and sprain *your* ankle wading through everything."

It wasn't as bad as he let on, and she found the crutches without difficulty. When the twenty minutes were up, his ankle looked marginally better, and so she put the ice pack back in the freezer.

"Now if you wouldn't mind fetching my work boots—or rather boot—I'll get started on chores."

"If you tell me how, I'll do them for you."

"Feeding beasts properly requires a knowledge of agri-science, but I suppose I can let a non-professional assist."

"I'll try my best to measure up. And when we're done, I'll show you the Garretson Fort. I can't wait for you to see—"

"No, that's all right."

"Oh, sorry. You probably want to rest. Just call me when your ankle's—"

"No, I mean I can't ask you to endure any more bloodshed and violence. At least not on my behalf."

"It's not always like what we saw this weekend. Don't worry. Your Garretsons had plenty of boring hours for us to look in on. I promise I'll skip anything involving blood."

"Then in that case, let's go time-surfing."

"What about the beasts?"

"They can wait. I can't."

When he was booted up, she handed him the crutches and he tried them out.

"How are they?"

"Not bad. I just hope the soil's not too soft or I'll get stuck and you'll have to call a tow-truck."

"What about the path to the fort your Aunt Nelda was going to put in?"

"It's on my to-do list."

His dependability was one of the things she liked most about him. But things like that always stuck in her throat.

"I'll start on the path the very day that old skin-flint sells the land to her."

"I thought Ogle sold the land and moved to Florida."

"Most of it. Not his house and not the parcel of land the fort sits on. He started holding out for more money once he realized how much Aunt Nelda wanted it. Heard he only plans to spend winters in Florida, so she'll be blessed by his presence in the neighborhood for most of the year. Lucky her."

"Then we had better lock Duke inside so he won't call attention to our trespassing. And don't worry. I can get you within forty feet of the site."

"You want to drive my Jeep?"

"Now's not the time for me to learn to drive a stick shift. Besides, my Subaru is already so beat up that a few more scratches won't hurt."

"Hey, my Jeep is not afraid to see action."

"You can tell me about all its adventures on the way."

He should have looked foolish swinging along on the crutches, wearing shorts and a single dusty work boot, but he didn't. She shook her head in wonder. No matter what the man wore he managed to look like a male model. It was another thing she liked about him. It was not even close to being one of the most important things, but still nice.

※※※

She took her Subaru SUV as far down into the woods as she thought prudent. They got out, and after she shouldered her backpack and he got his crutches in position, they started toward the fort.

The air was cooler under the leafy canopy than in the full sun. The smell of last year's leaves turning into loam came up with each step they took. A pair of blue jays flew across the path in front of them, expressing angry disapproval at their invasion.

But it was too beautiful a day to waste a minute being angry. A shining bubble of joy rose in Merrideth's throat, and for a moment she thought she might actually giggle. Brett was with her, and they were going on an adventure. She had someone to share her find with. Someone who shared her curiosity for knowledge. And she was about to give him the gift of meeting his ancestors first-hand.

"Last time I was here it was pitch black and snowing," she said.

"And to think I was only minutes away, relaxing after a turkey dinner in front of Aunt Nelda's TV."

He didn't say it in a condemning way, but still it had to hurt that she had not trusted him with her software. "I kept wishing you were here."

There. She had given him a compliment. And it had not killed her. From his expression, he was as surprised as she was. She expected him to say something smart-aleck about her finally sharing her feelings, but he didn't. Before he looked away she saw that the surprise had turned to some other emotion, sadness maybe, and she was puzzled by what that meant.

"It must have been scary, being alone in the woods," he said.

"The thing I worried most about was my fingers freezing to the computer. Oh, and being mistaken for a deer and shot in the back."

"Don't worry. It's July, not November. Even Odious Ogle obeys the hunting laws."

"We'd better keep quiet, all the same. He's not fond of trespassers."

Brett stopped, put a finger tip to his temples, and closed his eyes. "Shh! I'm getting a telepathic message."

"What, that you're going to drop your crutches and fall flat on your face?"

"I'm serious." He paused. "I sense that Aunt Nelda is up from her nap. Yes, she's stepping outside. She sees our cars and wonders where we are."

Duke came bounding down the hill behind Merri, panting and yipping, proud that he had found them.

Merri bent and ruffled his ears. "I hope you're right, Amazing Kreskin. Because you and Aunt Nelda are going to have one pesky dog if Duke figured out how to turn the door knob."

Brett laughed. "He's smart, but not that—"

"Shh," she said, putting her finger tips to his mouth. "You'll hurt his feelings."

His eyes went from laughing to smoldering. He wanted to kiss her. She saw it in his eyes. Her own eyes had to be unwisely projecting that she would let him—that she was eager to kiss him right back. Yet he only gave her a quick kiss on the top of her head and then turned away.

"We'd better hurry," he said, "or Aunt Nelda will worry."

Well, that certainly proved neither of them were mentalists, or at least she wasn't.

For a moment, she watched him swinging along on his crutches, then she adjusted her backpack and followed, figuratively scratching her head and trying not to feel like a little girl who had just been kissed by her daddy.

Duke followed them for a minute or two and then saw a squirrel and went crashing through the trees after it. The soil grew too soft for Brett's crutches and he was forced to leave them propped against a tree and lean on her for the last few yards.

Since she had last been there, Nature had landscaped what remained of the stone foundation of the Garretson family's blockhouse fort. Clumps of violets grew at the base of the foundation. They weren't blooming, but they would have been beautiful in the spring. And a vine trailed down the wall, which was a nice touch except it looked suspiciously like poison ivy.

Brett stood on one foot and leaned against a nearby tree while she got a stick and pushed the poison ivy away so they could sit on top of the wall without fear of taking home an itchy souvenir. He sat sideways so he could keep his leg up. She sat beside his foot and opened her laptop. Then she clicked on the *Beautiful Houses* icon, and handed him her laptop. "Here. Let me know when you get to the fort."

"How will I know?"

She grinned. "You'll know."

She got out her notebook and began thumbing through the pages. "I jotted down the date and time co-ordinates for some of the key moments. I'm not sure which ones to show you."

Then he yelped. "There it is!"

Merrideth got up and went to stand beside him. Yes, there it was, just like the first time she had seen the fort. The cabin was two stories tall with its upper floor projecting over the lower. The stockade wall on either side of it was made of upright logs still wearing their bark.

"But it's so sunny there," he said. "Where are all the trees? Oh, wait, I get it. They cut them for the stockade pickets."

"And they would need a clear view of people approaching anyway."

"So how do we get inside the cabin?"

She pointed to the screen. "You can toggle between interior and exterior there." When he reached for the touch pad, she grabbed his hand. "Wait! That's exactly what we don't want to see."

"What?"

"Look at the date. I may not be good with them, but *December 10, 1788* is burned into my brain. Right about now, the Garretsons have their dead son Samuel laid out on the kitchen table. Their dead *scalped* son."

"Good save, Dr. Randall."

"Thanks, Dr. Garrison. Let's rewind."

He held the computer out for her.

"No, you do it. You might as well get familiar with the controls."

"Okay. When?"

"I recall a time earlier in 1788 before the tragedy in December. The family was all cozy inside their cabin, happy that James Lemen had come to visit them. I'm not sure how good a look at James Garretson we'll get, but at least there won't be any gore."

"He'd be about fourteen then."

"If you say so," she said, thumbing through the pages of her notebook. "Ah yes, here it is. Type in November 21, 1788. And set the time to five o'clock."

He entered the co-ordinates and switched to interior. The screen scrambled and then they were inside.

Merrideth's breath caught. It was bittersweet to see the family again. She had trouble remembering her students' names, but the Garretsons' names came to her now, as familiar as if they were her own friends. They were all chatting and smiling happily, totally unaware of what was going to happen.

"That's James Garretson, Senior. And that's his wife Isabelle. You can see the tip of her spinning wheel at the edge of the screen. She was spinning wool before they all came in for dinner."

"My alleged eighth great grandparents."

"Not having your ginormous brain, I'd have to look up the number of greats, but yes. The older girls are Jane and Sarah and the little ones are Bella and Mary. And that's sixteen-year-old Samuel." In only a little while he would be dead. Her throat seized up and her eyes threatened to start leaking again.

But Brett sensed her distress and put a comforting arm around her waist. He might not be the Amazing Kreskin, but his touch was obviously magical. She no longer felt the least need to cry. Instead, another bubble of happiness rose in her throat, and she told herself to be sure to remember the moment.

"That leaves two males," he said. "Please don't tell me you think I look like the guy with the big nose."

When she finally came out of her daze enough to understand what his words meant, she said, "Oh, no, he's James Lemen. *That's* him," she said, pointing to the screen. "They called him James Kyle to distinguish him from his father James Garretson, senior. Zoom in and see what you think."

He complied and then scrunched up his eyes to study the image. "I think he's a teenager with dark hair and acne. One of millions who have lived on the earth."

"His hair is black, just like yours, and you know it."

"So?"

"Okay, I admit that at this point I didn't see that he looked like you—or rather that you look like him. But when he was a few years older the resemblance was striking. I first saw it was when he was visiting the Indian village."

"Okay, what do I do? Fast-forward?"

"Let me give you the co-ordinates for it. I know I wrote those down." She flipped a few more pages. "And you'll have to lock onto James first. Ah, yes, here it is. August 17, 1795."

"That's seven years and four months after this. He'll be twenty-one years old."

Merrideth grinned. "It's going to be so handy having you along when I time-surf. I may not have to take notes at all."

He gave her as much of a bow as he could while sitting with a bandaged foot on a wall. "At your service, madam." He typed in the date, and again the screen scrambled to take them where they wanted to go.

When the image settled, James Kyle Garretson was riding a bay horse down a path through a sun-dappled forest much like the one they now sat in, cautiously scanning the trees on either side of him.

Brett grunted in surprise and Merrideth laughed at the expression on his face.

"There," she said smugly. "Is that not you, Professor Garrison, in buckskins? The shape of his face is the same. Same nose, and he definitely has your black hair. Even the shape of his ears. I laughed my butt off when I saw him."

Brett paused the action and zoomed in to study the man on the horse closer. "I think his eyes are green, too."

"They are. The exact same shade of emerald green."

Brett sat there as if stunned, watching his ancestor riding along on his horse.

"Well, say something," Merrideth said.

He turned from the screen and looked at her. "I don't know what to say. I've believed for so long that I am not a true Garrison. I want it to be true. But I still don't see how it could be."

"You should talk to Nelda."

"Maybe."

Duke came back from his explorations with no indication that he had caught any squirrels. Still, he laughed up at them, happy to share the day with them. He put his front paws on the wall, and Brett patted him absently.

"You could switch to virtual if you want to hear James Kyle preach to the old Indian chief he's going to see. Or we could go back and follow James Lemen to Fort Piggot."

"No, we should get back to the house before Aunt Nelda comes looking for us. But I expect you to come back with your magic computer as soon as humanly possible."

"And just think of all the other wonders we'll see, Brett! The McKendree campus alone should be rich with historical data to be mined."

"And all those old houses around Lebanon."

"I haven't had the time to explore much, but I've made my bucket list. You should make yours, too."

"Oh, I will."

"Do you have any idea yet about how this works?"

"No, but you can bet I'll be thinking about it." He swung his leg off the wall and stood leaning against it.

She put her laptop away and grinned at him. "This was so much more fun with you by my side."

He put his hands on her cheeks and tipped her face up to his. "I loved every minute of it."

And she loved *him*.

How about that? Only an hour before she had still been telling herself they were just friends. But here, now, the truth insisted on being recognized and accepted: She loved him. She felt remarkably lighter, as if everything good and important in life was within her grasp. She had only to reach out and take it.

It was possibly the best, most romantic setting in the world in which to discover that one was in love. Leafy walls and ceiling enclosed them in their own private world, and fingers of sun sneaked through in a million spots, making everything they touched glow. She saw herself reflected in Brett's green eyes and knew with certainty that he was finally going to kiss her.

He clasped her to himself, as if he could not wait a moment more, then lowered his head and put his lips to hers. She leaned in to savor the taste and texture of them. It was definitely no sympathy kiss. No friendly little peck. It was the real deal, and it made her heart gallop and her legs threaten to melt into a blob of rubber. She reached up to put her arms around his neck so she could get a little closer.

Just as he pulled away.

He smiled down at her and patted her cheek. Patted her cheek. "Do you hear all the bleating, clucking, meowing, and barking?" he asked cheerily. "The beasts are calling for their supper."

"Well, we can't have that," she said as if she had not just been cast out of Paradise.

***

All the way back, she tried to analyze what had just happened. Granted, she was not the best judge of human communication, but surely she had not been reading Brett's signals all wrong for the past year. No, he had made it quite clear that he wanted more than a friendship. She was sure of it. And she was sure, too, that he would never knowingly hurt her. That she *was* hurt could only be attributed to her damaged, overly sensitive ego. She was learning to make allowances for that, to not assume the worst about people.

Obviously the timing was all wrong. He was in a hurry to get his chores done and get inside to check on Nelda. Besides, after the weekend they had endured, Brett's brain had to be as mushy as hers was. She sure couldn't think straight.

It did not help that every few minutes Duke, having decided he would prefer to ride in style in her Subaru rather than take his usual shortcut through the woods, stuck his snout between her seat and Brett's to give them doggy kisses on their necks and arms. To distract him, Merrideth lowered his window halfway, and he finally turned his attention to the view outside his window.

She parked in front of the barn to save Brett the steps and lowered her own window. "I don't hear the beasts."

"You will. Just give it a second and you'll hear a chorus of hungry pleas."

A second later two bleating pygmy goats came excitedly out the open side door, their hooves clicking on the brick patio as they rushed to the fence to greet them. At the same time, chickens came running from the four corners of the property and rushed *into* the barn's front door.

"Don't you worry about coyotes or other varmints getting them?" Merrideth said.

"You're referring to Rancho Garrison's free-range chickens? Well, not to worry. Every evening, Duke, the famous chicken-herding dog, gets them rounded up and tucked into the coyote-proof roosting pen I made for them. It works so well I'm thinking of patenting the design and retiring young."

Not waiting for Brett to extricate himself from the passenger seat, Merrideth got out and went to the fence for a closer look. "Oh, they're adorable. Hello, Lilli and Mini. Do the chickens have names, too?"

"Only two of them do," Brett said, joining her at the fence. "That buff colored one is Miss Cluck, and the rooster is Chanticleer."

"Ah, continuing in Aunt Nelda's literary vein, of course."

Lilli and Mini continued bleating at the fence.

"Don't believe a word they say," Brett said in mock disgust. "We do too feed them every day, and they are not starving."

"What do they eat?"

"They love vegetables and fruits. But mostly they eat hay."

"Can I pet them?"

"Sure."

"On second thought, maybe I'll wait until after they've eaten. I'd hate for them to mistake my fingers for carrots."

"Good idea."

"The patio is even more glorious in person than the photos you showed me, but what on earth is that contraption?" Someone, presumably Brett, had sunk four posts in the ground and built a wooden platform six or seven feet off the ground. One of the posts pierced a series of plywood rounds that formed a stairway to it.

He grinned. "Oh, didn't I mention Lilli and Mini's new jungle gym? It wasn't even on Aunt Nelda's to-do list, but I decided it should be, because as they say, a bored goat is a naughty goat. They play king of the mountain on it."

"Will they perform for us?"

"Not until they've eaten. Come on, and I'll show you where everyone's food of choice is."

When they went into the barn a calico cat streaked down from the loft as if it had wings. "That's Cat in the Hat," Brett said.

Cat in the Hat twined herself around Brett's leg and purred, lovingly. "There's also Cheshire Cat, The Black Cat, and—"

"As in Poe's story?"

"Yes, but he's not the least bit scary." A yellow tabby arrived and began meowing for his supper. "And that's Smelly Cat, but he's not."

"Sorry, I don't think I'll be able to keep them all straight. You know how I am with names."

Brett grinned. "Don't worry. They all have the same nickname."

Merrideth thought for a moment and then laughed. "Cat?"

"Makes it simpler all around. They'll be here as soon as you rattle the bag of cat food. But first we'd better fill the chicken feeders."

Those turned out to be more of Brett's inventions. He had built three small wooden boxes, and rigged them so that their lids only opened if a chicken—or other chicken-sized animal—stepped onto a lever in front. It kept mice out of their feed and, more importantly, the goats, which were too tall to simultaneously step on the lever and put their heads into the boxes to gorge themselves silly.

"I told Aunt Nelda I could probably fine-tune it so that only hens that actually laid eggs, not mentioning any names, would be able to activate the mechanism. But she voted me down."

"How socialist of her."

Brett sat on a bale of straw to rest his leg while she forked hay for the goats and put cat food into bowls. Then it was time to gather the eggs.

"Don't bother looking in the nest boxes I built for them out of prime-grade, knot-free pine," Brett said. "They prefer to lay their eggs in various and sundry locations throughout the barn, the more improbable the better."

"How lucky for you, Dr. Garrison. You get to have an Easter egg hunt every day."

He gave her a plastic ice cream bucket and told her to knock herself out. He made a game of it, telling her *warm, warmer, hot* until she had found all the hens' usual hiding spots. Afterward, smiling in excitement at her success, she sat down on the straw bale next to him to show him the five large eggs she had collected.

"I'm picturing you as a little barefoot girl in overalls and pigtails." His smile faltered and he looked away.

But then no wonder. His ankle had swollen up again. He was probably in too much pain to play at farming with her.

"Up you go, Tiny Tim," she said. "It's way past time to get ice on that."

CHAPTER 18

Nelda saw them coming up the sidewalk and had the back door open for them. "It's so good to see you, Merri, and I'm going to have a million questions about what you've been up to. But first, what happened to you, Brett Alan Garrison. You told me it was a safe cave."

"It is. I was in the parking lot, not the cave, when I sprained my ankle. Tripped over a *Fat Boy*."

"Brett!" Nelda said. "That's not nice!"

His laugh filled the kitchen. "It's a motorcycle, Aunt Nelda. Not a person. I got my foot tangled up in its spokes and we both came tumbling right down."

She laughed, as he had intended. "That's really the name of it? Fat Boy?"

"Yes."

"Your face looks awful. I supposed you sprained it too."

"Don't worry. It doesn't even hurt. Much."

He gave Merrideth a look that she interpreted to mean that he did not intend to tell Nelda he had been hit over the head with a beer bottle. Good. Merrideth saw no reason to worry her with the attack in the cave either.

"How did you manage your chores—or I should say *my* chores—with the crutches?"

"Other than almost falling because the cats wanted to use them as scratching posts, it was fine. Merri did all the work. I just supervised."

Merrideth gave Nelda a sad smile and whispered confidentially,

"He's clumsier than you'd think, isn't he?"

"I heard that. Sorry, I got manure on them. The crutches, not the cats."

"Brett! Don't come traipsing in on my clean floors with chicken poo."

"Hey, I wasn't born in a barn! I washed it off."

Nelda took the bucket of eggs from her. Merrideth pulled out a chair for Brett, and he sank into it gratefully and pulled another out to put his injured ankle on.

"I'll make an icepack for you," Nelda said. "Make that two icepacks. One for your ankle and one for your poor face."

"Don't need one for my face, and Nurse Merri already made one for my ankle. It's in the freezer."

Nelda got it out and put it over Brett's ankle. "That looks horrible."

"Only because I've been on my feet too much."

"So how are you, Nelda?" Merrideth said. "Brett says you haven't been feeling well lately."

"Just a little tired. The doctor tells me I'm anemic. We're working on that."

From her pallor and the look on Brett's face, Merrideth suspected the doctor had a lot more to say on the subject of her health than that. But it was crystal clear that neither of them wanted to talk about it, so she kept her questions to herself.

"Sit down, Merri, and tell me about your trip to Cave-in-Rock while I get dinner on."

"Now don't go thinking you need to whip up a five-course Sunday dinner," Brett said.

"Definitely not," Merri added. "Not on my account."

"I won't need to today," Nelda said. "Mrs. Ashe brought a nice casserole when she came by with the rent check this afternoon."

Brett smiled. "I suppose you won't tax yourself too much putting a casserole in the oven. Mrs. Ashe and her husband Neil lease Aunt Nelda's tillable acres. They live just beyond Odious Ogle, the poor souls."

"I'm glad to hear all your neighbors aren't...well, odious," Merri said.

"Definitely not," Nelda said. "Julia's the sweetest thing. About your age, Merri."

"Does Julia go around giving random people casseroles?"

"She said a little birdy told her I wasn't feeling so hot, which I suppose means the church prayer chain has been sending out smoke signals just because I missed a few services lately."

It had to be nice to have friendly neighbors who actually worried about you when you were sick. Still, Merrideth would not want to belong to a church where nosy members kept track of everyone's attendance and then blabbed about it when they missed.

Nelda took the foil-covered casserole out of the refrigerator and slid it into her oven. She set the timer and then took the bucket of eggs to the sink to wash. "Five big ones. I hope you told the girls thanks, Brett."

"I did."

"Do you need help, Nelda?" Merrideth said. "I could set the table."

"No way. You're company. Now tell me what you learned about the cave—and especially the pirates."

While Nelda set the table and put together a salad, Merrideth told her some of what they had learned. Nelda's curiosity was as enormous as her nephew's. It was an indicator of their intelligence, of course, but her endless stream of insightful questions kept Merrideth on her toes coming up with answers that did not reveal the existence of the software. Brett helpfully fielded questions, too, and Merrideth tried several times to change the subject to Nelda's interests—her jewelry and craft making or poetry—but Nelda invariably turned right back to the pirates and their victims.

"Sit down and rest while we wait for the casserole," Brett said.

"I think I will," Nelda said. "Lately I get tired over the littlest things."

Her face was paler even than when they had first come in, and Merrideth wished she had ignored her rule about company and helped her.

"So how's your genealogy consulting coming along, Merrideth?"

"I've been too busy to take on any new clients lately."

"Then I thank you again for taking the time to help us with ours," Nelda said. "I suppose your relatives are grateful to have a genealogist in the family."

"I haven't done our tree," Merrideth said. "I'm sure the Randalls aren't very interesting. Not like your heroic Garretsons."

Nelda couldn't know it, but it was a sore subject for her. Abby had been nagging her for ages to do it. She claimed that it was ridiculous for a professional genealogy consultant not to have her own family tree, for a sales tool if nothing else.

Merrideth could not bring herself to explain that putting the names of her living relatives on a genealogy chart would only be a reminder of their absence in her life. And as for time-surfing back to learn about earlier ancestors, well, that would not work.

From what her mother had told her, no one on either side of the family had ever lived in anything but small rented houses. Even if any of them were old enough for the software to work in, which they weren't, they wouldn't yield any useful information, given the transient history of her family. But she had not said any of that to Abby, and she sure wasn't going to say it to Brett and Nelda. It was too pathetic. The tale would elicit either disdain or pity, neither of which was palatable.

Merrideth realized that the conversation had ground to a halt as if Nelda had sensed her reluctance to talk about her family. So she smiled and said, "Brett's head for dates and details was a big help with my...research this weekend."

It turned out to be the wrong thing to say, because it fired up Nelda's matchmaking genes, and she was off and running on the topic of Brett's wonderfulness and how much he and Merrideth had in common. Brett was embarrassed by the attention and the obviousness of his aunt's schemes and tried to steer her to other subjects. Merrideth was grateful for the assist, figuring any moment Nelda would start talking about china patterns and whether Merrideth should wear a veil or flowers in her hair She was tempted to tell Nelda that one thing she and Brett had in common was a parent who abandoned a child for an addiction. His mother had died an alcoholic, and her dad had been hauled away in handcuffs and was serving time for making and selling drugs.

But then, thankfully, Nelda's oven timer dinged.

"I've been hoping to hear that sound," Brett said.

Merrideth hid a smile at the double meaning. "The casserole smells good."

Nelda rose slowly from her chair, grimacing as if in pain. She quickly covered it over with a smile. But Brett watched with concern as she brought the casserole to the table.

It was very good, and Brett tucked in like he had not eaten in a week. In between bites he watched his aunt push her food around on her plate. But he put a determined smile on his face and said, "Merri, tell Aunt Nelda about your new friend Trevor."

Nelda looked decidedly disappointed. Merrideth wondered if it was Brett's intention to pre-empt any more matchmaking.

He smiled mischievously. "Trevor was in Cave-in-Rock for the weekend with some of his other biker friends for the Hellhound Homecoming."

"Dare I ask what that is?"

"Think biker gangs and Woodstock. Only with punk rock music. And crack cocaine and heroin instead of marijuana."

"Well, how about that?" she said brightly.

Merrideth smiled to herself. It was obvious Nelda was trying not to be judgmental about her "friend Trevor."

"Trevor has the coolest tattoos," Brett said. "I've been thinking about getting some myself."

"Well, stop thinking about it right now," Nelda said.

"He's just teasing you," Merrideth said. "I think."

He laughed. "Hmm, you never know. Merri's friend Trevor is with CMA, the Christian Motorcycle Association. They were there to minister to the Hellhounds."

"Wow," Nelda said. "That must take a special calling."

"Or insanity," Merrideth said with a short laugh.

"Well, the Lord calls us all to different things," Nelda said. "And gives grace for the task. And whatever we must go through." No one said anything for a moment. Brett's expression turned solemn and he frowned at his plate.

Nelda smiled gently at him. "Brett, you mentioned the cats, but you didn't say anything about Lilli and Mini. Were they happy to have you home?"

He smiled again. "They did their happy dance. But since they do that for everyone, I didn't let it go to my head."

"Do you remember the way Butch used to dance on his hind legs when you got off the school bus every day?"

"Sure I do. He was our third dog, a huge shepherd mix," Brett said for Merrideth's benefit.

"Ugly thing, bless his heart," Nelda said. "But loyal to the bone."

"Not as scruffy as Scruffy. He was the first dog I ever owned. When I was three."

"You remember the dog you had when you were three?"

209

Merrideth said.

Nelda snorted. "He remembers every dog, cat, chicken, and guinea pig he ever owned, what year he got them, what they looked like, all their ailments and foibles, and the exact day they went off to the great beyond. Same for all his friends' pets."

"You forgot the snakes and lizards. I don't count the baby raccoons we had for eleven days."

Merrideth laughed. "I should have known." For the next few minutes Brett regaled them with funny stories about his various pets. He got Nelda to laugh, which was surely his purpose, and she even told a few funny anecdotes of her own. But by the time they were finished eating, it was clear Nelda's strength was failing.

"Why don't you two go sit in the living room?" Merrideth said. "I'll clean up in here, Nelda."

Nelda sighed. "Even though you're company, I guess I had better let you. Isn't she a sweetheart, Brett?"

"Indeed, she is." He smiled at his aunt, then he turned back toward Merrideth and let her see his gratitude. He probably did not realize that she also saw the sadness he was keeping at bay.

"Thank you, Merri," Nelda said. "But hurry and come back. There's something I think you might find interesting. I came across an old photo album I had tucked away. Wait until you see what a cute little guy Brett was."

"Now that's a surprise." Merrideth shook her head as if mystified. "Too bad about how he turned out."

Nelda chuckled.

"Ha!" Brett said, following his aunt out of the room. "And you thought she was sweet?"

✧✧✧

When Merrideth went in the living room a few minutes later, Nelda and Brett were side by side on the couch with their feet up on the coffee table studying an oversized photo album. Nelda's expression was nostalgic. Brett's was, too, although his also held a touch of displeasure.

Brett looked up and smiled at her. "Thanks, Merri."

"Not a problem." She sat in the easy chair next to the couch.

Nelda turned the photo album so Merrideth could see that they were looking at an eight by ten studio photo of a young dark-haired woman.

"This is Brett's mom, Jodie."

"She was beautiful."

"Yeah, well pretty is as pretty does," he muttered half under his breath.

Nelda lifted his hand and kissed the back of it. "I wish you wouldn't be so hard on her, Brett."

"I've forgiven her, you know. Just can't seem to pull off the forgetting."

"That's the hard part, honey." Her eyes grew clouded, and she stared off into space as if seeing the past. "They were so happy together, Brett. Not at first. They had a couple of really rocky years. Your father wouldn't listen when Dad quoted II Corinthians 6:14 to him—*at* him. Nolan was madly in love with Jodie and determined to marry her. But he soon learned what Dad had been warning him about. He and Jodie were on totally different pages about nearly everything. But when Jodie became a believer everything changed for them. They were so close."

Nelda opened her eyes and looked tenderly at Brett. "When your dad died, she was devastated. She just couldn't seem to get over it. No one knew how much she was drinking until it was too late. The alcohol had gotten its talons in her and wouldn't let go. Before that she was a good mom. You couldn't ask for a better one. And don't you forget that, Brett Garrison."

Brett studied the portrait of his beautiful, perpetually young mother. "I know."

"Did Jodie have a career or was she a stay-at-home mom?"

Nelda smiled. "She was home while Brett was little. They did everything together." Nelda flipped through the album and then turned it again toward Merrideth. "We were just laughing at this one before you came in."

In the photo, Jodie and a miniature version of Brett sat at a dinette table, each proudly holding up creations made from brightly colored Play-Doh for the cameraman to admire. Merrideth laughed. "You *were* a cute little guy, Brett."

He rolled his eyes and then went back to studying the photo. "Those are space monsters, in case you were wondering. Mom and I had contests to see who could come up with the most outlandish creatures. I called them Kookabonchers." He smiled fondly. "We invented a different species for each planet in the solar system.

These are typical examples of Monsterius Plutorius."

Merrideth laughed. "I could tell right off."

"This was taken shortly before Brett went off to kindergarten. Then Jodie resumed her research career with Monsanto."

"My mom always worked some job or another," Merrideth said. "Nothing you'd call a career. But she was the one who put food on the table and paid the rent while Dad...It seemed like she was never home, but of course I'm grateful she had a job."

"Brett's dad was gone a lot, too. He traveled all over Europe for his job. It's hard on a child."

"How did they meet? Jodie and Nolan?"

"They met at St. Louis University when she was getting her BS in microbiology, and he was simultaneously working on a BS in computer science, with certification in information systems security, and a BS in finance." Nelda chuckled. "How they ever had time to date, I'll never know. As if all that schooling wasn't enough, Nolan was making plans to get an MBA, but SysCom snatched him up right after college to be their Information Systems Security Officer. He was promoted to Chief Financial Analyst two years later."

"I wouldn't have thought being a CFA of a company would require much traveling," Merrideth said.

"Well, it did. He traveled throughout Europe on loan from SysCom."

Merrideth was surprised by Nelda's sudden change of tone. She sounded defensive, almost angry. Maybe Brett was right about her hiding something. "Can I see a picture of him?"

Nelda flipped a few pages forward. "Here's the last one we have of Nolan."

It was another studio photograph. A sandy-haired thirty-something man smiled at the world. He was a very handsome man, but Merrideth could not see any resemblance to Brett.

"Obviously, I didn't take after my dad's side of the family," Brett said, sending Merrideth an *I told you so* look.

Merrideth ignored it and spoke to Nelda. "The Garrisons are brainy about math. You with your accounting career and Nolan with his finance degree. And Brett, too. With his father's aptitude for math and his mother's for science, it's no wonder he became a physicist."

He raised his eyebrows to let her know he knew what she was

trying to do. She raised her own eyebrows back at him and smiled sweetly. "Did you also inherit that memory for numbers and patterns you have from your dad?"

"What do you mean?" Nelda said sharply.

"You know. Like he did with the pets. Yesterday he recited all the makes and models of the motorcycles in the parking lot."

Brett smiled self-consciously. "As far as I know, neither of them could do my little parlor trick."

"It must have been Jodie." Nelda let the photo album slip out of her hands, and Brett took it and set it on the coffee table. She closed her eyes and leaned back on the couch. "I apologize for being a rude hostess," she said softly. "But I think I'd better rest for a while."

"Where are your pills, Aunt Nelda?"

Nelda's eyes flew open. "You know about the pills?"

"Yes."

"In that case," she said, closing her eyes again, "they're in my bedroom. On the dresser."

"I'll get them for you," Merrideth said.

Brett smiled his thanks. "It's the first door on the right."

There were no prescription bottles on top of Nelda's dresser nor on her chest of drawers. Merrideth wasn't about to look *in* the drawers, but she didn't think Nelda would mind if she checked the bathroom medicine cabinet. There was one prescription bottle, but it contained hemorrhoid suppositories. She hurriedly put it back, feeling guilty for seeing something so personal. She was about to go back and ask Nelda where else the pills could be when she remembered that she had seen an orange plastic bottle in one of the kitchen cabinets when she had been trying to figure out where to put away the various dishes.

She finally found it in the spice cabinet next to the cinnamon. The label said, "Vicodin," and the date was recent. She filled a glass with cold water and grabbed the bottle of pain killers. Just before she reached the doorway to the living room she heard Brett say, "We're just friends, Aunt Nelda. That's all. Just friends."

Merrideth immediately pivoted, moving herself back around the open door out of sight. It had been an instinctive decision, like TV cops when they were preparing to enter a potentially dangerous room. Only she held a bottle of pain killers instead of a gun.

"But you want more," Nelda said. "It's obvious you do."

"I've wanted more from the moment I first met her."

"I knew it. So now you'll settle down. Have a family. I'd like the chance to hold a little baby Brett—or Bertha, your call."

"Aunt Nelda. Please."

"Why can't I say it? What's the hold-up, Brett? Merrideth's obviously crazy about you."

"No, what's she's crazy about is the idea that she can't date fellow faculty members. Marla White put that notion in her head."

"So convince her she's being silly."

"I've been trying. Making progress, too. But now I suppose I'm going to have to stick to being friends. It's what she wants anyway."

"Why?"

Brett lowered his voice and said something Merrideth couldn't catch. Apparently Nelda didn't either.

"I said she's not a believer."

"Oh, Brett. What were you thinking? I just assumed she was."

"As did I."

"Because you wanted her to be."

"I suppose so."

"What does she say?"

"I haven't had a good opportunity to talk to her yet. At the moment we're both exhausted."

"Then what makes you think—?"

"Trevor said she believes a Hellhound only needs to *get his act together* in order to be converted. As if it were possible for us to save ourselves by trying harder to be good. And she all but came out and told him she doesn't know Jesus. Didn't seem to understand that she even *could* know him. So no, she's not a believer."

Merrideth put a hand over her mouth to stop the gasp that threatened to burst out of her mouth. How dare Brett and Trevor discuss her! How could they say she wasn't a believer? She had always believed in God.

They always said a person who eavesdrops never hears good things. But she had been so blasted curious to know what he thought of her, and of their relationship. Well, now she knew. She wasn't good enough. She had always known that, but she had not realized it would come down to not being able to pass some Christian litmus test. Would it have made a difference if she had prayed aloud at the cave, groveling in her unworthiness? Maybe if she'd thrown in a *thank you, Jesus* and a few *amens* and *hallelujahs?*

Brett and Nelda had stopped talking. They were probably afraid she would walk in on their little discussion. Meanwhile, she stood on the other side of the wall, feeling like a fool. Well, she wasn't going to pretend she had not heard. What was the point of that?

Merrideth stepped into the doorway, walked briskly to the coffee table, and set the glass of water down. "Here are your pills, Nelda. Sorry it took me so long. They were in the kitchen, not the bedroom. Actually, I guess I should apologize for not taking longer so you and Brett could finish dissecting me."

"Merri!" Brett said, coming awkwardly to his feet.

"Hope you feel better soon, Nelda."

Nelda cried out and Brett gathered his crutches and started toward her.

She didn't even bother to look at him. "You should keep your foot elevated, Brett. I can see myself out."

"Wait a minute. You don't understand."

"Oh, I think I do. Finally." She walked away. He came squeaking along behind her. When she opened the back door, he let one crutch clatter to the linoleum and grabbed her arm. "Merri, don't go. We need to talk."

"I'm all talked out, Brett."

"We can be friends, right? It's what you always wanted."

"But are you sure *you* want that?"

"Of course I want that."

"Goodbye, Brett. Take care of Nelda. I'll see you in September."

She kept her stride casual in case he was still watching her out the window. And she even managed to drive away normally, when her inclination was to floor it and spew gravel all the way down Nelda's drive.

So *now* he wanted to be friends? What exquisite timing! While she had stood under the dappled trees reveling in his kiss, realizing she loved him—was *in* love with him—Brett was regretting the kiss and deciding he had better call a halt to what was turning into a romance. That's what he must have been thinking back at the lodge. He had wanted to kiss her several times but had turned away.

Noble Brett Garrison, descendant of heroes.

But, of course, she really should direct her anger at God. He was the one pulling the strings, not Brett. She had finally worked up the courage to trust a man again, to quit worrying about her career and take the prize staring her in the face. And then just when she had it in her grasp, God had pulled it away like a cruel schoolyard bully teasing a little kid with candy he had no intention of sharing.

And she was being paid back for faking a headache to Trevor. The ache in her head was very real now, and a perfect accompaniment for the one in her heart. She got home without remembering the drive, and parked her old car in back of the house next to the Oswald sisters' gleaming red convertible. Seeing their car reminded her that she needed to get the oil in hers changed. She dreaded taking it in, because the mechanic would hound her again about getting new tires. In the lobby, she pulled three days' worth of mail out of her mailbox. Her phone rang, and she dropped half the mail juggling her backpack, purse, and suitcase to get her phone out of her pocket.

It was Brett. She snorted. As if.

Inside her apartment, she flipped on the light with her elbow and set everything down to go through the mail. There were three bills, oh joy, but most of it was sales flyers for stores she could not afford to shop in and political ads for the latest batch of crooks trying to get a head start on next spring's presidential primary. A hand-lettered, unstamped envelope was the only thing remotely interesting. She tore it open and read the letter inside.

Oh great. It was from her ancient landlord Mr. O'Connor, regretfully informing her that he was selling the house and moving to Florida to be nearer to his son. "I hope you end up next door to Odious Ogle," she muttered. The return address may have said *Mr. Gilbert O'Connor*, but it was really another message from God. She went to her window and looked out onto the front yard. Light from the porch revealed an Advantage Realty sign sticking out of the grass. Her mother had to know about the house going on the market. But then maybe she had not even recognized the address as hers. After all, she had only visited twice since she had lived there.

She got a bottle of cold water from the refrigerator and then went to the medicine cabinet for aspirin. She swallowed two, then decided to live dangerously and swallowed two more.

Somewhere on her sagging bookcase in the living room was the Bible Abby had given her years ago. She found it on the third shelf between *The God Delusion* and *Free Thinkers: a History of American Secularism* where she had put it on another occasion when she was mad at God.

She sat on her lumpy couch and turned to the table of contents, surprised that the reference Nelda had thrown out was still stuck in her head. Second Corinthians was in the New Testament, cleverly located right after First Corinthians. The fourteenth verse of chapter six read:

Be ye not unequally yoked together with unbelievers: for what fellowship hath righteousness with unrighteousness? and what communion hath light with darkness?

So she was unrighteous and dark, was she? It figured. She closed the Bible and tossed it onto the coffee table.

Her phone signaled an incoming text. It was Brett: *Let's talk, okay?* No, let's not. He could call every hour on the hour, but that did not mean she was obligated to talk to him if she didn't want to. And she did not want to. Not yet. Maybe in a year or so.

Who needed friends, anyway? She had her students and her book. They would be her friends. Her children, even. The thing to do was get busy with her work and not think about him. Then in September when he came back to campus, the hard shell would be firmly back in place, and she would be able to resume an appropriate professional relationship with him, just as she had intended all along. She would not cry. Not now and definitely not when she saw him around campus. No siree, Bob. She would not have any embarrassing emotional meltdowns that would get her fired. Marla White would be proud of her.

Her phone bleeped again. She turned it off without looking to see who was hounding her and went to unpack her backpack. The suitcase could wait. Her brain could not. She would transcribe her notes while she still remembered what she had scribbled. Then she would rough out an outline of what she wanted to include about the pirates of Cave-in-Rock in her book. She might even get in a little online research to answer some of the questions time-surfing had brought up.

By then she should be exhausted enough to sleep through the night without thinking about him.

CHAPTER 19

Merrideth was trying to follow a History Channel program about the Aztecs when the doorbell rang, startling her so much she nearly fell off the couch. She sat up, putting her hands to her head to keep it from exploding. Her headache was better now, but for a while her head had pulsed as if a sword were lodged in her brain. The doorbell rang again, and she hauled herself up and stumbled to the door, barely avoiding tipping over a stack of books.

Through her distorted fish-eye peep hole Abby and the girls smiled blearily at her. She opened the door. "Hey, you guys. What's up?"

"Hey, yourself, Merrideth," Abby said. "I've been trying to get a hold of you for three days. I tried calling, texting, and emailing."

"I turned my phone off. Kept getting nuisance calls."

"Well, turn it back on, would you?" Abby was holding a brown box. It looked heavy, but before Merrideth could take it from her, she sailed into her apartment, the girls following. "And turn the light on, for crying out loud. It's dark in here."

Merrideth slammed her eyes shut when Lauren went for the lamp.

"We brought *Frozen.*"

"What, honey?" Merrideth cautiously opened one eye and saw that Natalie was holding a CD case six inches from her face. "Oh, drat. It's movie night. I'm sorry, girls. I completely forgot."

"That's all right, Aunt Mewwi," Natalie said, patting her arm. "Mom said we can't stay 'cause you're sick."

"We brought you dinner, too," Lauren said.

"Mom said you don't deserve it," Natalie said.

"I'm sure I don't, but it smells good." That was an assumption because everything Abby cooked was awesome. But to her tortured senses whatever was in the box smelled like vomit.

"It's psketti and meatballs," Natalie explained.

"It's leftover," Abby said. "It would have tasted a lot better if you'd eaten it with us the first time around. If you'd answered your phone you would have gotten the invite."

Merrideth took her phone from the coffee table and made a production of turning it back on. "There. Does that make you happy?"

"It's a start." Abby strode toward the kitchen like Mary Poppins come to take charge of a bad situation.

Merrideth stuffed the phone in her pocket, gathered the girls in a quick hug, and then followed their mother into the kitchen.

Abby set the box on the counter and flipped on the light. It was even brighter than the lamp. Merrideth put a hand up to shield her eyes.

Abby studied Merrideth suspiciously. "You girls go play in the living room. I want to talk to your Aunt Merri."

"But we want to hear about the pirate cave," Natalie said.

"Yes, we do, don't we?" Abby said snarkily. "Wouldn't you think Aunt Merri should have known we were waiting to know all about it?"

"I'll tell you in a minute, Bugs, but you had better go watch TV for a while. I think your mom wants to yell at me."

The girls left the kitchen, dragging their feet. Squinting, Merrideth tried unsuccessfully to interpret the look on Abby's face. "What's wrong?"

"You tell me. When I couldn't reach you, I called the college and they said yes, you were still alive, but that you called in sick this morning. You look terrible. Have you been sleeping in your clothes?"

"Thanks for the morale boost. And it's a free country, Abby. I'll sleep in whatever I want to."

Abby glanced toward the living room and then whispered, "Are you hung over?"

"What?" Raising her voice had been a mistake. The throbbing in her head reached a new peak. "Of course I'm not hung over. I have a headache." The headache was only a minor part of her misery, but it was easier than trying to explain the miasma hanging over her world. Most people, normal people, didn't understand and told you to snap out of it. It was best to just hide out until she got the Brown Cloud out of her system.

"Sorry. But I have to say you look like you're hung over. And this place is a complete shambles."

"Thank you very much. You try keeping up with things with a sword in your head. Besides, I've been busy researching for more info about the pirates. Before my brain broke, anyway."

"Are you hungry? I mean for real food," Abby said with a disparaging look at the pizza and cereal boxes littering her counter.

"Not even for your famous psketti and meatballs. But when this headache goes away I will be. Thanks for thinking of me."

Abby took a casserole dish and a bag of salad from the box put them into the refrigerator. It reminded Merrideth of Nelda and that made her stomach hurt. Abby started gathering dirty dishes to take to the sink.

Merrideth leaned against the counter, closed her eyes, and put her hands to her ears. "Could you stop the clattering, please? And for Heaven's sake, don't scurry around like that."

"Okay, I'll stop scurrying and clattering. If you'll tell me what's really wrong."

Merrideth forced her eyes open. "I have a headache. That's all."

"Professor Randall is far too career-oriented to miss her classes for a headache. And she is far too weight conscious to binge on junk food."

"If you must know, the big D dropped in for a visit, bringing his friend the Brown Cloud."

Abby glanced out the pass-through to make sure the girls were still watching TV, then took her by the hand and dragged her down the hall to her bedroom.

Merrideth threw herself onto her unmade bed. "Good. I need to sleep."

"Okay, give." Abby shut the door and turned on the bedside lamp.

"I don't feel like talking."

"Too bad. Talk. You know it's the best way to extricate yourself from the Slough of Despond. Hiding out here incommunicado is the very worst thing."

Merrideth's throat grew tight, and tears threatened, drat it. She pulled the covers up over her head so Abby would not see. "I know."

Abby sat on the edge of the bed and patted at what she obviously thought was her shoulder. "I'm sorry, kiddo. The attack in the cave triggered it, I suppose."

"That didn't help, but I think it was watching the pirates that initially set me off. There was this family from Pennsylvania—the Hoffmans. I can still see them." She swallowed and tried to banish the images from her mind. "They were murdered, every last one of them. Samuel Mason just stood there and shot Mrs. Hoffman while she…crawled…"

"Don't think about it," Abby said.

"I can't stop thinking about it. And Mason was a choir boy compared to the Harpe brothers. They called themselves Big Harpe and Little Harpe. I forget Little Harpe's real name, but Big Harpe's was Micajah."

"I'm relived his mother didn't actually name him Big."

"You'll love this—*Micajah* is Hebrew for 'who can know God?'"

"I think it's safe to say he didn't."

"They got what they deserved, though. The settlers finally got fed up and hunted them down. They decapitated them and put their heads on pikes as a warning to other outlaws. Serves them right. They were evil."

"We're all sinful, Merri. Ever since Adam and Eve in the Garden."

"But not like Samuel Mason and the Harpe brothers. What they did was beyond garden-variety sin. Why didn't God send someone to help them—like Matthias Frailey helped White Dove and the Cherokee? Like he sent Trevor to help me in the cave. Why not the Hoffmans?"

"I don't know, Merri."

Merrideth stuck her head out from the covers. "And here's another question for you: why did this software land in my lap instead of someone else's? Why am I the lucky one to see all this?"

"That's a question John and I have asked ourselves. I feel terrible we weren't there with you—for you."

"No, I'm so glad you didn't come with me on this trip. No sense in anyone else seeing what I saw. And you should have seen the women and babies, Abby."

"You're contradicting yourself, Merri."

"At least they got away. Eventually. But the Hoffmans…" Merrideth choked back the knot in her throat.

"Try not to think about it."

"No," Merrideth said fiercely. "Someone needs to remember them."

"Then tell me about them."

Abby seemed to genuinely want to know, so Merrideth attempted to gather her thoughts. "The older couple was Lars and Martha Hoffman. It was his idea to leave their farm in Pennsylvania and go west to the frontier. He wasn't a very strong man, but he was a good man. He just wanted to better his family. He didn't deserve to be…."

"Tell me about the rest of the family. Help me see them."

"Martha was a proud, cantankerous old thing, but she loved her cow. I can still hear her singing while she milked Daisy. And they had beautiful horses. I was surprised by how many animals they fit on their flatboat."

"Good. I'm beginning to picture this. Were there other people?"

"Yes. They had a teenage son named Tobias. And their older son Erich and his family were there." Her mind tried to make her see what the Harpes did to Erich, but she pushed the image away. "The wife Anna was so sick. I think she had malaria. And no one knew it, but she was pregnant. I heard her tell Mason. She and Erich had a little girl named Julianne. She was so sad when her doll fell in the river." Merrideth swallowed the knot in her throat.

After a moment Abby said, "Where are they buried, Merri? Maybe we can go there and put flowers—"

"That's just it. They don't have proper graves. When I left off, the pirates were going to throw their bodies in the river like fish guts. I was going to see if I could find some of the Hoffmans' living relatives and let them know what happened, but that's hopeless."

"Why do you say that? It's what you do. Very well, in fact."

"With their luck, the relatives they left behind back in Pennsylvania were probably wiped out by a monsoon or a herd of bears or something."

"Monsoon? In Pennsylvania?"

"Whatever."

"If the Hoffmans are no more, and I seriously doubt that, then you'll tell their story. So people won't forget. To your students first. And then you'll write about it in your book, and lots more people will know. And you should come give a talk to my classroom when I do my Illinois history unit this fall."

"Are you kidding? I won't pollute their minds with what I saw."

"Well, of course not. I figured you could tone it down enough for fifth graders."

"I can't imagine how I could. I probably won't be in the area anyway."

"Why not?"

"If I get another job at all it will no doubt be in some remote place. Juneau maybe. Or Timbuktu. Some place where they're desperate enough for teachers not to be too particular about who they hire."

"Why would you leave McKendree? I thought you liked it there."

"Because I'm going to get fired. I know that now. Just like Marla White warned. I thought I could be all cool, but I can't."

"Merri, you know how this goes. The Brown Cloud is temporary. You'll feel better soon, I promise. Remember, this is not who you are. It's not reality."

There was a timid knock at the door and then Natalie said, "Mom?"

"Yes, honey?"

"Are you done yelling at Aunt Mewwi?"

"Not yet. But soon."

"Okay."

Abby drilled Merrideth with her sternest look. "There you go, Merri. Two reasons why you are going to get up out of that bed and get back to your life. Go out there and tell the girls about the pirates. Or I swear, I'm going to let them go to that Pete-the-Pirate BBS—I mean VBS."

"I can't be around them right now. What if the Brown Cloud is contagious?"

"I hear Pete the Pirate has a whole line of action figures and dress-up clothes, which I might be forced to buy for the girls."

"Abby, I can barely breathe, much less talk."

"You've been doing a pretty good job of it so far."

Merrideth covered her head with the quilt again.

"Merri, they love you. More, they need you."

She heaved a disgusted breath, threw the covers aside, and got out of bed. "You really know how to hit where it hurts, don't you?"

"Go wash your face with cold water. And comb your hair, for Pete's sake."

"Do not mention him."

When they got to her combination living/dining room, Merrideth nearly fainted. Lauren and Natalie were not watching TV. Instead, they were at the table avidly watching something on her laptop. She sprinted to them. "What have you got there, Bugs?"

"We're looking at the houses, Aunt Merri," Lauren said.

"My favorite is the pink one," Natalie said.

"I haven't picked mine yet," Lauren said.

"Let's not look at that now." After an alarmed look at Abby, Merrideth shut the laptop. Two minutes more and the little geniuses would have figured out how to send *Beautiful Houses* into *miracle mode*.

"That reminds me, Abby. I'll be picking out a new house myself. This one is being sold out from under the tenants."

"You'll find something better." Abby studied Merrideth's laptop. "Is that new?"

"Yes. I had it express mailed—for an extra fifty dollars and change in shipping—when the other one started going on the fritz. Timmy Tech's working on it."

Abby's eyes bugged out. "What about—you know?" She glanced at the girls who were listening intently.

"Don't worry. I wiped it after I got—you know—safely installed on this one."

Merrideth pushed aside some of the papers and books covering her table so she and Abby could sit down. And then she worked up a smile for Lauren and Natalie. It felt stiff and fake, but it was the best she could manage. "You remember the cave we saw in the movie last week?" Both girls nodded their heads. "Well, I got the chance to go down there and see the actual Cave-in-Rock. I spent the whole weekend there."

"In the cave?" Lauren asked, wide-eyed.

Merrideth smiled. "No. In a very nice room at the lodge."

"When can we go see it?" Lauren said.

"I'll take you. Some time when your mom and dad can go too."

"And see the pirates?" Natalie asked.

Merrideth shuddered. "No, you can't see the pirates. They're long gone from the cave." Except for the occasional modern-day type, and she prayed they never ran across that kind. "One of the pirates was named Samuel Mason."

"And he had a pirate ship, right?" Lauren said. "Not like the movie."

"Sorry, no pirate ship. And no eye patches, or wooden legs. He looked quite ordinary."

Merrideth hurried on before the girls thought to ask how she knew that. "Samuel Mason was so clever he didn't need a pirate ship with cannons. He had men stationed along the Ohio river who would tell him when a flatboat was coming. Then he tricked the settlers into stopping their boats at the cave so he could rob them."

"That's mean," Natalie said.

Merrideth put an arm around her shoulder. "You're confused, right? I'm telling you pirates were bad guys, but this Pete the Pirate person is nice."

"He sings about God and Jesus."

"That's because Pete the Pirate isn't a real pirate. He's just a regular man dressed up as one. But trust me, Bug, real pirates were—are—bad guys."

Abby smiled excitedly. "Hey, you could write two books about the pirates. One for historians and one for kids."

"I wish I could." Merrideth gestured toward the mess on her table. "I've spent the last three days trying to organize my notes, but didn't get very far. Not with a broken brain."

"You should have come home when you felt the Brown Cloud coming on. Or called me. I would have found some way to go down and head it off before it took hold."

"Brett came down."

"I'm glad you called him. I suggested it to John, but—"

"I didn't call him. He just showed up."

"Bet that complicated things."

"You have no idea how it complicated things."

Abby stood up. "Girls, go watch TV. I have to talk to Aunt Merri again."

"Don't yell at her anymore, Mom," Natalie said. "She's sad."

"I'll try not to."

Merrideth started toward the bedroom, but then she came back and snatched up the laptop in case the girls decided to go house hunting again.

Abby closed the bedroom door and faced her, hands on her hips. "I meant Brett coming down must have complicated your ability to time-surf. What did *you* mean?"

"I meant that Brett found out about *Beautiful Houses*. Sorry, but I couldn't very well keep it from him since Trevor was in on it. I really liked Trevor. You would have been happy—well, not about his tattoos—but happy that I finally met a man I could consider dating."

"He has tattoos?"

"There's nothing immoral or illegal about tattoos, Abby. But don't worry. Nothing came of it. I'm not sure Trevor was ever interested in me. He rode off into the sunset on his Harley without one look back."

"Harley? He's a biker?"

"Yes, didn't I tell you?"

"What's the matter with you? Did you hit your head in that cave?"

"Of course not." Merrideth closed her eyes. No, it had just been a stab wound. And it was to her heart, not her head.

"Then are you sure you haven't been drinking? Why on earth would you be interested in a biker with tattoos when you had Brett right there?"

Merrideth lay back on the bed and fluffed her pillow. "Hey, don't knock Trevor. He's more my speed than the heroic Brett Garrison. We have a lot in common. Trevor would have made the perfect husband. He's all stocked up on dysfunctional, and as an added bonus he already knows the proper protocol for prison visits. He could have kept me company when I visit Dad. He probably would have enjoyed it, now that he's on the other side of the bars."

"Trevor was in prison?"

"Yes, and for drugs—just like dear old Dad. I always have trouble keeping the conversational ball in the air, but I bet he and Trevor would have chatted their heads off. But I suppose it's just as well things didn't work out. I couldn't possibly marry him, anyway. Think of our kids, Abby. With an ex-con for both father and grandfather, who knows how they'd have turned out?"

"Cut the nonsense, Merri, and tell me what happened."

"Nothing gets past your radar, does it?"

Abby sat on the bed beside her. "Come on, you might as well cough it up. You know I'll hound you until you do."

"He wants me—since the first time he saw me. I heard him tell his aunt so."

"Trevor?"

"Duh. Brett."

Abby laughed. "And this depresses you? Most women would be giddy to know Dr. Brett Garrison had the hots for them."

"Oh, but we're just friends. He said so himself." Merrideth tried to hold the tears back. She covered her head with the quilt and swallowed hard.

"Talk to me, Merri. Because I'm confused. You've been telling me since forever that you would not date Brett because he's on faculty with you. That you wanted him only as a friend. So this is good that he sees it that way, right?"

"Not if the reason is because I'm not good enough for anything more. Like maybe marrying him." And then the dam broke and she wept. "Now I can't have him for a friend either. I thought I could live without that, but I can't."

"Are you kidding me? He stood there and told you that you weren't good enough for him?" Abby thrust a wad of tissues under the covers. "Wait until I get my hands around that handsome throat of his."

"Not... to my face. It's worse. He told... his Aunt Nelda, so... it must be true."

"You were eavesdropping?"

"I couldn't... help it."

"Well, what was it that didn't measure up to his exacting standards? Wait a minute. He found out about your dad, right?"

Merrideth popped out of the covers and wiped her eyes with the tissue. "He's not like that, Abby. He's known Dad's in prison almost from the beginning."

"Then what?"

"Apparently, I don't *believe* enough to suit him."

"I should have known," Abby said, wiping Merrideth's cheeks with the sheet. She opened her mouth to speak again and then shut it.

The bedroom door creaked opened and the girls peeked in.

"Mom," Natalie said, "does Aunt Mewwi need more hugs?"

"In a minute. Go watch TV."

Lauren turned to look at her sister. "Man, it must be serious if Mom's actually *making* us watch TV."

"But I want to stay," Natalie said.

Lauren shut her off with a "shhh," and then the door creaked closed.

"What did you mean?" Merrideth said, sniffing. "You should have known what?"

Abby's brows furrowed. "I guess John and I haven't been thinking about this from Brett's perspective. We've been so thrilled that he came into your life. We kept hoping that—" Her voice trailed off.

"What?"

Abby looked at her cautiously. "Merri, the Bible commands Christians not to be unequally yoked to unbelievers. It sounds like Brett's finally getting around to remembering that."

"I know. Second Corinthians 6:14."

"You do?"

"Yes. But it doesn't apply because I believe in God."

Abby didn't answer.

"So you think I'm not good enough, either? That I'm *unequal* to Brett? Thanks a lot, Abby. I believe in God. You know I do. I keep the ten commandments. I don't lie or steal. And Heaven knows I don't indulge in bed-hopping."

"Of course you're good enough. Good enough for anyone, Merri." After a pause she added, "You say you believe in God. What exactly?"

"That he made the world and then sits up there watching us screw it all up."

"Sounds like you're taking the Deist position, then, Merri. Like Thomas Jefferson. God's the great Clockmaker who created the world, wound it up, and let it go. God exists, but he doesn't give a rip about his creation."

"No, not that exactly. But when I see him, I'm going to give him a piece of my mind for not doing something to fix the mess we're in."

"He did do something to fix it, kiddo. But tell me, Merri. What makes you think you *are* going to see him? Why should God let you into Heaven?"

"Because he loves me, doesn't he? At least you claim he does."

"It's good you know that, Merri. I realize it's difficult for people with your family background to see God as a loving Father. But don't forget that he's also holy. He is absolute goodness and purity. Heaven wouldn't be worth going to if it turned out to be tainted with sin like this world is. But thank God, sinners don't get in to mess it all up. No, Heaven is one hundred percent pure like God is."

"Then I guess that leaves me out," Merrideth said bitterly.

"It leaves us all out, Merri. You said you keep the ten commandments. What about that one about loving God with all your heart, soul, strength, and mind?"

"Okay, I admit I'm not doing so hot on that one at the moment."

"So, you do understand that you're a sinner?"

"Of course I am. Just because I don't go around groveling in it, doesn't mean I don't know that."

"Thank God!"

"What brought on the hallelujahs this time?"

"I'm happy that you know you're a sinner, because it is the first step to understanding you need a Savior."

Merrideth had a sudden mental picture of Trevor saying the very same thing about the Hellhounds and Road Hogs.

Abby smiled. "I wouldn't use the word *grovel*, but you do need to give up your pride."

"Pride? How can you say I'm proud? I'm not exactly known for my high self-esteem, you know."

"It's pride that makes us think we can get to Heaven on our own. Pride that deludes us into thinking we can save ourselves by our good works, by not being as bad as other people."

"That's what Trevor said." And then she saw Samuel Mason assuring Floss that God would let him into Heaven because he was not as bad as the Harpes.

"Good for Trevor, tattoos and all!"

The door creaked again. Two little blond heads were visible in the crack. Merrideth wiped her eyes and put on a smile.

"I guess that means it's time for more hugs," Abby said, waving the girls in. "But listen to me, Merri. God's at work in you. It's as clear as the nose on your face. And when he goes to work on someone, he never comes home empty-handed, but brings every lamb into his fold. He'll make it all clear to you. In his own time. I believe that with all my heart."

The girls jumped onto the bed and wrapped their arms around her. Merrideth swallowed back yet more tears and breathed in the sweet smell of their hair. "That's just what I needed, Bugs. You should bottle and sell your hugs and kisses. It would be so much better than Prozac."

After another tight squeeze, the girls released her and lay back on the bed beside her

Merrideth's phone rang. She tugged it out of her pocket. "It's Brett. He keeps calling and texting. He wants to be *friends*," she said sarcastically. She laid the phone on the bedside table and stared at it while it continued to ring.

"Then let him be your friend. God sent him to you. Just like he sent Trevor to rescue you."

Merrideth sniffed. "I miss him so much it hurts. My heart actually hurts."

Natalie patted her cheek. "Don't be sad, Aunt Mewwi."

Abby smiled tenderly. "Yes. Don't be, Aunt Mewwi. Answer your phone."

"Here, I'll help you." Lauren grabbed the phone, clicked the *Talk* button, and put it up to Merrideth's ear.

She exhaled a breath and said, "Brett."

"Thank God!" His voice went from relieved to sarcastic. "So you're not dead, then."

Her heart leaped at the sound of his voice. "No, I'm alive. Sort of."

The girls climbed over her and got down from the bed. Abby shooed them out of the room, then after a smile and a little waggle of her finger tips, she left, closing the door quietly behind herself.

"How's Aunt Nelda?"

"She seems somewhat better. Mrs. Ashe has been coming over to do a few things around the house, so that helps."

"How's your ankle?"

"It's finally better. The doctor told me to stay off it, or I'd have come pounding on your door. Listen, Merri, I know you're mad at me, but I need to talk to you."

"I'm not mad at you, Brett. Not anymore."

"You're not?"

"No." She wiped her eyes with the corner of the sheet.

"You have no idea how happy that makes me. I couldn't stand it, thinking you—"

"Me, too."

Brett cleared his throat and then there was silence. After a moment, he said, "Did you know you missed the faculty meeting?"

"Oh, drat. That was tonight, wasn't it?"

"Yep. It just ended. Finally."

"Did I miss anything important?"

He chuckled. "What do you think? But that's not to say I didn't pick up lots of interesting tidbits for your delectation. How about we go to the 1828 Cafe so I can fill you in? On second thought, we'd better make that somewhere off campus. How about the Tapestry Room?"

"Okay. If it's just coffee."

"Then we'd better go somewhere else, because I won't be able to resist their coconut cream pie."

"Oh, all right. Maybe one piece of pie won't hurt."

"Good. You can tell me how your book is coming, and I'll fill you in on the latest adventures of the beasts."

The danger was past, and they were back on solid ground. Merrideth could hear him smiling and pictured him looking solid and uncomplicated. His life was an open book, and he would never feel the need to have tattoos inked onto his body to remind himself of some horrible past. She needed that wholeness in her life. She needed him. And she would take him however she could get him, even if it were only as a friend.

"Did you know there's a for-sale sign in your front yard?"

"Brett?"

"Yes?"

"Where are you?"

"Sitting on your front step, waiting to get the courage to come up."

"Do not come up! Wait there. Just give me fifteen minutes to shower and change, and I'll be right down."

"I'll wait as long as it takes, Merri."

She knew he intended more than just the surface meaning of his words, but with her brain in the state it was, she could not quite grasp it. Hopefully, Abby was right, and everything would be as clear as day to her soon.

One thing was already clear. No matter what she thought of

that Bible verse in Corinthians, he believed it, and she could not expect him to violate his conscience. But Brett Garrison was not the only one who could be noble. She would be his friend. Even if it killed her. Maybe that would count for something with God while she figured out how to believe in him enough.

THE END

ABOUT THE AUTHOR

Deborah Heal, the author of the *Time and Again* History Mystery Trilogy and the Rewinding Time Series, which have been described as "Back to the Future meets virtual reality with a dash of Seventh Heaven thrown in," was born not far from the settings of her novels ***How Sweet the Sound*** and ***Every Hill and Mountain*** and grew up just down the road from the settings of ***Time and Again*** and ***Unclaimed Legacy***.

Today she lives with her husband in Monroe County, Illinois, not far from the setting of ***Once Again***. She enjoys reading, gardening, and learning about regional history. She has three grown children, five grandchildren, and two canine buddies Digger and Scout.

All Deborah Heal's books are available on **Amazon .com**.

A NOTE FROM THE AUTHOR

I grew up hearing about the pirates of Cave-in-Rock and always thought it was a fascinating tale. Now as an adult, I enjoyed researching more of the historical details. I couldn't cram it all into *How Sweet the Sound* so be sure to visit my website for more information about Samuel Mason and the Harpe brothers.

You'll find it under the "About my Books" tab on my website: **www.deborahheal.com**. Scroll down past the description of *How Sweet the Sound* for the following articles:

> *The Real Pirates of Cave-in-Rock: Samuel Mason*
> *The Real Pirates of Cave-in-Rock: the Harpe Brothers*
> *Flatboats on the Ohio*
> *Poor Mrs. Hoffman and the Calomel*

Acknowledgements

My sincere thanks and appreciation goes out to everyone who helped me with *How Sweet the Sound:*

My "editor-in-chief" Michelle Babb, who roots out a million typos and glitches every time.

My beta readers, who did so much to help me polish the story: Barbara Woods, Susan Steingrubey, Peter Wilson, Brenda Casto, Dana Mohr, Emily Kopf, Janelle Bailey, Marcia Dillard, Meagan Myhren-Bennett, Sonya DeBerte, and Janelle Bailey.

Kris Huckshold, Christian Motorcycle Association, for information about CMA's ministry to bikers.

Marty Kaylor and Kim McDowell, Cave-in-Rock State Park, for kindly answering questions about the cave when I couldn't get there to see it again for myself.

And Patsy Ledbetter, author/editor of *The Way It Was in Hardin County*, who called with interesting information about the region.

Let's Keep in Touch

Thanks for supporting independent authors!

I'd love to hear what you think of *How Sweet the Sound*. If you enjoyed it, please write a review for it and post it wherever you can, especially on Amazon and Goodreads. Or if you're not a member, you could post your review in the comment section of any of the articles on my website.

And sign up to get my newsletter **V.I.P. Perks** (in the right sidebar of my website). You'll get my free short story "The List" just for signing up. Then you'll be among the first to hear when new books in the series are released (Six planned in all!) You'll also get information about contests, giveaways, and when my books are scheduled to be free or reduced.

I'd really appreciate it if you would "like" and "follow," or otherwise connect with me.

www.facebook.com/DeborahHeal

www.twitter.com/DeborahHeal

www.goodreads.com/deborahheal

BOOK FOUR IN
THE REWINDING TIME SERIES
(coming Christmas 2015)

Merrideth and Brett meet literary giant Charles Dickens who visited their town in 1842. They get to know the man behind the masterpieces and solve the mystery of the ghostly appearances that have plagued the Mermaid House Inn ever since Dickens slept there.